AUDREY, WAIT!

For my mother, who always says,
"You have to have faith."
And for my brother, who always has.

AUDREY, WAIT!

by

ROBIN BENWAY

raz**O**r
bill

Audrey, Wait!

RAZORBILL

Published by the Penguin Group
Penguin Young Readers Group
345 Hudson Street, New York, New York 10014, U.S.A.
Penguin Group (USA) Inc., 375 Hudson Street, New York, New York 10014, U.S.A.
Penguin Group (Canada), 90 Eglinton Avenue East, Suite 700, Toronto, Ontario,
Canada M4P 2Y3 (a division of Pearson Penguin Canada Inc.)
Penguin Books Ltd, 80 Strand, London WC2R 0RL, England
Penguin Ireland, 25 St Stephen's Green, Dublin 2, Ireland
(a division of Penguin Books Ltd)
Penguin Group (Australia), 250 Camberwell Road, Camberwell, Victoria 3124,
Australia (a division of Pearson Australia Group Pty Ltd)
Penguin Books India Pvt Ltd, 11 Community Centre, Panchsheel Park, New Delhi – 110 017,
India
Penguin Group (NZ), 67 Apollo Drive, Rosedale, North Shore 0632, New Zealand
(a division of Pearson New Zealand Ltd)
Penguin Books (South Africa) (Pty) Ltd, 24 Sturdee Avenue, Rosebank, Johannesburg 2196,
South Africa

Penguin Books Ltd, Registered Offices: 80 Strand, London WC2R 0RL, England

10 9 8 7 6 5 4 3 2 1

Library of Congress Cataloging-in-Publication Data

Benway, Robin.
    Audrey, wait! / by Robin Benway
        p. cm.
    Summary: While trying to score a date with her cute co-worker at the Scooper Dooper,
sixteen-year-old Audrey gains unwanted fame and celebrity status when her ex-boyfriend, a rock
musician, records a breakup song about her that soars to the top of the Billboard charts.
    ISBN 978-1-59514-191-0
    [1. Dating (Social customs)—Fiction. 2. Fame—Fiction. 1. Title.

PZ7.B4477Au 2008
[Fic]—dc22

                                                2007023912

Printed in the United States of America

"Muses work all day long and
then at night get together and dance."
—Edgar Degas

"Oh, baby, here comes the sound!"
—My Chemical Romance, "Give 'Em Hell, Kid"

1

"Don't you just love goodbyes?"
—Mew, "156"

THE DAY I BROKE UP with my boyfriend Evan was the day he wrote the song. You know, *the song*. I'm sure you've heard it. Maybe you danced to it at prom or sang it in your car on a Friday night when you were driving and feeling like you must be inhuman to be this happy, the windows down and nothing but air around you. Your mom has probably hummed it while cleaning the dryer's lint trap, and your grandpa has most likely whistled a couple bars. If he's the whistling type.

According to the poll on the front page of *USA Today*, sixty-three percent of Americans blame me for the breakup, so let me clear the air right now: They're right. Sixty-three percent of Americans are no fools when it comes to knowing about my love life, a fact which is really creepy and isn't helping me sleep well. But it's true: I broke up with Evan, and eight hours later, he had a song in his head and a guitar in his hand and it snowballed from there.

It took me forever to decide whether or not to break up with him, I can tell you that. It wasn't like I just woke up one morning and was like, "Hey, let's liven things up!" Please. I have enough on my plate without all this. I'm a junior, for God's sakes! It's not like I have to take the SATs this year or anything. But I had been thinking about it—breaking up—for a while.

"Make a list," Victoria had said. She's big on lists and has a folder full of them. They have titles like "Six Colors to Dye My Hair Before I Shrivel Up and Die" and "Five People to Banish From the Face of the Earth" (Evan, according to her, is now *número uno*). So the day I did it, I sat at Victoria's kitchen table and wrote down the reasons why I should stay with Evan.

1. He's a singer/songwriter with a band and actual talent.

2. He has excellent oral hygiene (That one is so important, I can't even tell you. I can't imagine ever kissing a non-flosser. So gross.).

3. He says he's going to write a song about me.

And then I wrote the cons:

1. He smokes too much pot.

2. He's always "practicing" or "gigging" with his band, the Do-Gooders, especially when I need him.

3. He says "gigging."

4. He's mellow about everything. *Everything.*

5. He makes me be the one to get condoms from the school nurse's office.

6. He sucks his teeth after he eats, which makes horrible squeaking sounds, like a mouse dying.

And so on. I wrote so many cons that I needed a new piece of paper, and by the time Victoria saw me start a fresh page, she took it away and shook her head. "Audrey," she told me, "save a tree."

"Well, can we still be . . . I don't know, friends? Or something lame like that?" Evan had been cross-legged on his bed when I broke up with him. I was on the opposite side of the room in his desk chair, sitting backwards. We were both crying, but he was the only one who needed tissues. Still, we passed the box back and forth.

"Friends would be great," I said, and relief flooded through me. Friends were *fantastic*, friends were not angry at each other and wouldn't reveal sexual secrets about each other in locker rooms. Friends still talked. Friends drifted apart. "I'd really like being friends."

He fell on his bed for a minute before sitting back up. "Steve finally got the A&R guy to come to a show of ours. He set up a one-off tonight. You're really killing my vibe."

"I'm sorry," I said, and I meant it. I really did.

"Will you still come?"

"If you want me to, sure." *Anything to make this conversation end,* I thought.

Evan nodded and hugged his guitar tighter to him, and I have to admit that in the eleven months we were together, that guitar practically got more action than I did. (Reason number fourteen on the list of cons, by the way.) "You sure you want to do this?"

"Yeah," I whispered. "I'm sure."

We didn't talk for a few minutes, and then I got up and said, "I'm going now." When he didn't respond, I left the room and was halfway downstairs before I heard him say, "Audrey, wait!" But I kept going, pretending I didn't hear him calling for me.

That night, I enlisted Victoria and her boyfriend, Jonah, to come with me to the show for moral support. "Like I wasn't already going?" Victoria said when I asked her. "I've already gotten about fifty million texts and thirty million Facebook bulletins about it. And besides," she added, "I want details."

During the drive over to the Jukebox in Jonah's car (he has an awesome sound system with a subwoofer), she made me recount the breakup word for word, with Jonah wincing every few minutes. "Harsh, man," he kept saying. "That is so *harsh*." Victoria finally whacked him on the shoulder. "Can you please be more sensitive to Audrey's situation?" she hissed.

"Sorry, Aud." Jonah smiled at me in the rearview mirror. "Sensitivity controls now engaged."

"And could you not sound like a dork when you do it?"

"It's one or the other, babe."

"Don't worry about it, Jonah," I told him. "It's all good."

Victoria just shook her head and hung over the backseat. "Either way," she said, "I cannot believe you agreed to go tonight."

Half an hour later, packed like sardines inside the Jukebox, we were still talking about it. "Did Evan actually say 'kill his vibe'?" Victoria asked. By now, she was on her third Diet Coke and I could see the caffeine starting to shoot out of her eyes.

I crossed my arms in front of me and stood by the side of the stage, hoping the Do-Gooders would hurry up and play so we could go home and skip the traffic. "Those words exactly," I told her. "Plus some other choice phrases."

"What? Like, 'Fuck you'?"

"No, more like, 'How could you do this to me?' 'I thought we were gonna be together forever.' That kind of stuff." I stirred my melted ice with my straw.

Victoria rolled her eyes in solidarity. "Please. He must be a closet romance novel reader. I'm surprised he didn't break out a lute and try to woo you."

"If he had done that, I would've been more interested." I took her drink from her and set it down. "You're making me nervous with all the addictive stimulants. Don't you know that NutraSweet can give you cancer?"

"So can sunlight." She took her drink back and made a big deal out of slurping the rest with her straw. "I hope Jonah's getting me another one of these."

"I hope he's also getting you a side of tranquilizers." I looked over my shoulder and saw a third of our class standing behind us. No one seemed too interested in me. Yet. "Do you think people know we broke up?"

"Have you told anyone besides me and Jonah?"

"Nope. But Evan might have."

"You've totally ruined the pool that people had going for Cutest Couple in the yearbook, by the way. Not to guilt you out or anything."

"What?"

"Not me, I mean. *I* saw this one coming a long time ago. But people were laying two-to-one odds that you and Evan would be Cutest Couple."

"People are betting on yearbook superlatives? Really?"

Victoria nodded. "Now the smart money's on Dan Milne and Janie Couper. She's worse than static cling."

I was about to comment on Janie Couper's static-clinginess, but just then I saw Sharon Eggleston across the room. Even if you've never met Sharon, you know her. Every school, I'm sorry to say, has a girl like her. She's pretty or hot or whatever word you want to use, and she has this weird ability to make every guy worship her.

Every guy, that is, except Evan.

At least, that was the scuttlebutt (PSAT word) when Evan and I first hooked up. Sharon had apparently set her sights on him, he set his sights on *me*, I set my sights right back on *him*, we got together, and Sharon found herself on the outs before she was even on the ins. As you can imagine, she wasn't thrilled. Even to this day, she still shows up to all the shows and smiles at Evan in the halls and generally is an annoying little gnat. And when I saw her across the room at the show that night, she smiled and did that little wave thing that showed off her French-manicured silk tips.

"What are you looking at?" Victoria asked, craning her neck to see, but luckily Jonah elbowed his way back to Victoria and me with her Diet Coke and my cranberry juice with lime. "See, now, Evan wouldn't have done this," Victoria pointed out as she took her drink. "He wouldn't have noticed that you were even thirsty, much less that *I* was. I mean, you could both be walking in the goddamn Sahara desert and you'd be dying of thirst and he'd be like, 'Hey, Aud, I've got this killer idea for a song.' Totally useless."

I swirled my ice with the straw. "Evan used 'killer' last year. This year, everything's 'fool-ass.'"

"Okay. Audrey? Let me introduce you to something called The Point. You are missing it."

It should come as no surprise that when Victoria is asked to spell her name, she says, "Like the queen." She was on a roll now. "I'm just saying that you've been really patient with Evan. More patient than I would've been—"

Jonah snorted and then became really interested in his drink.

"—and I think you just deserve someone who makes you feel special and wonderful and all those good things that you see on TV."

"I thought you weren't watching TV anymore."

Victoria shrugged. "I fell off the wagon."

If you ever meet Victoria, do not call her Vick, Vicky, Victor, Victrola, Vicious, or anything other than Victoria. If you're feeling both immortal and bored, though, call her Vicks VapoRub.

Onstage, Jon, the Do-Gooders' drummer, started to do a half-hearted sound check. If there is a hell, there will be a drummer sound-checking there, I guarantee you. "Oh, God, kill me now." Victoria rolled her eyes again.

"I'm a weak, spineless girl, what can I say?" I was quickly downing the cranberry juice and wishing it had a kick to it. The problem with the Jukebox is that it's so local the bartenders know all of us and, more specifically, how old we are, so alcohol's not happening. Which is why everyone gets wasted in their driveways afterwards. "Plus, the A&R guy's here and Steve kept promising that he would come and I want to see him in person."

A word about Steve: Three months ago, the Do-Gooders played a show at the Jukebox, the one where part of the ceiling caved in during their set and it knocked out their amps and they kept playing anyway. (Maybe you saw the article in the local paper. I was there too, and if you look closely at the picture, you can see my hand in the bottom part of the picture—I was cheering them on with the rest of the crowd. I spent the rest of the night picking insulation out of my hair.)

Anyway, Steve was at the show that night. Steve was a freshman at UCLA who smoked tons of weed, went to class occasionally, downloaded MP3s, and had an uncle who knew someone who did A&R at a record label. Steve thought the Do-Gooders were "a-*may*-zing dude, fucking a-*may*-zing!" and after the ceiling collapsed and the amps gave out, they all went and hung out at Steve's dorm room, where they dreamed big, bet each other $20 to drink the bongwater, and agreed to let Steve manage them. As far as I could tell, though, getting the A&R guy to come to the show was the first managerial thing that Steve had done for them.

It wasn't the first time that someone from a record label had shown up at the Jukebox. I mean, every third person in our school is either in a band, starting a band, managing a band, or breaking up with his or her band. Most of those bands, however, suck. A couple of years ago, there were three seniors who were way into ska and managed to get signed to some tiny label in San Francisco, but I heard the trombone player started doing way too much cocaine and sold his trombone for a couple of grams of something that killed him.

This fame thing isn't all it's cracked up to be. Take it from me and the trombone player.

"Do you think they comp the A&R guy's drinks?" Jonah wondered.

"Of course not," Victoria replied. "He blows the bartender like everyone else."

Both Jonah and I cracked up and Jonah looped his arm around her neck and pulled her into him. She is so tiny that when they hug, you can barely see her. She has to stand on the very tips of her toes just to squeeze his neck. "My crazy, slutty girlfriend," Jonah said, then kissed the top of her head, and for the first time since I broke up with him that morning, I missed Evan. Not that he would've kissed me in public, especially before a show, but sometimes it's just nice to know there's potential.

I knew Evan was backstage now, or at least what passes for "backstage" at the Jukebox: the loading dock behind the venue. It always smells like beer and piss and garbage, but there's something exciting about being back there, adrenaline and nerves rushing around and cramming into your heart. Whenever he was about to play a show, Evan's hands would shake and he'd hold them out to me and I'd see his fingers vibrate like hummingbird wings. "You're fine," I would tell him. "You're gonna be great." Sometimes I lied when I said it; other times, I meant it so much that it killed me more than lying.

I was about to say something to Victoria about it, something about how weird it was to be in the crowd before a Do-Gooders show rather than backstage with Evan, when she grabbed my arm. "Space!" she cried, and shoved me about six feet toward the speaker.

If you really want to know something about me, you should know this: I like my music loud. I mean *loud*. I'm not talking the kind of loud where your parents knock on your bedroom door and ask you to turn it down. Please. That's amateur hour. When I say loud, I mean you-can't-hear-your-parents-knocking-and-the-neighbors-are-putting-a-FOR-SALE-sign-on-their-house-and-moving-to-another-block-because-they-can't-handle-the-constant-noise-anymore *loud*. You have to turn it up so that your chest shakes and the drums get in between your ribs like a heartbeat and the bass goes up your spine and frizzles your brain and all you can do is dance or spin in a circle or just scream along because you know that however this music makes you feel, it's exactly right.

If you are not this kind of person, then I don't think we'll be great friends.

Victoria and I always turn things up to ten. In fact, it's getting to be a problem because we've already blown out the speakers in my car. Twice. The first time, my parents took pity on me and replaced them, but now I have to dig up the cash to fix it. So Victoria and I use Jonah for his car, or we just ride in mine and sing really loud until we laugh so hard, we want to throw up, and Jonah ducks down in the backseat and pulls his hoodie tighter around his head and looks like he wants to just *die*.

The lights finally went out and the crowd started whistling and clapping. Next to me, Victoria was grinning and wriggling around. She lives for this moment at shows, when the lights are cut and all you can see is the dim outline of a stage and empty mics waiting to be picked up and abused. When the Do-Gooders came out, shaggy and skinny with their heads down, the applause got louder. Even I let out a few whistles.

"Here comes trouble," Jonah muttered behind me when Evan came out, and I could see Victoria plow her elbow into his ribs from the corner of my eye.

My resolve took a little nosedive when I saw Evan. God, he was cute. Not even cute: hot. H-A-W-T, hot. His hair was shining under the stage lights and he was wearing his beat-up shoes, the ones that looked horrible and smelled worse. I could see him looking out at the crowd and I didn't know if I was supposed to make eye contact with him or smile or pretend that I couldn't see him.

Was Evan looking for me, though? His eyes scanned across stage left and never stopped, and I didn't wave. Next to me, Victoria reached down and squeezed my hand twice.

Seriously, I love her.

"Hi, we're the Do-Gooders," Evan said into the mic, and you could hear some girls giggle and swoon. I had never been jealous of them before, but now I felt a small twist in my stomach. *Just get this over with,* I begged silently. "The name's ironic." Ha ha, hee hee. Oh, Evan, you're a riot. Please. Stop. My sides.

They played through six songs and the crowd danced and sweated on each other and the bass shook the floors under our feet and the roof over our heads. The Jukebox was approximately the size of my parents' kitchen and the walls would get slick from the humidity of too many people too close together. Onstage, Evan kept shaking his head back and forth in time to the music, his hair pinwheeling and sending little blue drops of sweat toward Bob, the rhythm guitarist, and Daniel, their bassist.

Here's something you don't know about Evan: He used to practice that move in front of the mirror. I'm just saying.

Between songs, I finally saw the A&R guy standing next to Steve. Steve had this big, dopey grin on his face (totally high) and the guy next to him was wearing really expensive jeans and enough product in his hair to make it crunchier than celery, and was texting someone. Was he interested? Was he just returning a favor by coming out to see the band? I nudged Victoria and pointed him out, and she looked back at me and twirled one piece of hair around her finger. "Product!" she mouthed over the crowd noise, then wrinkled her nose. Not that Victoria's hair is naturally spiky or anything, she was just anti-gel for men. Jonah avoided this problem by shaving his head every month or so, which Victoria greatly appreciated.

Evan's voice pulled me back toward the stage. "This is usually the point where we go backstage and you clap and we do our encore, but we're gonna skip that middle part tonight and get straight to the music."

One more song, I told myself. *One more song and then I can go to the In-N-Out drive-thru with Victoria and Jonah and get a grilled cheese and a chocolate shake and blast music until my ears want to fall off and Jonah takes me home. One more song and then I can be a normal, average girl without a boyfriend.*

"This is a new song for us; I wrote it tonight."

A new song? Everyone in the crowd was talking a little. The Do-Gooders hadn't written a new song in at least four months, and we already knew all the words to their stuff. The encore was usually just a cover of Oasis's "Don't Go Away," and I already wasn't looking forward to watching Evan go all emo with the lyrics.

But new song? This wasn't in my grilled-cheese-and-loud-music plan.

Victoria, I should point out here, is very smart. Sometimes she's smarter than me. "Uh-oh," I heard her say, but before I could turn my head to see what "uh-oh" was about, Evan kept speaking.

"My girlfriend Audrey broke up with me today and—"

Uh-oh.

You know how in movies, the room will be really crowded and noisy and someone will say something that causes everyone's heads to whip around and stare at that person? Let me tell you something: That happens in real life, too. And it happened to me when Evan said that. Two hundred people in the room, four hundred eyes (actually 399— Jake Myers lost one in a fishing accident when he was six), and all of them were burning into me.

Evan hadn't shut up yet. "Yeah, she broke up with me right

before the biggest night of my life—"

"*Harsh,*" whispered a voice behind me. Guess who.

"And I always said I'd write a song about her and, well, I hope it's not too late. This one is called 'Audrey, Wait!'"

Have you ever had brain freeze? That's what it felt like when I heard the title of the song. I remembered walking down Evan's staircase, pretending I didn't hear him. I had made a huge fucking mistake. I hadn't listened then, so he was making sure I was listening now.

(Okay, so I also have to admit, I was a little disappointed the song wasn't titled "Audrey, the Hottest Girl I Ever Met," or "Audrey, That Time Upstairs at the Party (Was Amazing)" or something like that.)

The bass drum pounded hard, just like my heart, and a thin guitar line sizzled up and sliced through the stage, setting the whole band off. It was like nothing they had ever played before. Evan was changing chords so fast and I thought for the briefest moment, *Is that how he loved me? Did he really love me like this?* I began imagining our reconciliation scene, making out after the show and giggling about how stupid I was for breaking up with him and—

He started singing.

"You said your piece and now I've got to say mine! I had you and you strung me on the *liiiiiinnnnnneeeeee!*"

What?

"We said we loved and it was a lie! I touched your hair and watched you die! You crucified my heart, took every part, and hung them out to *drrrrryyyyyyy!*"

Oh. My. God.

"'It's all good!' you always say! But save it for another day! 'Cause now I'm watching you walk *awaaaaayyyyyy!*"

Here's the worst part: The song was *good.* I mean, you obviously know that by now—I'm not revealing some big secret or anything. But at the time, the whole crowd was about to have a collective heart attack, they were dancing so hard. Even the bartenders, the mean bartenders who are bitter about life and water down the Cokes, had stopped pouring and were drumming their fingers on the bar top. Even the kids who don't dance, the ones who refuse to show any emotion about anything but still show up at the Jukebox just for *something* to do, they were nodding their heads to the beat like they were issuing a mob hit. I could see the A&R guy tapping his foot and watching the stage, hungry. Steve was completely bug-eyed and gaping—he'd had no idea this band could produce this song.

Neither had I.

And then the chorus started. Sing along if you want.

"Audrey, wait! Audrey, wait! You walked out the door and I want you to see me slam it shut! Audrey, wait! Audrey, wait! You can say all you want, but I want you to know that this is the cruelest cut!"

I swear, if that song hadn't been about me, if I had never met Evan, I would've been on that stage shaking what my momma gave me, it was that addictive. But instead I was rooted to the floor and my jaw was somewhere around my knees. Victoria was next to me, her eyes wide, and Jonah was bopping around behind us, a little unaware of how dire the situation was. I mean, Evan was standing on the stage and *singing about me in front of our entire school*! If I had been quicker, I would've run up onstage and yanked the wires out of the amp, and while I was at it, body-slammed Evan or knocked over the drum kit or something. But I couldn't move; I couldn't cry or cheer or talk. Really, it was like being buried alive, the weight of everything in the world crushing my chest, and Evan had the shovel.

"Audrey, wait! Audrey, wait!"

Now people behind us were singing along, and Evan was totally getting off on the crowd interaction. He used to talk about these kinds of moments sometimes, when we were in his bed underneath his California Angels sheets, the afternoon sun peeking in through the shades. "I want to hold the crowd in my hand," he whispered, and I had giggled and said, "One day you will," but I mean, come *on*. The Do-Gooders had only written three songs by that point. Evan wasn't exactly at the front of the Rock God line.

Until now.

I finally turned my head to look at Victoria, who kept glancing from Evan to me. "Holy fuck," her mouth was saying again and again. But even her foot was tapping the floor. She saw me looking and stopped. I was trying to send her messages with my eyes, like, "I think I'm going to die and I want to leave now, please," but she wasn't getting it. The place was too dark and too loud. Damn those speakers. Why couldn't we listen in the back? Why couldn't I have broken up with Evan tomorrow? Why couldn't I be a procrastinator like Victoria?

I bet he lied about flossing, too.

"Audrey, wait! Audrey, wait! Audrey, wait!" The music had stopped now—it was just Evan and a roomful of his new friends, screaming the words at the top of their lungs. The rest of the band was watching the crowd surge back and forth with the kind of look little kids gave Jonah when he took a part-time job as Santa Claus last Christmas. *Are you really real?* (Side note: Jonah in a Santa costume = Best Christmas Ever.)

"Thank you, we're the Do-Gooders!" Evan shouted, putting his fist in the air as he pulled his guitar off. The rest of the band walked offstage, but Evan? I swear to God, he *strutted.* Just like a chicken.

"Is this really happening?" I grabbed Victoria's hand and held it in front of me. "Is this a dream? Am I dreaming? Are you about to turn into a Cadillac or is a unicorn gonna run through the room?"

"No, you're awake."

I closed my eyes and then opened them wide. "Could you please just lie to me?"

Victoria, without taking her eyes off me, pulled on Jonah's sleeve. "Uh, you might wanna start leading us out of here, sweetie."

"Is Jonah dreaming? Am I in Jonah's dream, maybe?" Jonah was holding on to Victoria's hand, and she had mine, and we were making a little train through the crowd of people.

"No, you're having a meltdown. You're going Chernobyl on me. And make your eyes normal—you look like a fish."

"Is it a bad thing that I can't feel my feet?"

"Now you're just being dramatic."

"Um, excuse me, did you not just see what happened?!"

"Hey, Aud, that was an awesome song!" Kids waved at me as if I'd written The Song. As if I *would* write it!

"Good thing you broke up with him!"

"Audrey, wait! Audrey, wait!"

I heard that one every time I took a step. Everyone was flushed and excited, like they had just come out of a revival and been saved and had to go tell five friends about what they had seen.

"I'm going to kill them," I told Victoria.

"No, you're not." Jonah tugged her to the left and I zigzagged behind them.

"You're right," I agreed. "I'm not going to kill them. I'm going to kill *Evan*."

"That would make a fantastic college entrance essay. 'I Killed My Boyfriend and Still Managed to Maintain a 4.2 GPA and the Lead in the Spring Musical.'"

"Audrey, wait! Audrey, wait!"

"Fuck off, Pete, you asshole!"

"You would never write a song about me, would you, Victoria?"

"I wouldn't write a song like *that* about you, that's for sure."

"The spring musical?" I was momentarily pulled back from the edge. "When have I ever starred in the spring musical?"

"Fuck if I know. Do we even *have* a spring musical?"

"They did *South Pacific* last April."

Victoria laughed through her nose. "I don't think I had to be there to know how it went."

By the time Jonah got us back to the car, I had pulled my hair over my shoulders so that it hung toward my stomach and hid my face. "Buckle up, Cousin Itt," Jonah said into the rearview mirror.

"Now would be a good time to engage those sensitivity controls again, Jonah."

"Got it."

Victoria climbed into the backseat with me and we sat facing each other. "So do I kill myself now, or do I wait and do it in front of Evan so he feels really, really, *really* bad?"

"You're not going to kill yourself. Remember in health class, when they talked about how adolescents drink to mask pain? *That's* what you're gonna do."

"Did they talk about dismembering ex-boyfriends, too?"

"I don't think we'll get to that until anatomy next year."

I laughed as the car lurched forward into traffic. Everyone was looking into our windows and then turning to each other in their cars. I could practically hear what they were saying: "There's the girl who broke up with Evan! Her, right there!"

"Look," Jonah said from the front seat. "Don't worry about this, Aud. It's just some song. It's not like those people weren't gonna find out you broke up, anyway."

"Listen to the man," Victoria agreed. "He speaks the truth."

"Damn straight," Jonah said. "He's gonna be so high later that he probably won't remember the lyrics, anyway."

"Amen," Victoria added. "You wanna go to In-N-Out?"

I rested my head against her shoulder and nodded. She knows me so well it's scary. "Yes. But I have no cash."

"Neither do I. Jonah, Audrey and I have no cash."

"Why aren't I surprised?" he muttered while merging into the intersection.

So while we were in the drive-thru line, while Jonah was yelling our order into the teeny-tiny speaker box, while they were making me a strawberry milkshake instead of the chocolate one I ordered, you probably know what Evan was doing. I mean, he's talked about it in every single interview he's ever given. The A&R guy came out onto the Jukebox loading dock and shook all their hands and said things like "You guys rocked!" and dropped some names of label heads and invited them to the office on Monday morning. "Get ready," he told them. "Your lives are about to change."

No one told me that *my* life was about to change, though. They didn't tell me about paparazzi and magazine editors and publicists and the lawyer my parents would have to hire. They certainly didn't tell me that all of you people would know my name by the end of the year.

And that's all you really know: my name.

But not anymore, kiddos.

Here's my side of the story.

2

"You can always see it comin', but you can never stop it. . . ."

—Cowboy Junkies, "Bea's Song
(River Song Trilogy: Part II)"

DESPITE THE INSANITY OF THAT SHOW, things calmed down pretty quickly. It's like when something horrible happens to you and you wonder, How will I ever live another minute without freaking out about this? And then a minute will go by without you thinking about it, and then an hour, and pretty soon your life goes back to normal and you can't even remember what had you all upset.

Apparently, everyone else at that night's show had the same reaction, too; Evan's song died down by the time school started, thank God. People weren't even talking about it by the first day, because Jennifer Epstein threw up in the girl's bathroom three times before lunch, and people were convinced she was either pregnant or bulimic. Either way, it was exciting, and now when people said, "Audrey, wait!" in the hallway, they meant just that. No irony required. (Oh, and it turns out that Jennifer just had some bad sushi the night before.)

Evan and the Do-Gooders never showed up to start their senior year, and I heard a bunch of rumors about that. No one said anything to me directly, since Victoria had made it clear that Evan was *persona non grata* in our little world, but still, you know how rumors are. They slip around corners and slide under doors. Someone said that he and the band had dropped out of school and moved to Japan to record their first CD, and they were already famous there. Others said that the A&R guy had signed them that night, then dropped them on Monday morning after his free drinks wore off and he came to his senses.

But the prevailing view was that the band had dropped out of school and were being tutored at home so they could rehearse more. I was curious, I admit, but mostly just relieved that I didn't have to see Evan in the halls every day. It's like every breaker-upper's dream that the other person will just magically disappear so you never have to have an awkward moment with them, and except for that one night and that one song, Evan was gone. (Confession time: I did Google the Do-Gooders a couple of times, but nothing new ever came up besides their outdated MySpace page that Victoria had helped them create.)

Anyway, I managed to survive the first few months of school with a minimum of drama (save for a stupid computer that managed to delete my entire paper on *Death of a Salesman* the night before it was due).

Then the Saturday before Halloween, Victoria came over for two reasons: (1) I was gonna help her dye her hair hot pink. Not the whole head, just a landing strip down the middle of her scalp so it would look like she had a Mohawk. Victoria is brave and awesome and all of that, but shaving part of her head held no appeal for her. Hair dye would have to suffice.

And (2) it was a year to the day that I had first talked to Evan at Charles Hurty's Halloween party. I know how Ev likes to explain it in interviews. Everyone and their mother likes to mention it to me when he talks about me in public, which is just wonderful. Like I don't know what happened in our relationship? But yeah, Evan likes to tell this part:

"We were at a Halloween party. She was standing in front of me and our eyes met and it was like . . . *wow*."

Sweet, right? So ideal and romantic and exactly what a million girls are secretly hoping will happen to them one day when they're the lucky ones to meet Evan.

All I can say is this: Bring Handi Wipes.

Our eyes met as he bent over to puke foamy keg beer on the boots that perfectly matched my go-go dancer costume. *That's* how it happened. And Victoria never got over the fact that the boots were ruined. "They were *vintage!*" she moaned for six months afterwards.

My dad was carving a pumpkin when I came downstairs to wait for Victoria, nearly tripping over our cat, Bendomolena, and killing myself. I guess you could say that Bendy is a cat, but she's not so much a cat as a hair ball the size of a suitcase. I'm not kidding. The mailman is terrified of her, which is so ridiculous because (a) she's not a pit bull; (b) she weighs approximately twenty thousand pounds (Bendomolena couldn't lunge for his ankles even if she wanted to); and (c) she's scared of everything that didn't originate in our house. One time Victoria brought her pet hamster Charlotte (the last in a long line of hamsters) over to run around in her little plastic ball, and oh my Lord. I don't want to go into details, but let's just say that Bendomolena had to temporarily go on anti-anxiety medication and Charlotte the Hamster refused to set paw outside of her plastic ball ever again.

"Bendy, away from the stairs!" my dad yelled as I managed to catch myself before falling to my death.

"Did you want her to move any time soon?" I asked. "Because it probably won't happen until Christmas."

"Ha ha, Miss Comedy." He looked up from the pumpkin he was carving and straightened his glasses. "Nice shoes."

"You think?" I did a little twirl in my flamingo slippers. They were so big that I had to waddle everywhere. Just like Bendomolena.

"They're stylin'."

"Dad, if you never say 'stylin" again, it'll be too soon."

"Can I still say things are cool?"

"Not around me, please."

"That's cool."

I sighed. "Where's Mom?"

"Out buying candy for when the neighborhood kids come begging tomorrow night."

"Um, she left you alone with the pumpkin?" My dad, well-meaning as he is, has almost been forced to retire from pumpkin carving, thanks to the dramatic and colorful Massive Blood Loss Incident of Halloween Three Years Ago. Let's just say one should never carve a pumpkin while watching the Steelers lose.

As an answer, I got the Dad Look.

"I only ask because I love," I told him. "How are we on Band-Aids?"

"Isn't Victoria coming over?" *Stab-stab-stab, slice.*

"Any minute." I sat down at the table and watched for signs of blood. "Y'know, I can make a tourniquet using a shoelace. I learned how in Girl Scouts."

"I thought you dropped out of the Girl Scouts."

"Not before the lesson on first aid. Besides, the uniforms were itchy."

"Of course they were. How's the pumpkin?" He turned it so I could see its triangle eyes and nose and crooked mouth. He's a traditionalist like that. "Does it look even?"

"It's just gonna get smashed in the street like every year," I said as I ate some pumpkin seeds off the cookie sheet.

"Humor me, Aud."

"Best pumpkin ever!"

"Your lack of faith is very distracting," my dad pointed out.

I eyed the pumpkin, which had a few unintentional gashes where its ears should have been. "Believe me, Dad, I can tell."

Victoria let herself in and came into the kitchen just as my dad accidentally shaved off one of the pumpkin's teeth. "Hey, I thought your dad wasn't allowed to carve pumpkins anymore."

My dad pushed his glasses back up on his nose. "Hi, Victoria."

"Hi, Mr. Cuttler." My parents have asked Victoria a bajillion times to call them Henry and Carol, but she says it would feel too weird. "Still got all ten fingers?"

I waved the phone in her face by way of greeting. "Did you bring it?"

She pulled the bottle of Marvelous Magenta out of her bag. "Ready and waiting for you, my dear."

"Dad, I'm going upstairs so we can dye Victoria's hair. If anything happens, just remember to raise the cut above the heart, okay?"

Victoria was peering around my shoulder. "Does that pumpkin have *ears*?"

"Battle wound," I told her.

"Oh. Pretty hard-core, Mr. Cuttler. I like that."

But my dad was too busy trying to fix the pumpkin's now-toothless grin to respond, so I grabbed her arm and pushed her toward the stairs. "Goodbye," I told my dad. "We're going far, far away from here."

"Take Bendomolena with you," he said as we trooped up the stairs, stepping over my land mass of a cat.

I love my room. Victoria loves my room, too, but she'll never admit it. My parents don't exactly love it, but they've decided to accept its fate as eternally messy. Well, not so much messy as busy. I have a very *busy* room. CDs are in every corner and on every surface, and there's a bunch of cut-up magazines all over the floor, where I put them after hacking them up and making collages of all my favorite bands. I thought it would be really cool to have one whole wall be a huge collage, and about one-fourth is covered so far. I can do whatever I want in here, and sometimes when it's the middle of the night and it feels like no one else in the world is awake but me and I'm cutting up another picture and an amazing song comes on the stereo, I could die happy.

Evan always said that my room creeped him out, that the walls were watching him or something. That's so like him to think that everything's watching him, waiting to see what he'll do next. What an egomaniac. I hate him.

Victoria still hated him, too. "So . . . I believe it's officially a year to the day since you met Fuckhead?"

I sighed. "You're the most indelicate person I've ever met."

"You mean except for the guy who *ruined* those *beautiful* vintage boots"—she still wasn't over it—"and wrote a mean song about you?"

"The Song of Which We Must Not Speak," I reminded her. "The Song That Will Die an Obscure Death and That No One Will Ever Hear Again."

"Of course. So are you gonna burn anything in effigy to commemorate the day Ev puked on your boots? A Ken doll? Anything?"

I put on the gross latex gloves that came with the hair dye and shook the bottle a couple of times. "Nope. I have to work. You know that."

Okay. I've been trying to avoid this part, but it's not a secret anymore. It's true. I work at an ice cream shop—excuse me, *shoppe*—at the mall. That in itself is not so bad, except for three things: (1) I hate the mall; (2) I hate all the customers; and (3) I'm forced to wear a bright pink hat and T-shirt that say . . . are you ready for this?

Scooper Dooper.

If there is any justice in the world, the first major meteorite to ever strike the Earth will score a direct hit on the Scooper Dooper. I might even become an astrophysicist just so I can help move that plan along. But until then, CDs and concert tickets and gasoline aren't cheap, and my parents are into that whole "earn it!" mentality, so I work.

My job sucks the most suck that has ever sucked.

"Maybe you could burn the Scooper Dooper and pretend it's Evan," Victoria offered.

"That would require a lot more planning than I have energy for," I said. "Tilt your head back."

She did. "I can see up your nose."

"Ew, gross! Stop looking!"

She squeezed her eyes shut and giggled. "Jonah and I are gonna go see *The Exorcist* downtown. You should blow off work and come with us."

"Nah, I don't like paying money to watch heads spin. Or to be the third wheel."

"Shut up, you're not the third wheel."

"If you and Jonah were a school dance, I'd be the parental chaperone."

"Yeah, except for the fact that you let us make out in front of you."

"Which is great fun for me."

She opened her eyes. "Do we make you uncomfortable?"

Kinda. I don't know. Maybe just lonely. "No, it's cool. Besides, someone has to be there in case one of you swallows the other one."

Victoria started to laugh. "Rest assured that there has never been, nor will there ever be, swallowing. *Ever.*"

"Oh, Jesus Christ, Victoria!" I cried. "So many details that I don't need!" I tried to cover my ears but my gloved hands were covered in Marvelous Magenta.

"You love it—you know you do." She was still laughing.

Have you ever been through a breakup while your best friend is, like, practically engaged to the guy she says she's gonna marry? It's awkward. I mean, on the one hand I love Victoria and Jonah to pieces and I'm excited to be a bridesmaid and buy little kid-sized drum sets for their sure-to-be adorable babies, but on the other hand . . .

There's no nice way to say this: It blows like hurricane season.

"We just need to get you a date," she decided after calming down. "You need to go up to someone in the hallway and make out with them on Monday."

"Oh, yes, because the options are limitless in our school. I don't know why it didn't occur to me sooner."

"Hey, school is where I met Jonah!" she protested.

"One out of fifteen hundred. What fantastic odds."

Victoria settled back in the chair and I could see the wheels spinning in her head. Never a good sign. "What about James?" she finally said.

"James? James, the guy I work with?" She was too funny. "James who takes ice cream scooping more seriously than anyone should? James who almost had a nervous breakdown when the chocolate and rainbow sprinkles accidentally got mixed together? That James?"

"He has a good work ethic," she countered. "And he's cute."

"Hello, I'm not thirty. I don't want a good work ethic yet. I just want someone who can form complete sentences."

"Which he can totally do! I've heard him! He says, 'Hello, how can I help you today at the Scooper Dooper?' It doesn't get much more complete than that, Audrey." She paused. "And he's cute."

"He's a smidge of cute," I acknowledged after a minute.

"No, Aud, he's *cute*. One hundred percent cute."

"If he's so cute, then why don't *you* make out with him on Monday morning?"

"Because, as I've pointed out, I'm already with the best guy in the world."

I laughed through my nose. "That's fabulous news for the rest of us."

3

"She started shakin' to that fine, fine music!"

—The Velvet Underground, "Rock & Roll"

THREE HOURS LATER, Victoria had a sorta-kinda Mohawk that she proclaimed her best hairdo ever; my dad had finished carving the pumpkin with only a small flesh wound; my mom had brought a dozen bags of grossly misnamed "Fun Size" candy bars home; Bendomolena had moved half an inch on the stairs; and I left for work with strict instructions to bring home a pint of Coffee Dream ice cream for my parents. (They seem to be the only ones benefiting from my employee discount, which is just another cruel irony in my life.)

The Scooper Dooper was empty. It was the end of October, it was starting to rain outside, and anyone with any sense was getting hot chocolate or coffee from the food court upstairs. Nobody wanted Misty Moroccan Mint in a waffle cone that day. (And between you and me, they shouldn't want it on any day, because it's just plain disgusting.)

"I already cleaned out the water wells and reorganized the overstock," James said to me as I clocked in and tied on my apron. He always tucks his work shirt in, which makes me a bit nuts.

"And a happy hello to you, too," I said.

"And I think we're low on waffle cones, so I left a note for the manager to reorder some on Monday morning."

"What a relief."

My sarcasm wasn't registering with him at all. "I *know*," he replied. "You know how customers are about waffle cones."

"It's one of the great injustices of my life that I *do* know, James." Okay, I even out-bitched myself on that one, I admit it.

It's not that James is a bad guy. I mean, he's not at all. He's always polite and nice to little kids after they drop their double scoops on the floor. When the old people come in at five o'clock for their dessert, he always speaks loud into their hearing aids. But he's just really quiet and only talks about work at work. I tried to fish around when I first started working with him, asking him about movies and books and stuff, but he just stuttered and stammered and finally said, "I think we need more butter pecan."

What am I supposed to do with that?

He's really skinny, too. Like, super model skinny. And super tall. Once I saw him running down the hall between second and third periods and I thought his legs would snap out from underneath him and he would shatter into pieces that would slide all the way down the hall to my locker. It's kind of sad, though. I don't think he has any friends. If I didn't work with him, I wouldn't know who he was. He's the kid in the yearbook who everyone sees and says, "Who's that? Does he even go to our school?"

But what can you do, you know? I tried to talk to him and all I got was "butter pecan." There's not a lot to build on.

So when I work with James, I try to pick tasks that play to our strengths. My job is Music Supervisor. He is In Charge Of

Everything Else. We're allowed to play the radio there, so I always switch it to KUXV, the college station that plays the good music. We're supposed to keep it on the adult-contemporary station, but I can't work at the Scooper Dooper and listen to Céline Dion at the same time. It's just not gonna happen, I'm sorry. I have my limits.

I flipped the station as soon as I put my hat on, and I could see James already getting twitchy about breaking the radio station rule, but he didn't say anything (just like always). Pretty soon I was humming along with the Ramones and "Blitzkrieg Bop"-ping to the register whenever somebody wanted a room-temperature Coke with a non-bendy straw. These customers are nothing if not picky.

We worked pretty much in silence for the next couple of hours as the sun set outside and the mall got more crowded with couples and families coming out of the movie theaters next door. Judging from the number of guys practicing their karate moves on each other, most of them had seen some kung-fu movie. The DJ on the radio was doing a good job of playing decent music, and James and I stayed at opposite ends of the store. A whole gaggle of kids and their parents came in around eight forty-five, fifteen minutes until the mall closed at nine. (It never fails that people will walk in at the last possible minute. I suspect it's a major conspiracy to annoy me.) It was a normal Saturday—nothing too exciting, nothing crazy.

I really miss normal Saturdays.

The kids and their parents were all wearing bright blue T-shirts that said YOUTH CHOIR GLEE-A-THON! on the front, which just goes to show how little parents love their kids, if they're willing to let them wear a shirt like that in public. James, who lives for this sort of scooping action, was already reaching for sugar cones, and I was about to ask the first customer if he wanted a free sample (said with a Scooper Dooper smile, naturally) when I heard my favorite sarcastic DJ talking through the speakers.

"Okay, someone just put this in my hand. It's a new single— we got it on Friday. Local band, the Do-Gooders, blah, blah, blah. Call in and tell me if you hate it. I haven't heard it yet. It's called 'Audrey, Wait!'"

The ice cream scoop fell out of my hand and hit the floor so hard that the handle broke. I could hear the first chords and even though I had only heard them strung together once before, I knew the song by heart.

"You said your piece and now I've got to say mine! I had you and you strung me on the *liiiiiinnnnneeeeee!*"

When I first heard the song at the Do-Gooders show last summer, I thought that was the worst moment of my life. Wrong-ola. *This* was the worst moment ever.

"Straw-berr-eee! Straw-berr-eee!" The kids were starting to chant in a non-gleeful way, completely unaware of the fact that I had gone numb. My Scooper Dooper smile was still plastered on my face and I couldn't force it to go away.

James gave me an odd look, handed me another scooper, and said, "Scoop now, think later."

"But . . . are you *hearing this?*" How could he be so calm! It was outrageous. "Do you know what this is?"

"Um, no. Just scoop now, think later," he repeated, like he was the Dalai Lama of frozen dairy desserts or something. I wondered if he wasn't aware of the whole dramatic situation and was just sharing his personal credo with me. "Hi, sir, how can I help you?"

I turned to the first kid in front of me and I could tell I was freaking him out. "What flavor?" I asked through my teeth, even as Evan's words were spilling out of the radio and falling all over me.

"Audrey, wait! Audrey, wait! Audrey, wait!" It sounded as good on the radio as it had that night at the Jukebox. Goddamnit.

"Straw-berr-eee! Straw-berr-ee!" The kids were now singing the words in time to the chorus and I suddenly understood why people sometimes show up to work with a gun and a grudge. "Dad, this is a good song!" one of the littlest girls said, her pigtails flying every which way as she clapped her hands.

"It is," her dad agreed.

"You crucified my heart, took every part, and hung them out to *drrrrryyyyyyy!*"

"I've heard better," I offered.

"Excuse me?"

"Nothing. What size cone, sir?"

Three minutes and forty-nine seconds later (yes, I counted), the song was over and the Gleeful People were halfway served. I could barely hear the DJ over their noise. "Wow," he was saying. "I gotta tell you, we get a lot of crap here at the station, but this was good. And you're all calling in right now, too. I like this. I like this a lot. We're gonna play it again next hour, stick around."

So there I was, my ex-boyfriend on the radio, chanting my name like it was an insult; a gaggle of Glee-People in front of me; wearing a hot pink hat and shirt that had the words SCOOPER DOOPER written across my chest-in-training, with ice cream sticking to my wrists and arms.

My cell phone was ringing in the break room—Victoria's ring. I'd have known it anywhere. James kept giving me funny looks and

I kept my head down, cheeks on fire, trying to scoop and serve and get everyone the hell out of there. *"She couldn't believe what she heard at all!"* I heard Lou Reed and the Velvet Underground singing on my cell phone. *"You know her life was saved by rock and roll!"*

Lou Reed, you liar.

By the time James and I got everyone served and out the door, I was ready to take up smoking and drinking and whatever vice I could get my hands on without being arrested. "Oh my God!" I screamed at him, and he took a step backwards. "What was *that*? Did you hear that!"

"It sounded pretty good," he offered. "That's cool your name's in a song. My mom's name is Mandy and so everyone always asks if that one Barry Mani—"

"It's not just my name, it's *about* me!" I shrieked. Two customers who looked ready to enter the store saw me freaking out and turned around to leave. Wise move on their part. "And it's on the radio!"

"Oh."

"It's my ex-boyfriend's band and he wrote it about me and it's on the radio and *I'm wearing a Scooper Dooper T-shirt!*"

"Um, do you think maybe you should sit down?" James pointed to the stool by the register. "You look a little upset."

"I'm a ball of rage right now, James," I told him. "Sitting isn't gonna do much."

"At least it's a good song," he pointed out. "It's really catchy. I liked it."

"How many people do you think were listening?" I asked him. "Like, a thousand? Ten thousand?"

"Maybe more."

"More?"

James looked like I was about to shoot him. "It's a popular show. Maybe fifteen thousand?"

"*Fifteen thousand???*"

"Maybe?" Then he actually winced. Perhaps he was waiting for me to explode all over the Scooper Dooper.

All I can say is this: Thank God for Victoria. Across the mall and out the glass doors, I saw Jonah's car swoop up to the curb. Victoria jumped out and started running toward me in all her pink-Mohawked glory. And let it be said that Victoria does not run. She failed P.E. freshman year because she refused to run the mile. Maybe if her house was on fire or something, she'd hustle, but it'd take an act of God or nature to make her move her ass.

Or a song on the radio.

Her boots were clomping on the mall floors as she came running, and James's eyes widened. "Wow," he said. "She's on a mission."

"Audrey!" Her face was flushed as she charged into the store like she was in Spain, the bulls nipping at her heels. "Did you hear that?"

"James here thinks that fifteen thousand people heard that!" I cried.

"I tried . . . calling . . . and you . . . didn't answer. . . . Why?" She bent over to catch her breath and I heard her wheeze a quiet "Fuckin' . . . hell . . ."

"I was scooping for the Glee People," I told her.

"The . . . *who* . . . People?"

"Some choir thing. Do you need water?" Leave it to Victoria to get winded and possibly pass out during my crisis.

She waved off the water and sank down in a chair. "This is huge," she said once she caught her breath. "Everyone at school heard it."

I sank down next to her and pulled off my hat as Jonah ambled into the store. "I just got the *el presidente* of parking spots," he announced. "Hey, Aud. Pretty fuckin' crazy about that song, huh?"

"Um, Audrey, I think we gotta close soon and I don't think they're allowed—"

"No worries, kid, we're not here to take the loot," Victoria said over her shoulder. Then she turned back to me and whispered. "Did you hear all those complete sentences?"

I feigned amazement. "You're right, Victoria," I whispered back. "Now would be the perfect time to pick up a guy. Will you focus for a minute, please! How do you know everyone heard?"

"I got, like, a million IMs and two million text messages. It almost crashed my computer." Her eyes were wide and shocked. "Audrey. It sounded so good on the radio! You're going to be famous!"

"No, I'm not," I hissed. "It's just a little college station—"

"They stream their broadcast live online," she pointed out.

"No one outside of our school is going to care that it's about me."

Across from us, Jonah was eyeing both the ice cream bins and James. "Hey, man, what's up?" He offered his hand to James for one of those complicated guy-handshake things, but James had no idea what he was doing and got it all muddled up. Someone could have lost an eye.

Lucky for him, Victoria missed the whole exchange. "Sharon Eggleston texted me that she was up visiting her sister's sorority house at USC and they all heard it and Sharon told them that she was friends with you and everyone started freaking out."

I paused. "There's so much wrong with that sentence that I don't even know where to begin."

"Like?"

"Sharon Eggleston's sister got into USC?"

"I know, right? Apparently her parents are alumni."

"And when did you start texting with Sharon?"

"Just today. I guess she got my number from someone else after she couldn't get ahold of you."

"Sharon told her sister we were friends?" I asked.

"I know, it's crazy, she obviously drank an entire keg last night or something. But Audrey! People really love that song!" Victoria's eyes were shining just like Sharon's lip gloss. "I bet your cell phone exploded from all the messages. I could barely get through half the time."

James was scurrying around behind the counter, rinsing scoopers and starting to close the register. "I gotta help him," I told Victoria.

"Just think," she said, sinking back in her chair, "everyone is gonna be kissing your ass at school."

"Oh, joy."

"And Sharon Eggleston is gonna go batshit crazy." Victoria clapped her hands together with glee. "Oh my God, I cannot *wait*. Monday is gonna rock."

"Sharon Eggleston?" James said. "That's the girl that always comes in here."

Victoria and I glanced at each other. "She always comes in here?" I asked. "Really?"

"Yeah, usually on your days off. She's the one with the . . . I don't know, the flippy hair, I guess you could call it." James mimed tossing his hair over his shoulder.

Victoria and I exchanged another look: *Oh, really?*

I snorted as I went around the counter and began counting the change in the register. "Sharon Eggleston had a huge crush on Evan before I started going out with him," I told James. "She's probably plotting my imminent demise. Be prepared to find my body in the freezer."

"Uh . . ." James's eyes widened.

"I'm *kidding!*" I told him. Apparently the word *sarcasm* had never entered his lexicon. "Only kidding, I swear."

"Aud has a weird sense of humor," Jonah pointed out to James. He was still eyeing the ice cream and I stopped counting my register long enough to scoop him a cone of Choco-Nuts-a-Lot. "Awesome." He grinned. "Thanks, Aud."

Then I threw a rag at Victoria. "Here," I told her. "Please do something useful so I can get the hell out of here."

She wrinkled her nose, but started wiping down tables anyway. And when she was in the middle of the third table, and after I counted the change in the register twice and it still wasn't balancing out, the song came on the radio again. "This song is already on its way to being number one on tonight's countdown," the DJ said. "And you heard it here first on KUXV, 98.5!" But we only heard the first few bars because I reached up and turned the stereo off.

The silence in the store was even louder.

After we closed and locked up and James almost got the key stuck in the front door and we had to wedge it out, I walked with Victoria and Jonah to our cars. "So, the second-most exciting thing that happened today?" Victoria said. "James."

"James?" Jonah and I both asked.

"He was really talking to you a lot," Victoria pointed out, and nudged me in the ribs. "At least he can say he knew you before you were famous, right?"

"Vic-tor-ia!" I cried. "I'm not famous! Remember that one girl last year who got a perfect 2400 on her SATs and she ended up in that article in the *L.A. Times*? She's more famous than me."

"Perfect 2400? Pfft." Victoria waved her hand in front of her face. "I could do that in my sleep. Besides, cool sells better than brains."

Jonah laughed and nodded. "She's right."

Victoria grinned and linked her arm with his. She *loved* being right. "Anyway, I'm just saying that James kept looking at you all night."

"I think it's his lazy eye."

"Did he talk to you out of his lazy eye, too?"

Okay, that one made me laugh, I admit it. "When the song first came on the radio," I told them, "I totally froze behind the counter and he came up to me and said, 'Scoop now, think later.'"

"Words on a bumper sticker," Jonah said, nodding his approval.

"Embroidery on a hand towel," Victoria added. "See, he's very calm, very Eastern philosophy, very Buddha-like."

"He couldn't be more Irish," I pointed out.

"Buddha-like in *spirit*. When everyone asks you how you stayed humble, you can say it was because of James."

I shot her a look, but couldn't really hide a smile. "How I stayed *humble?*" was all I said.

"Gimme a break, I'm still giddy with excitement. I'll come up with a better example later."

After they walked me to my car, I got in and locked the doors and waited to see them drive off. I could see that Victoria had scooted closer to Jonah and he had his arm around her shoulders, and he was laughing about something (probably the Buddha comment). They both looked so happy.

The inside of my car was really, really cold.

I reached into my bag and, for the first time that night, pulled out my cell phone. The message light was flashing like a strobe and I flipped it open and saw that my text message box was full. I only recognized half of the names, but they almost all started this way: "OMG HEARD SONG CALL ME!!!!! LOL!!!!!" I didn't even bother checking the voice mails.

But what I did do was scroll through my phone book and stop on one of the most familiar names in there. Evan Dennison. Although I hardly remembered any phone numbers besides my own, I knew all of his by heart. And then I wondered why I had never deleted him, why he was still taking up this space, why he was still everywhere.

I acted before I could stop myself. I dialed his cell phone number from memory, just to see if I could, and then I let it ring. My heart was in my ears and toes and everywhere except where it belonged, and after four rings, I braced for his message. I wondered if it was still the same, that low stoner laugh followed by the words "If you don't know who you've reached, don't leave a message. Otherwise, talk."

But that cold animatronic voice came on: "The number you have reached is no longer in service." And my hands were shaking and for some reason—or maybe for too many reasons—I wanted to cry.

So I did.

Afterwards, I drove myself home in silence past Halloween decorations and lit pumpkins and dried my face and checked my eyes in the rearview mirror before going inside. My parents were on the couch and Bendomolena was still in the exact same spot on the staircase. When I walked in, everyone except Bendy looked at me expectantly. "Well?" my dad said.

Oh Jesus, they had heard the song. They had heard the song and listened to the lyrics and then got totally paranoid and hacked into my email account and figured out that Evan and I had slept together, and now I was going to have to sit through some intervention where my parents talked about sperm and condoms and responsibility and teenage pregnancy statistics. And then they'd probably ship me off to one of those wilderness camps where they give you a name like Little Running Bear and make you scavenge for food to build up your self-esteem until you swear to be abstinent for the rest of your natural life.

I'll tell you this right now: me and nature? Not so much.

"Um, yeah?" I said. I kept my coat on just in case there were two burly men waiting to drag me off to some nameless desert camp.

My dad held up a spoon expectantly. "Where's the Coffee Dream?"

Oh. Ice cream.

Right.

4

"Making islands where no islands should go . . ."

—Death Cab for Cutie, "Transatlanticism"

I SPENT MOST OF SUNDAY not returning any phone calls, not writing emails or text messages, or on that note, doing any of my homework. Instead, I ate whole-wheat pancakes with my mom, sat in my room and cut up two magazines, then made a very explicit playlist and CD case for my "Suck It Up!" mix. A random sampling:

Track 3: No Doubt, "Just a Girl"—You can never have too much sarcastic girl anger too early in the morning.

Track 11: Jay-Z, "99 Problems"—Unlike Mr. Z, I only had one problem, not 99 of them. (But either way, it's super awesome for driving.)

Track 8: Bob Marley & the Wailers, "Trenchtown Rock"—Because the opening lyrics are "One good thing about music / When it hits, you feel no pain." I mean, c'mon. Do you really need me to explain further?

All of this took some time because my phone kept ringing every two minutes or so and of course I had to look at the caller ID. By the fifty-seventh ring, though, I realized that I barely recognized any of the numbers, so I turned it off. Victoria knew my parents' n u m-ber, so if something urgent happened, like if Sharon Eggleston lost all her hair in a tragic oil spill or if Evan got nominated for a Grammy, I knew Victoria would know how to find me.

Bendomolena waddled into my room later on and settled herself on top of a pile of magazines, suffocating the cover photo with her stomach. "Why couldn't you do that to Evan?" I asked her. "You had plenty of opportunities."

Bendomolena never liked Evan. That was my first inkling that things weren't cool. My second inkling came during one of our marathon phone conversations. Actually, calling them "conversations" is generous. They were more like monologues by Evan, during which I said "yeah" and "uh-huh" and watched *Steven's Untitled Rock Show* on Fuse with the sound off while Evan went on and on about why his drummer sucked.

Finally, one night, I got bored. And fed up. And annoyed. So I did a little Evan experiment. "Hey," I said casually. "Bendomolena's on fire."

"Cool. So yeah, Jon wants to do a drum solo and we were just like, 'Dude, *no*.'"

I looked across the room at Bendomolena who was, quite obviously, not on fire, and was instead lolling on her back. "Wow, she's really flammable," I said, and Bendomolena opened one eye. "Who knew something that little could burn up so furiously?"

"I know, right? So get this. *He* said—"

"Hey, Ev, I better go get the fire extinguisher. She's toasty."

"What? Fire extinguisher? What the hell are you talking about, Aud?"

I sighed and avoided the stony gaze of Bendomolena, who

sensed she was a pawn in my game. "Nothing, I'm just kidding. But I gotta go, okay? My mom needs me for something."

So of course I called Victoria right after we hung up. "I told him that my cat was on fire and he didn't even *hear* me!" I cried. "On *fire*, Victoria! And he didn't care!"

She paused for a minute. "Aud," she finally said, "that is so fucking twisted that I don't even know where to start."

"Okay, I know, but it had to be drastic."

"That's not drastic, that's sadistic. You've got your *–tics* mixed up."

"Will you please focus on the issue at hand? Evan doesn't listen to what I'm saying!"

I could hear her sigh loudly. "And this is news?"

"Should I break up with him?"

"Do you want to break up with him?"

"I don't know." I did my best dramatic sigh. "Distract me from feeling miserable."

"Umm . . . ummm . . . I got new shoes."

"Woo."

"Wanna come over and try them on?"

I kinda did. "I'll be there in ten minutes," I said, and my trouble with Evan was forgotten for the moment.

Evan and I had spent hours on and in my bed while my parents were at work. Sometimes we'd sprawl opposite each other while he'd strum his guitar and try to think up words that rhymed with *Bendomolena*. The only time he actually succeeded was when he accidentally stepped on her tail and then spontaneously burst into song: "Bendomolena! / I didn't see ya!" And I was like, "Hi, you almost severed my cat's tail, thanks."

What kind of guy writes a song about stepping on your cat while she's yowling in pain? I should've known then.

But it wasn't all bad, of course. I mean, I had *loved* him, I really had. There were better times, the quiet moments when no one was talking and even our breath was the same, rising and falling under our tent of blankets like we were made to breathe with each other, for each other. It's funny how bed and pillows and covers can change a conversation. Words turn quiet and you mean more and say less. It's like you can build your own little world, Population: 2.

Evan would play with my hair and wrap it over his wrist and reel me toward him until our lips touched. They were small moments but I could only hold them like water in my hands before he was slipping away, pulled back by melodies or friends or rehearsals, leaving my hands empty and my heart too full to hold alone.

5

"To readjust you've got to trust that all the fuss is just a minor thing. . . ."

—Red Hot Chili Peppers, "Minor Thing"

ON MONDAY MORNING, I pulled a little illegal trick and drove to school wearing headphones so I could listen to the "Suck It Up!" mix as much as possible to psych myself up for the day. (My car's speaker fund was steadily being drained for the "Ooh, I want that CD!" cause.) I couldn't even handle the radio, since KUXV was playing "Audrey, Wait!" almost every hour. (Okay, I cheated a little and listened to the nightly Top 5 countdown—the song was number one—but you would've done the same.) The night before, when I was supposed to be sleeping but instead was lying awake looking at the glow-in-the-dark stars on my ceiling, I tried to think of how long the song's popularity would last. Maybe it was a one-week thing, a novelty that would wear off as soon as the next big band broke. It wasn't like Evan was on MTV or in *Teen Vogue* or anything like that, right? This was just a local thing, a hometown boy making good.

By 8:01 A.M., that theory was shot straight out of the water.

Victoria saw me walking out of the school parking lot and came running down to meet me. "Hi!" she said breathlessly. "You're not gonna believe this!"

"Based on the events of the past forty-eight hours," I told her, "I'm gonna believe it. And good morning to you, too."

"Whatever. Hi. You suck for not answering your phone, by the way. But I was talking to Chris Collins and his brother's a freshman at Rutgers and he said—"

"Hi, Audrey!" Sharon Eggleston called across the quad, waving to me with that perfect bone-china wrist of hers.

I blinked. "Did Sharon Eggleston just say hi to me?"

"Of course she did," Victoria huffed. "She's moving in on you. Prepare to be invaded. Did you ever call her back?"

"No, of course not. What am I supposed to say? 'Hi, you had a huge crush on my ex-boyfriend, let's be beffies and go shopping'?" We were walking toward my locker and I was painfully aware of the fact that many, many people were staring at me, including a group of freshman girls that sounded like they sucked helium. "Hi, Audrey!" they cried out as I passed.

"Hi . . . ?" I said, not sure how to respond to three people who looked like they were about to either spontaneously combust or eat my head.

Victoria, of course, kept moving forward. "So anyway, Chris Collins IM'd me last night and he said that his brother's going to school in New Jersey—"

"Why Jersey?" I interrupted. I couldn't help myself. "I mean, why didn't he go to New York and spend time frolicking in the city? That's what I'd do if I were him."

Victoria paused and I could tell she was trying not to smile. "Did you just say 'frolic'?"

"Is it not a word?"

"Who the hell says 'frolic'?"

I spun the lock on my locker and waited for it to stick like it always did on 33. "I say frolic," I told her. "And more people should."

"They should *say* frolic or actually frolic?"

"Both."

"Hey, Aud."

"Hi, Audrey."

"Audrey, wait!"

Victoria glanced at her watch. "Wow, ninety seconds before the first 'Audrey, wait!' I was way off."

I shoved my geometry book and copy of *The Awakening* into my locker and pulled out my American history text. "On a scale of one to ten, how hard do you think today's gonna be?"

Victoria bit her lip and leaned against the wall. "Honestly?"

"Like you've ever been anything but. C'mon, pretend you're the Russian judge."

"Pretty fucking hard."

"I don't think the Russian judge would say that."

"I believe the correct term is 'Soviet Republic'. And I'll say 9.8."

I sighed. "And tomorrow?"

"Worse."

I looked into her round eyes and I could tell that she knew something I didn't. "What, exactly, did Chris Collins tell you?"

She lit up like a Christmas tree. "Damnit, you and your frolicking got me all distracted! So his brother's in Jersey, right?"

"And not frolicking in New York."

"Right-o. But Chris did say that his brother emailed him yesterday to tell him 'Audrey, Wait!' is playing on the Rutgers radio station, too. I guess it's really popular because people keep requesting it and Chris said that his brother said you can hear it in all the dorm rooms when they party."

Now, I know that, physiologically speaking, my heart didn't stop when Victoria said that. I know that's impossible, because I'm still standing here today. But it did some flippy thing it's never done before, that's for sure.

Victoria mistook my silence as permission for her to continue. "And there was a picture and an article about the Do-Gooders in the local paper. That's how his brother recognized them, because he had gym one year with Evan. Was it gym? I can't remember. Maybe it was geology. Or geography. It wasn't geometry because—"

"Victoria!" I screeched. "Did you hear what you just said?"

"I know!" Her eyes were radiating a weird energy, like she had been initiated into a cult and wanted me read a pamphlet. "Isn't this amazing? I mean, they play local shows, whatever. But now they're *nationally known*! And so are *you*!"

"How old do you think you have to be to have a heart attack?" I asked her.

"At least thirty-five."

"I'm about to break the record."

"That's really not gonna help your anonymity."

"Did they talk about me in that article?" I squeaked. I suddenly wanted to be back in my bedroom with the door shut tight and my "Suck it Up!" mix playing on ten.

"I don't know. Good Lord, Aud, that vein in your forehead is about to burst."

I took a deep breath. (I happen to be very self-conscious about that vein. It's not exactly my best physical feature.) "Victoria, this is insane."

"No, it's not."

"Do you think they'll have that paper at the bookstore?"

"I dunno. Don't they have to, like, ship them here?"

"*We have to get to the bookstore!*" My skin was suddenly freezing while every muscle underneath it was on fire. "We can take my car."

"Okay, all right. At least wait until after third period. I heard a rumor about a pop quiz in bio and if I miss it, I'm screwed."

"You're in a three-way tie for the highest GPA in the school," I pointed out. "One quiz will not kill you."

"Yeah, but I'll be goddamned if Sharon Eggleston steals my best friend *and* my rightful spot as valedictorian."

"Okay, fine, but after third?"

"I promise."

I was going to add something about how Sharon Eggleston would never steal me away when I saw James walk past me, alone as usual. He had headphones on and was carrying the same black-washed-to-gray hoodie he always wears, and I moved to wave or say hi or something. I kinda felt like I should, since Mr. Scoop-Now-Think-Later had sort of saved my ass on Saturday. But he just kept going straight, cutting a clean line through the crowd. I wondered what he was listening to, why he always wore the same hoodie day after day, and I wondered why, when dozens of people I never talked to kept saying hello to me, why didn't he?

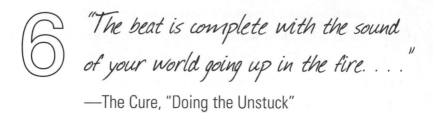

6

"The beat is complete with the sound of your world going up in the fire. . . ."
—The Cure, "Doing the Unstuck"

UNTIL THIS WHOLE BUSINESS with Evan and The Song and my nationwide fame started, Victoria held the record for Most Strife Ever at Jackson High. She came in one day with her hair royal blue (assisted by me, of course) and by the end of first period, she was in the principal's office and they were calling her mom. Here's the thing, though: Victoria's mom is even more kick-ass than Victoria. After her husband left her, she had this rebirth or something and went back to school and ended up becoming a lawyer, so when the school called, she swooped in like a hawk. I was in the nurse's office getting aspirin for a "headache" (i.e., eavesdropping), so I heard the whole thing. They were even threatening to suspend Victoria, but her mom was all like, "Yeah, nice try, bucko," and then threatened to sue them and call the ACLU if Victoria "is forced to miss *one minute* of *one day* of school because of something as inane as *hair color!*"

It was incredible and ever since then, our principal kind of hates Victoria and is kind of scared of her, too. It doesn't help that she always gives him this really big fake smile whenever their paths cross.

All this to say that sneaking out of school with Victoria is a real pain in the ass, which is why we ended up not going to the bookstore together. Instead, I made Victoria swear on her Nirvana box set that she would go and scour the shelves while I went to work.

In the meantime, though, three things happened:

(1) In second-period geometry, a girl named Tizzy leaned across the aisle toward me. We hadn't really talked before, despite sharing two classes, which was a conscious decision on my part. Let's just say the girl was aptly named. "Um, are you the girl that Evan Dennison wrote the song about?" she hissed over at me while we were getting our homework out.

"Um, yeah," I said. "What'd you get for number four?"

"Screw the homework!" Tizzy cried. "Oh my God, that song is so awesome! And you're Audrey! Oh my God! This is crazy! Just crazy!"

"How'd you get the name Tizzy, anyway?" I asked.

"What?"

"Never mind."

"So is Sharon nice? She seems really nice. What's it like dating Evan?"

"Um, we're not really dating anymore," I started to explain, but Tizzy wasn't interested in that answer.

"Hey, do you think I could meet the band? Their guitarist is really cute!"

"Well, I—"

"So you're not dating anymore? What a bummer, right?" I swear to God, her eyes were going in two different directions by this point.

(2) During fifth-period bio, apropos of nothing, Jared

Simmons turned around in his seat and handed me a CD. "Hey, do you think you could give my band's demo to Evan?" Well, a herd of giraffes could have run through the lab right then and I don't think anyone would've noticed because up until that moment, we had all thought that Jared was mute. No joke, we really did. So when he (a) talked, and (b) revealed he was in a band, the whole room came to a standstill. Even our lab teacher was like, "Holy crap." I was so surprised that all I could say was, "Um, sure," and he just nodded and turned back around in his seat like nothing had happened. Meanwhile, my buddy Tizzy was having kittens in the back row. "Did you guys just *hear that?* Oh my *God!* Audrey, you're like a miracle worker!"

(3) I made it a personal mission to track down Chris Collins, original source of the famous-in-New-Jersey story, which didn't happen until after the last bell. I was a wreck by this point, and over the day I ended up braiding my hair into all these little braids because I had to keep my hands busy and collaging wasn't really an option during history class. Plus, it gave me an excuse to not have to make eye contact with people.

Yeah, so finding Chris Collins took some time. Talking to him, however, was like talking to time suckage personified.

"Oh, yeah, that," he said when I prompted him about his brother's news. "That's right. Pretty fuckin' awesome, huh?"

"Totally. Best day of my life. So your brother told you about it? Did he say anything more?"

"Uh . . . I dunno. Not really."

"Like if I was mentioned in that article or anything . . . ?"

His eyes were heavy-lidded and I couldn't tell if he was just in a general haze or suffering a pot overdose. "I don't think so."

"Are you sure?"

"Uh, maybe? I don't really remember. I wasn't there."

"Of course you weren't."

"So that song's about you, huh?" Chris shoved his hair out of his eyes and laughed. "Wow, you really pissed him off. What, did you suck in bed or something?"

"Hey, I—" I stopped myself from giving Chris Collins a detailed outline of my sex life, limited as it was. "That's a really rude question to ask a girl," I finally said. I was trying to go for a cool, detached, Karen O vibe but I just ended up sounding like someone's pinched grandmother.

"Hey, it's a party!" Victoria came running up and grabbed my elbow. "Hi, Chris."

"Whatever, dude." Chris waved us both away.

"What crawled up his ass and died?" she asked as I took her arm and practically dragged her into the parking lot.

"Hopefully something sharp and poisonous."

She was giving me the fish eye. "What's up with your hair?"

"Oh, um . . ." I reached up and fingered a braid. "Nervous habit."

"It's sort of like Bob Marley meets Pippi Longstocking."

"That's not a compliment, is it?"

"Hell no."

I sighed and began unraveling my hair. "Can we go to the bookstore now?"

"I did better than that." She held up a printout from the computer. "I Googled."

I smacked my palm to my forehead. "Why didn't I think of that?"

"Nice facepalm. You trying to keep that vein down?"

I ignored that last bit. "Thank God one of us is good under pressure."

"Yeah, you caved like a wet noodle. So anyway, if I may." She held up the paper and began to read as we walked to the parking lot. I took her arm so that she wouldn't walk into a parked car or something. "Okay, it's titled 'Band We Love This Week,' exclamation mark. 'If "Audrey, Wait!" is any indication, the Do-Gooders are in for a long ride down the musical highway. Led by the vocal athleticism—'"

"It does *not* say that. You made that up."

She pointed to the paper. "Look, I highlighted it. Anyway, 'Led by the vocal athleticism of seventeen-year-old cute-as-the-boy-your-parents-warned-you-about Evan Dennison, this Los Angeles–area band plays its heartbreak song the way you want to hear it: loud, fast, and hard, with—"

"Oh, good Lord," I sighed. "Please, stop, I get the idea."

By now, we were at my car. "Yeah," she said. "Not exactly award-winning journalism, but yeah." Victoria pushed a hand through her freshly pink hair. "So are you going to work?"

"Yeah, just a normal day, you know. Wake up, hear about my love life on the radio, read a college newspaper article about my ex-boyfriend, then go scoop Double Bubble Gum for strangers. The usual."

Victoria grinned. "Can I have a ride home? Jonah's got something after school."

"Like detention, maybe?"

"Maybe."

We smiled at each other over the roof of my car. "What can I say?" she shrugged. "First period is not his friend."

"Get in," I told her. "I just have to stop by the house first and get my shirt for work."

"Scooper Dooper!" she replied, and ducked away before I could punch her shoulder.

Judging from the way my day went, it was only fitting that my Scooper Dooper shirt was on the floor of my bedroom. Laundry is not always at the top of my to-do list, as my mother will attest. I gave it a quick sniff, deemed it acceptable, and was mid-change on the stairs when my phone started to ring. "Can you get it?" I yelled to Victoria, who was flipping through the new J.Crew catalogue on the kitchen table.

"Okay, who comes up with these color names?" she asked, waving the catalogue. "Pool? Celery?" She answered the phone even as she ranted. "I mean, Christ, it's a sweater, not a—Hello, Audrey's phone. She's currently suiting up for a soul-deadening hourly job that provides no benefits, how may I help you?"

"Dead to me," I hissed at her, but she was no longer paying attention. Her eyes were getting wider and wider and she kept saying, "Uh-huh . . . uh-huh . . . okay, hold on." Then she covered the mouthpiece of the phone and pulled it away from her ear. "Aud!" she hissed. "*Audrey!*"

"I'm right—*oof!*—here," I said, trying to pull the shirt over my head. "Who is it?"

"It's the *L.A. Weekly!*" she said. Pool-colored sweaters were no longer her biggest priority that afternoon, I could tell.

"What do they want?"

"They want to talk to you!" She was jumping up and down like she does at shows during our favorite songs. "Here, talk to her! She's a reporter!"

I backed away from the phone even while stuck inside my ugly work shirt. "No way," I told her. "I'm already late for work."

"Audrey." Now Victoria was using her please-don't-fuck-with-me-or-so-help-me-God-you-will-regret-it voice. (She's gonna make an awesome mom one day.) "Get over here and talk to her. She's a reporter, not a Dementor."

"*Harry Potter* nerd."

"Whatever. Take the damn phone."

I sighed and did as she said. "Hello?" I answered while trying to squeeze both my arm and my head into the shirt at the same time. "Ouch! Sorry, hello?"

"Um, hello, I'm looking for Audrey Cuttler, please?"

"You found her." Either my head had grown or the shirt had shrunk while decaying on the floor.

"Hi, my name is Isabella, I'm a reporter over at the *L.A. Weekly* and—"

"Where?" My head was so constricted that I couldn't hear, so I pulled the shirt back off and realized that I had been trying to squeeze my head in through the armhole. "Oh, for pity's sake."

"Sorry?"

"No, sorry, it's me. You're a reporter from where?"

"The *Weekly*? We're doing a feature on local bands, and we wanted to put something in about the Do-Gooders, and I was wondering if you had a minute?"

"Um, sure, okay." I looked at Victoria and shrugged. She was still all excited and had her hands clasped in front of her mouth, but I beckoned her closer so she could listen, too. "How'd you get this number, anyway?"

"Their press agent gave it to me."

Press agent? Evan had a press agent now? My rage boiled up again and I glanced at the clock that hung over our kitchen sink. If this conversation took five minutes, I could get Victoria home and make it to work in two Cure singles (but not ones from *Disintegration*) and clock in one minute late. "I have plenty of time," I told her. "What do you want to know?"

"Well, for starters, what's it like to have a song written about you?"

"Oh, it's all good." I practically had to wipe my dripping sarcasm off the phone. "I love being singled out in public, it's the best."

She laughed and I could tell I was charming her. Finally, someone to hear my side of the story! "And did Evan talk to you about the song at all after he wrote it?"

"No, we were broken up by then. He didn't have the guts!" I laughed again and Victoria and I knocked elbows in solidarity. "You know guys—they say everything to their friends after you walk out the door."

"Tell me about it." I could hear her frantically typing on the other end. "What do your friends think about the song?"

"Well, there's a lot of 'Audrey, Wait!' being screamed in the hallways, and it seems like now everyone wants to be my friend, but that's about it." Then I thought about Chris Collins. "This one guy I know said that his brother heard it at his school in New Jersey. That was weird."

"Oh, it's all over the radio in London, too."

"You mean like the English London?"

"The one and only. They've released it in Europe, and according to the label, the U.S. is next. They're really giving it the full-court press."

My throat suddenly felt sort of tight. "Really? Wow. Fantastic."

"What's fantastic? Tell me!" Victoria whispered away from the phone, but I waved at her to shut up.

"Any plusses to the attention?"

"Uh, all the sex?" We both laughed and I forced myself to unclench my hands. "Not really, it's just a song about me, that's all." And even as I said the words, I started to believe them. I mean, I really did. "They were just words written by someone who didn't know me anymore. Maybe he never did, I dunno." I reached over so I could refill Bendomolena's water bowl. "I broke up with him and I hurt him and I guess he wants to do the same thing to me."

Seriously, Isabella must have been the world's fastest typist. "Any plans to release a song of your own?"

"Um, not right now!" I laughed. "I don't think that's ever gonna happen. I only sing along to the radio."

"And what do you think about music right now? Are you listening to local bands besides the Do-Gooders?"

"God, I'll listen to anything. I love music, it's like . . ." I sighed and put the water dish back down. "I mean, sometimes it's like the only thing that matters. Sometimes when I hear a great song, it means more than anything, like even my family or friends or anyone." Next to me, Victoria made a face that clearly said, *"Not more than* me, *your very best friend in the world."*

"Is that how it felt when you heard 'Audrey, Wait!' for the first time?"

Just then, the garage door opened up and my mom came struggling in through the door with groceries and cat litter. "Help . . . me . . ." she said, trying to keep the door from slamming behind her. "I'm too young to break a hip."

"Look, I have to go," I told Isabella. "Good luck with everything, all right? I hope it turns out okay."

"That's fine, I think I've got everything I need. Thanks for your time!"

We hung up and I ran to take the kitty litter from my mom while Victoria grabbed a bag of paper towels. "Thanks," she sighed. "Who was that?"

"Um, just someone from the newspaper," I said. In the grand scheme of house rules, I wasn't sure if talking to a reporter was a violation, so I decided to selectively edit.

"We canceled our subscription months ago!" my mom cried. "What, are they offering us another deal?"

"I dunno, I hung up."

She set down the groceries and pulled a bag of oranges out of the top. "For our still-life class," she said, her eyes shining.

An explanation: A couple of months ago, after the whole Evan breakup, my mom decided that we needed to spend more time together. I was all up for shopping and eating pasta lunches by the beach, but in her words, "Let's broaden our horizons, why don't we?"

So we signed up for tae kwon do classes, but that was doomed from the start. Partly because my mom, while not a pushover, is also not the violent type and apologized every time she hit someone or something. *Wham!* "Sorry!" *Pow!* "Sorry!" A superhero she is not. The other reason it was doomed was that whenever I'm supposed to be really serious about something, I get the giggles and can't stop. Seriously, it's embarrassing, but I can't help it. By the fourth class, I was practically turning purple and our teacher kept barking out orders until I finally lost it and doubled over with laughter while my mom alternately beat up the practice dummy and apologized to him.

"So," she said in the car afterwards. "How do you feel about watercolors?"

I looked at the oranges. "They're very orange-y, Mom."

"That's the best you can give me? Orange-y?"

"Orange-y like a brilliant sunset." I kissed her cheek and then one of the oranges for good measure. "See, I love them already. They're adorable. I gotta go. It's been fun and all that, but I'm late."

"And she's taking me home," Victoria said, slinging her bag over her shoulder and taking an orange from the counter. "It'll help prevent scurvy," she explained. "It's been going around school."

My mom just grinned. Victoria can do no wrong in her mind. "Do you think you can remember the ice cream this time?"

"Already etched onto my brain," I told her. "I'll put it in the car at the start of my shift so I don't forget, how's that?"

"Ha ha, funnypants." She smiled and gave me a squeeze good-bye. "Is your shirt dirty?"

"I can't hear you—I'm too busy remembering ice cream!" I grabbed my bag and car keys at the same time.

"Do your laundry!"

"I hear nothing but the demands of my customers!"

James was already behind the counter when I came running in, still holding my hat while diving to slide my time card. One minute late, just like I thought. I am nothing if not accurate. "Remind me to bring home a pint of Coffee Dream ice cream," I told him after (reluctantly) putting on my hat. "My parents are crack fiends for it."

"Okay." He was straightening the towers of sugar cones into

something resembling a skyline. "Do these look even?"

"Um, sure."

"You think?" He took a step back and eyed his handiwork.

"So . . ." I fiddled with the ice cream scoops in their well. "Way to say hi to me at school today."

To say we were both surprised by my comment would be an understatement. "When, today?" he said, heading back toward Sugar Cone Town.

The ship had already sailed: I might as well go with it. "Yeah, today. This morning. I was gonna wave at you and then you looked away so that I was doing that weird half-wave thing—"

"I hate when that happens."

"Yeah, me too." There was another awkward pause. I hated those even more. "So what were you listening to while you weren't saying hi to me?"

"Oh, um, just a mix my brother made for me."

"James!" I cried. "You're *finally* speaking my language! Halle-freaking-lujah, I live and breathe mix CDs. What's on it?"

He left the sugar cones alone and started refilling the napkin dispensers. I suspected James suffered from a mild form of OCD. "Just some Clash, some Dylan, y'know. The standard mix-tape stuff."

"You listen to the Clash?"

"You don't?"

"Not all that much."

"I could burn you a CD, if you want."

"Cool, thanks." I boosted myself up onto the counter and swung my feet against the cupboards, probably committing ten health code violations in the process. "What about new bands, do you listen to any of them?"

"You mean like the Do-Gooders?"

I never thought I'd see the day when James would make me blush. Thank God Victoria would never hear about this. "No, I just meant, like, *other* bands. . . ."

He smiled a little. "I'm just giving you a hard time."

"Because today hasn't been hard enough, thanks."

"Yeah, you're kinda famous at our school."

"I'm not *famous*, I'm just . . ." I fumbled for words. "There's a bump in my popularity numbers, let's put it that way."

He smiled and the back of his neck turned bright red, almost as red as his hair. Looked like I wasn't the only one blushing.

But when I turned around, I saw that I wasn't the only one making James blush. Sharon Eggleston was standing in front of the register, doing her patented flirty girl smile at James. "Hey, Aud!" she said, like she was surprised to see me, like it was some big secret that I worked at the Scooper Dooper. "What's up?"

"Um, hi," I said, while scanning the store for an escape route.

"You know, all the sorority girls at USC are totally into your song."

"It's not my song," I told her.

"Do you want to try a free sample of our latest flavor, Pumpkin Pie?" James offered her a tiny spoon with a bit of ice cream on the end. "It's seasonal." I kind of wanted to bop him on the head.

Sharon moved her eyes over to him and did that thing girls do where they tilt their head down and look up at guys through their lashes. "Wow, thanks," she said. "That's so sweet."

"Uh, no problem," James said, and Sharon did her full-on megawatt smile.

I tried not to roll my eyes and almost gave myself a migraine in the process. Why was my heart suddenly too big for my chest? Why was I mad? Why was James acting like a bumbling idiot around her? And why did I care? I mean, it wasn't like I had a cru—

Evan's voice on the radio suddenly cut through the noise in my head.

"Hey, this is Evan from the Do-Gooders, and you're listening to our new song 'Audrey, Wait!' on the world famous KROQ."

Holy shit.

"Did he just—?" I said to James as Sharon's mouth fell open.

"Was that—?" she said.

"I don't—" James tried to answer both of us at the same time.

"He did a promo for KROQ?" I squeaked. "Are you *kidding* me?"

"*We said we loved and it was a lie! I touched your hair and watched you—!*"

Sharon was honest-to-God squealing. "This is, like, the biggest station in L.A.! In California! On, like, maybe the planet!"

I mentally shot death rays at Sharon's head as James reached over and turned the radio off. "Wow," he said. "This is . . . uh, yeah. This is kinda big."

Sharon and I both looked at him. "Holy shit," I said after a minute. "Holy freaking shit."

7

"Can't help the feeling I could blow through the ceiling . . ."

—Radiohead, "Fake Plastic Trees"

IT TOOK TWO WEEKS for the *L.A. Weekly* article to come out, and to be honest, I wasn't really thinking about it. But the whole time before that, I was still trying to navigate the weird popularity circle that Evan's song had landed me in at school. I didn't know what Evan was doing anymore, but it's a safe bet that he was having a better time of it than I was.

"Audrey, Wait!" entered the Billboard Hot 100 Singles chart at number eighty-four, then zoomed to number forty-seven the very next week, which was apparently some big to-do that only a handful of bands had ever done before. I know all this because I started reading the Do-Gooders new website, which was all fancy-schmancy with a message board and photos of the band in a recording studio. Evan looked exactly the same, only with longer hair and a bigger smile, and okay, I admit it, I still thought he was cute. Maybe hot. But you didn't hear that from me.

Their message board was getting pretty popular, too, and I will shamefully admit to spending more than one late night clicki n g "refresh" on my computer screen to see what comments people were

posting. In this weird way, I was proud of Evan, like he was finally achieving all the success he had ever wanted, and then I'd read
some comment like "Screw that Audrey bitch, you're too good for
her!" and that would pretty much kill my benevolence. (That one
comment came from someone named "QTpie," by the way, if that
gives you an idea of Evan's new fanbase.)

Sharon Eggleston, never one to miss a party, kept saying hi to
me along with her gaggle of friends and telling me what she was
doing for the rest of the day. For example: "Oh, hi, Audrey! We
were going to go to Sbarro for lunch today, okay?" Translation: "If
you don't want to spend the rest of your life in Loserville Hell eating egg salad sandwiches, I suggest you eat lunch with us." I don't
even know who she thought she was kidding, since no one has ever
seen Sharon Eggleston eat anything in her life except butter rum
LifeSavers and the lemon wedges that she squeezes into her Diet
Coke.

But of course, I kept wimping out and saying, "Oh. Oh, okay.
But see, I have this orthodontist appointment/study
session/"Save the Whales!" rally I have to go to, so . . ." I really
wanted to wish Sharon a lifetime of frizzy hair and chin zits, but
that'd just be mean, and I couldn't be mean. At least, not yet.

If there was one thing that Sharon knew how to do, though, it
was hitch a ride on the Popularity Train and then take over as
conductor. If she couldn't date the guy, then she was gonna be my
friend whether I liked it or not.

Victoria, on the other hand, was less sympathetic than I was
and had plotted a cruel fate for Sharon that involved piranhas and
a chainsaw and wasn't for the faint of heart.

And then there was Tizzy, speaking of the faint of heart. She was on me like a barnacle, following me between classes, offering me food from her lunch *during* classes, which was making Victoria either jealous or irritated, I couldn't tell. I couldn't ask her, either, because unlike Sharon, you couldn't really hate Tizzy. She was well-meaning and probably a little lonely, which meant that she didn't show up on Victoria's radar. And besides, all Victoria wanted to do was talk about The Song and Evan and What Possibilities It Presented. Possibilities that I myself had yet to see.

"You sound like a guidance counselor," I finally told her as we were sitting on the grass during English two weeks after the song had come out on KROQ. We were supposed to be reading *Leaves of Grass* but instead everyone was just sitting in the sun and glancing at the book every once in a while.

"I'm just saying," Victoria began for the forty-sixth time, "that maybe—just *maybe*—you should look into getting some representation or something and try to make something out of this. This could be an opportunity, you know. We could go to movie premieres, get free swag at the Grammys—"

"Swag?" I asked.

"Swag."

I flopped down and watched the leaves flutter over my head. Whitman had been on to something with his "let's all love nature" philosophy, I had to admit. "And what am I gonna do in between the swag collecting?" I argued, also for what felt like the forty-sixth time. "What? Christen new strip malls? Tell knock-knock jokes as Evan's opening act?"

"Ha, yeah, no. Look, you're Audrey. You're my best friend, you're the most awesome person I know, and everyone is going to love you. Capital *L* love. L-O-V-E. All you have to do is just put yourself out there and be open to whatever opportunities might be available. Like, say, opportunities for free jeans."

I snorted.

She threw a handful of grass at me. "Why are you being a raging pessimist?"

"I'm not. I'm a realist."

"A real pessimist."

And so on. It would've kept going, too, but a shadow suddenly came over me and I opened my eyes to see James standing there, looking almost as tall as the trees. "Oh!" I said. "Hi!"

And if you don't think that the sight of James standing next to me didn't get the whispers going, then you haven't been paying attention.

"Oh, hey," he said, like he was surprised to be standing next to me, like it wasn't *him* who had walked over. "I, uh, I burned you a copy of that CD we were talking about. Remember . . . ? The Clash? I, uh, I put some other stuff on there, too."

Victoria sat up like an eager puppy, almost like she was expecting him to pat her on the head. Behind her, I could see Tizzy's eyes widening and Sharon Eggleston's narrowing. Every single copy of *Leaves of Grass* had been, well, left in the grass.

"Oh, yeah," I said. "Thanks, that's really cool." I took the case from him. The front cover was this awesome collage of black-and-white photos. "Did you make this?"

"Yeah, I . . ." He cleared his throat and was now turning as red as his hair. "Yeah, I did."

"It's awesome," I told him. "I do collage sometimes too, in my room."

"One whole wall of her room is almost covered," Victoria piped up. "You should see it sometime."

I looked over at her as James's eyes widened. "Um, I gotta go," he said, then held up the potted plant he was carrying, the instantly recognizable hall pass from Mr. Elson's U.S. history class. "Enjoy the CD."

"I will, thanks," I said, still pretty impressed by the collage. "Good luck with the plant. Don't forget to water it."

He smiled as he slunk away, and I held onto the case a bit tighter. Victoria leaned in close and whispered, "We need to talk!"

"What's there to talk about? He made me a CD."

"You're shitting me, right? He made you a mix CD and carried the fucking potted plant all the way over here just to give it to you." She studied me for a long minute. "Someone has a crush," she finally said.

"James does not have a crush on me," I told her. "It's just a CD."

"Yeah, well, you're blushing."

"I'm blushing because everyone's staring at me!" I hated when she was right, especially about this.

"Um, news flash, Audrey. Everyone's been staring at you for the past two weeks."

Sharon Eggleston wasted no time getting her two cents in. She and her friends found me as I was going toward the language arts building to get my stuff after class. (Side note: language arts? It's one or the other, people, not both.) Victoria had abandoned me for Jonah, who had some major project due for chemistry and needed someone to help him who wouldn't mind if her eyebrows got singed off. That's the kind of girlfriend Victoria is. I, on the other hand, happen to like having eyebrows on my face, so I left the two of them in the lab and instead got a faceful of Sharon and the Clones.

"I saw James talking to you today during English," Sharon said as she sidled up to me. "Did he give you something? I saw him hand you a CD."

"Oh, James?" I said, as if flocks of guys had been coming up to me all day and I was having trouble remembering who was who. "Yeah, James, he just gave me a mix CD."

"A mix CD?" Sharon repeated, like she was a mynah bird or something. I was trying really hard not to get annoyed. The situation wasn't made any easier by Sharon's posse, one of whom, Natasha, was a mouth breather and kept exhaling right over my shoulder.

"So is he your new boyfriend?"

"No!" I said a little too quickly. "He's *not.*"

"And that's why he gave you a CD? Because he's *not* your boyfriend." Sharon had this look on her face like she was trying to win something, like a game show contestant trying to guess the lowest price on cleaning fluid, and now I was annoyed. And then I felt annoyed at James for putting me in this position, and then I was annoyed even more with Sharon for making me annoyed at James, and then I just wanted to knock both their heads together and be done with it.

"Look, I have to go," I said, my hand on the door to the building. "I've got this oral report for Spanish in two weeks and I haven't done anything for it yet. I'll see you later, okay?" I ducked into the building and didn't get to hear where Sharon would be "eating" lunch that day.

I mean, *enough* already. Right?

So suffice to say when I went home at three, I was already in a pretty craptacular mood. I had this stupid Spanish report to do and I hadn't done anything for it yet because my best subject is and always will be Procrastination 101, but all I wanted to do was go play James's mix CD and read Evan's message board to find out what total strangers were saying about me. Besides, I had read rumors about a possible music video, and as much as I hated myself for being curious, I had to know what they were planning and whether or not I would somehow be involved.

The hopes of lurking the message board were dashed, however, when I pulled up to my house and saw both my parents' cars in the driveway. This never happens except on weekends, so of course I went to the first random thoughts that came to mind:

Oh my God, we won the lottery. Now, my parents don't even like going to Vegas, much less buying lottery tickets, so I don't know where that one came from. I chalk it up to either optimism or greed.

Then the next thought: *Oh, my God, Bendomolena finally attacked the postman.* Enough said.

Then, *Oh, my God, someone's dead.*

By the time I got into the kitchen, I was having a mild panic attack. "Ohmygodwhodied?" I said breathlessly as I skidded to a halt in the kitchen.

"Someone died?" my dad said. He and my mom were both standing next to each other with a pile of newspapers. The *L.A. Weekly*, to be exact. *Fourteen* copies of the *L.A. Weekly*.

Oh. Oh, dear.

"No one's dead," my mom interrupted. "But did you give an interview to a reporter?"

"Um, maybe?"

"Here's a hint," my dad continued. "There's only one correct answer, and it's not 'maybe.'"

I set my bag down very carefully on the floor, as any courteous and innocent daughter would do. "It was just this woman from the *Weekly*," I said, thinking of ways to make it sound like it was something that happened every week, like getting a manicure. "It was just a couple of questions."

My dad raised an eyebrow, then picked up one of the papers. "Ahem," he said, reading aloud. "'But Audrey has found a bright side to all the attention that her ex-boyfriend's song has brought her. The best thing, she says with a giggle "All the sex!"'" My dad set the paper down. "I can't believe I just said that sentence out loud."

Guess where I get my sarcastic streak from.

"*I* can't believe that *you* said that," my mother said, pointing to me. "What were you thinking?"

"I was *kidding*!" I shrieked. "Oh my freaking Lord, I was *kidding*! She didn't really put that, did she?" I grabbed a copy for myself and began scanning the article. "We were just talking about the song and . . . I was being *sarcastic* and . . ." I trailed off as I read another paragraph.

In "Audrey, Wait!" the Do-Gooders craft a three-minute-plus song of pop perfection that's so sweet, you can feel your teeth rotting as you sing along. It's a song for teenagers, written by teenagers, but damn if it doesn't remind you of the one that got away, of every girl who has ever done you wrong, put you down, kicked you out. And what does the girl think about that? "It's all good!" squealed sixteen-year-old Audrey, title heroine of the Next Big Thing. "I love being singled out in public—it's the best!"

Listen up, kids. This ain't your parents' rock and roll.

That bitch. I don't even like calling other people "bitches" but . . . that total *bitch*.

"I was kidding," I said again to my parents. "I was being sarcastic. She called me when I was late to work a couple of weeks ago and she asked if I could answer some questions and she was nice—she *was* nice—so we were joking around and—"

I was interrupted by the ringing phone, but my mom just waved it off. "Let the machine get it," she said. "It's the tenth call since I got home half an hour ago."

My dad pushed his glasses back up his nose and looked at me. "Audrey," he said in his I'm-not-mad-but-I'm-not-particularly-thrilled-with-your-current-life-choices voice, "the article was syndicated. The story ran in some newspapers."

It took a minute for me to realize what he had said. "Newspapers?" I repeated. "Plural?"

"Plural."

"How do you know?"

"Your mother Googled your name at work."

I chewed on my lower lip for a minute. "So the whole country didn't get the joke?"

"Your humor doesn't exactly translate in print, sweetheart."

"Which papers?"

My mom stepped in as my dad began rubbing at his forehead. "Mostly smaller papers," she said. "Local ones."

I tried desperately to understand the scope of the problem. "Like, how many?"

Suddenly the machine clicked on and a male voice came over the tape. "Hi, this is Michael Anderson, I'm a reporter over at *USA Today*. We are interested in speaking to Audrey Cuttler for a few minutes for a story we're doing on teenage celebrity and—"

I would tell you what else he said, but really, my mind shut off at that point. My skin felt fuzzy and warm and I knew I was doing that fish look again that Victoria can't stand. "So far," my dad continued, as if a reporter from *USA Today* wasn't asking about me on our answering machine, "we've had calls from the *L.A. Times*, the *New York Times*, the *Miami Herald*, the *Chicago Sun-Times*, the *Chicago Tribune*, the *New York Post*—they're insistent, three messages so far—ABC, NBC, CBS, NPR, MTV, and many other media entities with three letters."

"And *People* magazine," my mom added. (She will never confess to reading tabloid magazines, but I know for a fact that she tears through them when she gets pedicures.) "Audrey, what is going on?"

I sank down in one of our kitchen chairs and began creasing a corner of the *Weekly*. "It's like the article says," I sighed. "Evan wrote a song. After we broke up. About me. And it's good. People like it."

I could see my dad's eyes getting wider and wider until it looked like there were two golf balls in his head. "*You're* Audrey?" he said. "That's *you?*"

Now *my* eyes were pretty wide too. "You've heard the song? I thought you only listened to classical music in the car."

"I've been hearing that song every ten minutes," he said, ignoring that last bit about classical music. So my mom reads tabloids and my dad listens to Top 40 radio. This day was becoming more revealing every minute.

"How does it go?" my mom asked. "Hum a few bars."

Now, I thought my dad only listened to classical music in the car, but this day was becoming more and more revealing every minute. "Oh, you know," he said. Then he sang a few bars in a voice that, let me tell you, sounded nothing like Evan's. "Audrey, wait! Audrey, wait!"

"*That* song?" my mom gasped. I swear to God, she actually gasped. "I've been hearing it every ten minutes. That song is about *you?*"

If there was one small mercy in this whole debacle, it was that Evan never explicitly mentioned sex in the lyrics. I couldn't handle the mental image of my parents blithely singing along to a song that talked about me having sex. My brain would melt and run out of my ears. "It's me," I said. "Thanks for giving me such a catchy name that rhymes with every third word in the English language."

Now my mom was humming the song to herself. "Evan wrote that?" she said. "I can't believe it."

"Join the club," I told her.

The phone started ringing again. This time, we all listened, waiting to hear who it was.

"WHY ARE YOU NOT ANSWERING YOUR PHONE?!? OH MY GOD, DID YOU SEE THE ARTICLE? I AM *FREAKING OUT*, WHY ARE YOU NOT ANSWERING YOUR PHONE?!" Victoria took a deep breath and I could see her switching the phone from one ear to the other, like she a l w a y s does when she's so excited and her words can't come out fast enough. "Please call me, I'm starting to act like Tizzy around here. It's getting ugly. Oh, hi, Mr. and Mrs. Cuttler, in case you get this first. Everything's fine, I'm just trying to get ahold of Audrey. Okay, 'bye. AUDREY, CALL ME BEFORE I HAVE TO RESORT TO SKYWRITING."

We all looked at each other after Victoria hung up. "Why do I not have a hard time believing that Victoria actually would hire a skywriter?" my dad said.

"The odds are 70-30 in favor of it," I agreed.

My mom just shook her head and began restacking all the newspapers, even though they were already stacked. "Audrey," she said, "this is kind of a problem."

I didn't know what to say. I felt like I was going to cry—my parents were upset, Victoria was apoplectic, and now everyone was going to think that I was some groupie whore. I hadn't even finished reading the article yet, but I'd gotten a good idea of where it was going from that one paragraph. "I'm sorry," I said. "I didn't know that it would be such a big deal."

"Was this before or after you gave the interview without talking to us about it first?"

"Um . . . both?"

My dad sighed. "We're not mad, it's just . . . well, I don't know what it is." He looked to my mother. "Can we sue?"

She just rolled her eyes at him. I guess almost twenty years of marriage gives you the right to not take your husband seriously during serious moments. I filed it away for future reference. "Audrey," she said again. I was starting to hate the sound of my own name. "Your father and I aren't upset with you, but we just wish you had told us that you talked to a reporter. Or that Evan had written this song. Is there anything else we should know?"

I thought for a minute. *Should* my parents know some things? Like maybe the fact that Evan and I had had sex, or that we'd met because he was so drunk that he puked on me? Should they know about the time Victoria and I got sick off peach schnapps when we were fifteen?

Absolutely not. Like I needed more parental drama right then.

I faked innocence. "It says on Evan's website that they're going to shoot a video. Is that important?"

She blinked twice. "Are you going to be in it?"

"No one's asked me to be."

"Then I think we're fine." She glanced over at my dad. "Maybe?"

"What about the reporters?" he asked.

We all were flummoxed by that one. "Sic Victoria on them," I offered.

"That's what you should have done with this one," my dad said, shaking a copy of the *Weekly*.

"She's probably already on it," I replied.

Finally, my mother had an idea. "I'll talk to my friend who works in the PR department over at the magazine. She might have some ideas."

"Who?" my dad asked.

"What magazine?" I said at the same time.

"You know, Evelyn?"

Now it was my turn to blink. "Evelyn works at the senior citizen center!" I said. "Her 'magazine' is the *Leisure Ledger*! It covers things like golf cart repair and produce sales at the grocery store! And she *is* the PR department."

"You'll be a hit with the sixty-five-and-older crowd by the time all of this is over." My dad started to laugh. I could tell that he was much more content with that idea than one that involved male groupies.

"*In the meantime*," my mother said over us, obviously a little annoyed, "you"—here she pointed at me—"are not allowed to give any more interviews or appear in videos or sign autographs or do anything that will cause reporters to start calling our home and/or Grandma."

"Can I still go with Victoria to the concert next Friday?"

"What concert?"

"The Lolitas are playing with the Plain Janes at the Silver Cup in Hollywood. You said I could go last month," I added quickly. "The Lolitas are gonna be huge and this is my last chance to see them in a small venue before all the wannabe fans get ahold of them."

"No, that's fine, you can go," my mother said. "Just don't inspire any more love songs, all right?"

There was this weird silence then, which was strange, because my family's pretty chatty, in case you haven't noticed, and we don't really let things hang. But then the phone started to ring again and I just wanted to go up to my room. "Can I call Victoria back now?" I said, and when my dad nodded, I went upstairs.

I didn't call Victoria back right away, though, and not because I was curious to see if she'd follow through with the skywriting threat. Instead, I put my stereo on so I couldn't hear the ringing phone, then laid down on the bed and put one arm over my eyes, making the world as black as I could. So many people were going to read that article. My parents. Victoria. Jonah. Sharon Eggleston. Tizzy. Evan. James. My stomach cramped at the idea and I rolled over, taking my pillow with me.

A few minutes later, I felt something tugging at the edge of my comforter, and I rolled over long enough to see Bendomolena meowing at me from the floor.

I'll say this about my cat: She may weigh three hundred pounds and be a sloth, but she knows when I need her. So I lifted her up with an "Oof!" (me) and a "Meow?" (her) and put her next to me so we could lie nose to nose. Radiohead came on just then, and I sang "Karma Police" to her while petting her ears. Bendy's the only person who doesn't hate my singing voice, and I'm the only person who's allowed to pet her ears, so it's a fair trade. "For a minute there, I lost myself, I lost myself," I sang, and then the words began to pick apart my heart and I had to stop singing and just swallow hard for a minute and not think and put my hands over my eyes and make everything go black again.

And after it passed, after Bendomolena licked my face and I combed two tangles out of her fur, I took a deep breath, reached for the phone, and called Victoria. "Hi," I said when she answered. "Call off the skywriters. I'm still alive."

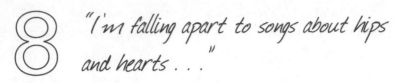

8 "I'm falling apart to songs about hips and hearts . . ."

—Fall Out Boy, "Get Busy Living or Get Busy Dying (Do Your Part to Save the Scene and Stop Going to Shows)"

SO HERE'S THE FUNNY THING about newspapers: Aside from this whole "syndication" thing, they can also write whole articles about you without your permission. Like the *New York Times*, for example, which put in its Sunday Styles section a whole paragraph about me and how I "represent all that is different about Generation Z. Their lives are entertainment, their entertainment is composed of their lives. All the world's a stage, if you will, with sixteen-year-old Audrey Cuttler in the role of Juliet."

We all know how that worked out for good old Juliet, don't we? (And Generation Z? That sounds like it should be the name of the world's lamest clothing store in the world's lamest mall.)

Victoria, in a move that shocked no one, had a theory about the whole thing. "You give good interview," she told me one afternoon when we were in my room, both of us cutting up magazines and newspapers. I was trying to finish one side of my collage, but Victoria was on an entirely different project: making a scrapbook of me. I'll say this much: It was pretty funny to look down at our amassed pictures and see pictures of me spread out next to pictures of rock stars.

Oh, yes. The picture. That's been great fun. On the Do-Gooders' online message board (which added 539 new members yesterday, in case you're keeping track like I am), someone posted my photo from last year's yearbook, which then caused a debate about whether or not I'm pretty. Apparently the jury is still out, but the words *sux* and *awww* and *ewww* got used with hearty abandon. I still don't know who posted it, but I guess it doesn't matter anymore, because some paper in Arizona saw it and ran it, which opened the floodgates just in time for all the other papers' Sunday editions.

Try reading the paper one morning while eating cereal and seeing last year's yearbook photo staring back at you. It'll take ten years off your life, I swear to God.

Plus, "Audrey, Wait!" was getting more and more popular. They were playing it in between innings at baseball games, according to different Do-Gooders fan websites, and potential video rumors were continuing to swirl around. "I heard they're filming it at the L.A. Zoo!" one person posted online, but that turned out to be untrue. (Thank God.)

Victoria was carefully trimming around said yearbook photo as she talked. "You give good interview," she continued. "All these writers and editors are sooo used to the same blah-blah-blah, and then here you come with your 'I love being famous!' routine—"

"I was misquoted," I interrupted.

"Of course you were. But who cares about that?" She reached for my glue and began outlining the back of the photo. "Evan's song is blazing and here you come with your can of gasoline and ka-boom! Instant news!" She scrutinized the article for a minute. "This is the best thing that could've happened."

"Easy for you to say," I muttered, making sure I had a second copy of *Blender* before I started hacking up the first one. (I'm obsessive about my magazines and always buy two copies, one for cutting up and one for safekeeping.) "You're not the one who's being maligned on every major Top 40 and alternative radio station in the northern hemisphere."

"If I was, though," she said, "I'd make damn sure that I was having some fun with it."

"Whatever." I grimaced and grabbed a glue stick to attach the photo to my collage.

"You are just so lucky," Victoria continued as if I hadn't said anything, "that they didn't use your freshman year photo. Your hair looks much better in this one."

I handed back the glue stick and pasted a photo of the Lolitas to the square of posterboard. "I'm seeing you tomorrow night," I told the picture, sort of desperate to change the subject. All I had done for the past week was talk about myself.

"Yeah," Victoria added, glancing over at the photo. "So don't suck."

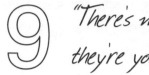 *"There's music and there's people and they're young and alive . . ."*

—The Smiths, "There Is a Light That Never Goes Out"

I LOVE THE DAY OF A CONCERT. I absolutely love it. Even when I was dating Evan and going to his shows every week, there was always a little zip in the air when I knew we were going out. Besides, I was ready to get out of my house and away from my parents, who were now totally paranoid that I was gonna start talking to every reporter who happened to wander down the street. They were none too happy when my yearbook photo got leaked, and didn't seem comforted by the fact that, as Victoria said, at least it wasn't my freshman year photo.

Other than school, though, all I had done was go to work and go to Victoria's house to eat greasy Chinese food and watch late-night videos on MTV so we could make fun of them. I couldn't help but notice that the Scooper Dooper was getting more crowded with each passing day, mostly with girls my own age who had this slightly dazed look in their eyes and kept staring at me. And I don't think they were just admiring my hair. They came to see me, which could bring them one step closer to Evan. "What, do you think he's going to drop in here?" I wanted to shout at them, but instead I just gave them really wimpy cones.

James, who—let's just be honest here—isn't great with girls, was suddenly all thumbs and could barely handle the soft-serve machine whenever it got crowded, much less the cash register. Which was kind of cute.

But I digress.

So yeah, the day of a concert has a certain electricity. I'm not one of those girls who wears tiny shirts and heels to a packed club show, but I like to look nice. Okay, hot. I want to look hot while I'm dancing around. If you're going to see a band called the Lolitas, you've gotta bring your A-game, know what I mean? However, when you're a laundry avoider, it can be difficult to pull something together at the last minute.

I was forced to forsake jeans, since my cleanest pair were too long to go with the boots I wanted to wear, which sent me into a crisis until I found a miniskirt that wasn't too short or too long, and a pair of black tights to wear underneath them in case I had to get pulled out of the pit. (I wasn't looking to give the whole theater a free show up my skirt.) Then I had a minor laundry miracle when I found a plain black T-shirt buried in the back of my bottom dresser drawer, and I ironed it with one hand while pulling on my dark red riding boots with the other. That still left the problem of my arms. It was late November and definitely cool out, but I didn't want to have to take a jacket, because then I'd have to carry it, or worse, tie it around my waist like a preschool dork.

And then I had an epiphany: tube socks.

Five minutes later, I had snipped the toes off a pair of my dad's socks and pulled them up over my arms so that only my fingers and upper arms showed. I wasn't sure if it was genius or a sartorial disaster, but I figured that Victoria would be quick to make the distinction.

When she and Jonah pulled up at four o'clock, I was ready. "Hi," I said, breathless as I fell into the car.

"You look hot!" Victoria replied, her eyes lighting up to see me. "Doesn't she look hot, Jonah?"

Jonah just laughed through his nose and backed the car down my driveway. "You're a lunatic if you think I'm telling you that your best friend looks hot."

"Hi, Jonah."

"Hey, Aud. Cool boots."

"I was there when she bought them!" Victoria said, leaning over the front seat so she could face me. "Are those socks on your arms?"

"Too much? I was trying to stay warm and be original at the same time."

"No, it looks good. It's like the girls' hockey team ran over Green Day."

"Um, thank you?" I decided the socks would stay on.

"Enough about socks. I'm already bored. Let's talk about you! You're actually leaving the house, this is so exciting!"

"I've left the house plenty of times," I protested. Jonah braked hard, apparently forgetting there was a stop sign at the end of my street, the same stop sign he'd stopped at hundreds of times before, and I reached for my seat belt. "I've been to work and to school."

"Those are required subjects," Victoria said. "You haven't been doing any electives, so to speak. You need some balancing out. A little yang in your yin."

Jonah grumbled a little in the driver's seat and Victoria rolled her eyes at him. "Jonah doesn't want to go tonight."

"Why don't you want to go, Jonah?"

"Because it's a chick show," he said, glancing at me in the rearview mirror. "It's gonna be all chicks."

"How lucky am I?" Victoria grinned. "My boyfriend's upset that he has to stand in a roomful of women tonight. He's the best!" She planted a wet kiss on his cheek with a hearty "mwah!" sound.

I swear, if they spent the entire freeway ride making out while we sat in traffic, I was going to throw myself under the wheels of the car. "A-*hem*," I said. "Audience of one back here."

Victoria kissed him one more time, then turned her attention back to me. "So now I want to hear about *James*." She had this way of saying his name like it was a super-special secret, all hushed and excited. "Did you work with him yesterday?"

I thought about what to tell her. Yes, we had worked. Yes, he spilt vanilla soft-serve and burned a whole batch of waffle cones. Yes, he had stood right next to me while I was ringing up customers, close enough that I could smell what laundry detergent he used.

But all I said was, "He spilt the soft-serve. It took forever to clean up." Then I started digging in my bag for my makeup kit, since it had taken so long to get dressed that I had no time to spruce myself up. "Here, tilt the mirror so I can see myself," I said as we merged onto the freeway. "Mommy needs to put her face on."

"Like this?" Victoria moved the rearview mirror, which reflected a sunbeam and nearly zapped Jonah's eyes out of his head.

"Because it's not like I'm driving or anything!" he cried. "Jesus!"

"Sorry, sorry," Victoria apologized. "Want me to kiss it and make it better?"

"You want to kiss my eyeballs? You'll get your sticky lip gloss all over them."

"Yeah, but it smells like strawberry. See?" She puckered up and stuck her lips under his nose. Meanwhile, I was trying to see myself in the rearview mirror, but no matter where I moved, all I could see was my chin, where I suspected a huge zit was days away from making its stage debut. "Great," I muttered.

Victoria turned back from kissing Jonah's nose. "Here, switch seats with me so you can see." She practically dove over the front seat and into the backseat, while I did the opposite and climbed into the front seat. And because we're both complete klutzes, we both managed to kick Jonah in the shoulder.

"Ow!" he yelled, and then two seconds later, "OW!"

I looked at him warily. "I don't have to kiss it and make it better, do I?"

"You *better* not!" Victoria said, her voice muffled. Her dive had taken a wrong turn and she had landed with her head against the door handle and one foot above the backseat.

I craned my neck to look at her. "My kingdom for a camera right now."

"I—goddamnit, that *hurt.*"

Jonah looked over his shoulder at her. "Why don't you kiss yourself with your strawberry lip gloss?" He looked smug, no doubt feeling justified after getting whacked in the arm.

I ignored both of them and turned back so I could do my makeup. Thank God the traffic was heavy—I didn't need Jonah's brake-happy foot making me stab myself in the eye with my mascara wand.

There are basically two rules I have about going to concerts:

(1) Wear waterproof mascara. I cannot emphasize this enough, especially if you're trying to meet the band by the busses afterwards and want to take pictures. Trust me on this one. It's going to be hot and sweaty and while you're dancing up a storm and singing along, your mascara will be somewhere around your chin and you'll look like a melted doll. And (2) do not—again, *do not*—wear any item of clothing that celebrates the band you're going to see. If you're seeing Band X, do not wear a Band X T-shirt. As Victoria says, "Don't be That Guy."

We ended up sitting in three hours of traffic on the 5 freeway, going past Disneyland and the spiky crown of Space Mountain at a colossal crawl. Getting to L.A. is always a freaking nightmare, and by the time we finally got off at Sunset, Victoria and I had to beg Jonah to pull over at Denny's so we could pee. Then we spent forty minutes at the In-N-Out drive-thru across from Hollywood High, then ate our food while we waited in line to park Jonah's car at the theater.

I had butterflies already and my hands were cold and I grabbed Victoria's arm and did a little happy dance with her. "We're going to the con-cert! We're going to the con-cert!" we sang together in the parking lot while Jonah just glanced back at us like we were strangers. Too bad for him, we were both sailing on sugar and french fries and adrenaline. We wouldn't be coming down for a while.

The inside of the theater was already warm and the line for the women's bathroom stretched down the stairs and around the corner. I was about to say something to Victoria about it, but then I realized that two girls I didn't know were staring at me. Like, *star-ing* at me. Ogling. And then they did the worst thing and t u r n e d their heads so I couldn't see their mouths as they whispered. It was the most freshman girl move ever, and I decided that I hated them.

Victoria saw my face and followed my gaze to the girls. "Hey, Aud, c'mon," she said, pulling at my arm. "Fuck 'em. Just . . . let's go, all right? Fuck 'em."

"Yeah, okay," I said and let her and Jonah pull me into the theater, which was already packed with people, especially up front. Usually that's not a problem—Victoria and I could teach a class on how to wiggle your way up the front barricade—but I suddenly realized that if I was going to walk through a crowd, people were going to see me. They were going to recognize me. They were going to say things like, "Audrey, wait!" and I was going to feel stupid and embarrassed and very, very small.

I do not like feeling small or stupid; *ergo*, I was about to turn around and walk out and go hide in the car when someone tapped me on the shoulder. "Are you Audrey?" he said.

It was a bouncer—the biggest, hugest bouncer I had ever seen. The kind of guy who's so built you know his friends at the gym call him "Tiny." He was actual theater security, too, not one of those hacks with the yellow jackets that don't help kids out of the pit when they're getting trampled. He was standing next to the stairs that led to the VIP loft, the one place that wasn't packed with people. Yet. "Are you Audrey?" he said again.

"Um, yes?" I replied, like there was a wrong answer to the question. *Please don't squash me like a bug,* I added silently.

Tiny was motioning with his walkie-talkie upstairs. "Yeah, management just radioed down to me and told me to have you wait. They want you upstairs."

Next to me, Victoria made a small noise in her throat, and I felt my adrenaline and sugar rush start to pick up speed. "Um, why?" I asked.

The guy shrugged. "Just said to have you wait, that's all."

I still wasn't getting it, which just goes to show how ridiculously dense I am sometimes. "Um, are we being kicked out?"

Tiny cracked a small smile. I guess I was a pleasant change from all the drunk people he had to corral every night. Either that, or he thought I was an idiot. "Naw, you're not getting kicked out. They want you"—he motioned upstairs with his walkie-talkie again—"*upstairs.*"

Victoria grabbed onto my arm. "Upstairs," she repeated. "The *VIP area!* They must have seen you come in. The security guards must have told someone!" I could tell that she was about to implode like a star; even Jonah looked impressed. No doubt he was thinking about the possibility of an open bar and bartenders who didn't check IDs.

"But why do they want me up there?" I whispered to Victoria, trying not to look at Tiny.

"Because you're *Audrey!*" she hissed back. "You're 'Audrey, Wait!' You're a celebrity!"

I gaped at her. "Do you think we might be able to go back-stage?"

She squealed and jumped around, and I grabbed her hands and squealed with her.

"So you're *that* Audrey, huh?" Tiny said. "That's cool. My kid sister likes that song. She's got a crush on that lead singer guy."

"That's her ex-boyfriend!" Victoria told him, jabbing me the ribs. "Evan!"

"Whatever, man. It's a cool song."

I decided that I could dig Tiny's Zen vibe about the whole thing. And as a man in a suit rushed down the stairs and introduced himself as Eric, the promoter of the show, I realized that this was *really happening*. My hands were shaking a little and I have no idea why, but I looked over to Tiny for support.

And God bless that man with the thick neck, he got it. "Hey, girl," he said to me under his breath as he lifted the velvet rope so we could follow the promoter back up to the VIP area. "Enjoy yourself, all right?"

"No worries, my friend," I told him. After all, my privacy hadn't been sacrificed just so I could sit at home in my pajamas and watch *Laguna Beach* marathons and wonder for the thousandth time why I hadn't told that Isabella reporter to fuck off. I looked awesome. No one else had my boots on. I had my best friend on one side of me and the love of her life was on the other side of her, and when the promoter guy came back with all-access stickers, I slapped mine onto my hip, exchanged grins with Victoria, and thought, *Let's dance.*

10

"Amazed to stumble where gods get lost . . . "

—Patti Smith, "Beneath the Southern Cross"

NO MATTER WHAT YOU READ in all the magazines or see in movies and TV shows, it doesn't give you a sense of what it's like to be in the VIP area.

It was just so *calm* that I couldn't believe it. I think it was the first time that I had been at a show and no one tried to climb over me or trample me to death in the pit. (That happened to Victoria last year at the My Chemical Romance concert and oh my God, we could barely get her up. They had to stop the show so she and a bunch of other people could get pulled out. Totally scary.)

But this? This I could get used to. Here Victoria and I had all the room we wanted, and there were free drinks in the corner, and we could actually talk to each other without screaming in each other's faces to be heard over the sound system. And the view of the stage was *incredible*.

Still, I couldn't help but notice something.

"Do you get the feeling?" I said into Victoria's ear as we leaned up against the railing, "that people are watching us?"

Victoria, subtle as she is, immediately started looking around to see if I was right. "Don't look!" I hissed. "Great, you're looking now. Never mind, you ruined it."

"How can I tell if they're looking at us if I'm not looking at them?" she shot back, then peeked over our shoulders. "Oh, yeah, they're definitely looking at you. Not us. *You*."

"Me?"

She sighed and rested her head on my arm. "Yes, you, *mon cherie*. They didn't invite us backstage because Jonah slipped the bouncer a twenty."

We watched the crowd for a few minutes, pointing out the drunk girls and the loner guys, when I suddenly saw a guy with longish red hair, tall and towering over the rest of the crowd. James. "Hey, it's—!" I started to say, but then he turned around and I realized that it wasn't James after all. His nose was too pointy. James had a cuter, more buttonish nose.

Too late, though. Victoria had seen me point. "Who?" she said, and followed my gaze. "Oh." Then she turned to me with a knowing smile. "*Oh*."

"Shut up," I told her.

"I haven't said anything yet!"

"Don't."

"How can I shut up if I haven't said anything?"

"I know you. You've got a monologue coming up."

"No, I don't." Then she paused. "But if I *did*, I would say that maybe you should ask James out and stop torturing the rest of us, and that James obviously likes you in a 'let's have our own pep rally under the bleachers' way, so you don't have to worry about rejection." Then she sipped at her water innocently. "But don't worry, I'm not saying anything."

I pretended to be annoyed and ignored her, but Victoria always had a way of saying what I didn't want to admit to myself. In the car earlier that day, I hadn't told her that after those girls came into the Scooper Dooper and James spilled the soft-serve, he and I had both cleaned it up, and I'd accidentally gotten some vanilla on my face—and he had wiped it off with his fingertip. The store had been so quiet and we were below the counter where no one could see us, and if this mom and her three kids hadn't barged in just then . . . well, I think something would have happened.

I think he would have kissed me.

I think I kind of wanted him to.

And I didn't know what to think about that.

"Audrey, please bring your tray table to the upright position," Victoria suddenly said. "You're zoning out. It's unattractive."

I looked past her to see Jonah talking to some guy near the bar. The guy was with his girlfriend, who I later learned had won some radio contest and brought him as her plus-one. You could tell that Jonah and this guy were each thrilled to have another guy to talk to, since all the other men backstage were wearing suits with baseball hats pulled low over their eyes. ("Industry types," Victoria said knowingly.) *They* were looking at me too.

Jonah waved and I waved back. Victoria blew him a kiss.

"Are you going to marry Jonah?" I suddenly asked her. It struck me that in this whole room, she could look at one person and know that they knew her, really *knew* her, while everyone who looked at me only recognized me. They didn't *know* me. Not at all.

Victoria put her head back down on my arm and said in her quietest voice yet, "Yes."

And I kind of wanted to cry.

But then the lights cut out and Victoria stood up straight and started doing her crazy whistle as the Lolitas walked onstage. They were the opening act, but they were the reason Victoria and I had gotten up early six Saturdays ago to get tickets to the show. Who cared about the Plain Janes? They were big last year, but then they released their horrible second album, and then their lead singer got caught with cocaine and a gun at Newark Airport, then went to rehab, and I kind of had the feeling that they had reached their creative apex. It was band infighting, tell-all exposés, and massive debt from here on out.

The Lolitas, however, were incredible. Evan and I used to spend hours listening to the demo that he'd downloaded off some website, and we would drive up and down the freeway at midnight, singing along at the top of our lungs while we held hands over the gearshift. Their choruses made you wish you could fly, and we drove so fast on those nights, the orange streetlights lighting our way, taking us home.

Also (and I didn't mention this part to Evan), it didn't hurt that the band was fucking hot. I mean, I was into their music and everything way before I knew what they looked like, but they had put their pictures in the CD insert and when Victoria and I got it, we were both like, "Why, *hellooooo* there." Plus, they were British. I'm a sucker for cute boys with guitars, as you may have noticed, but throw in a London accent and I'll happily sell my soul without a second thought.

The Lolitas took to the stage and for the next half an hour, Victoria and I were the only ones dancing upstairs. Below us, the floor was packed with moving, gyrating people, and it looked like an earthquake was rolling beneath our feet as kids climbed on top of the audience, as bouncers threw them back, as the Lolitas shook their heads and stomped their feet and made everyone believe. "They're so fucking good!" Victoria screamed at me as they started in on their final song, and I could only nod. Something happens during a concert like this, when people are packed into every corner of the floor, like you're all in on some big secret, like that night could be the one show people talk about for the next forty years, the show where everyone says, "I was there!" but only a handful really were.

I could already tell that I would remember this show for the rest of my life—it was that good.

After the last song, I pulled my hair up into a knot and then hugged Victoria while we jumped around excitedly, still high off the show. "This is so cool!" I cried. "Can we do this again?"

"Fuck that!" she yelled back. "We're doing this *every* time!" She glanced over my shoulder. "Hey, do me a favor? Dance your way over to the bar! I need water!"

I nodded and made my way through the suits so I could get over to the bar. I'm usually pretty good at sizing up bartenders to see if they're willing to let a little drink slide by, but us VIPs were into the open bar thing, so the line was long. Once I got to the front, the bartender was all business as he got out a bottle of water and sprayed Diet Coke into a glass, so I didn't even bother trying to finagle a little vanilla Stoli splasher.

Which was a good thing, because when I turned around, all four Lolitas were making their way into the VIP room.

Immediately, I felt a hot flush creep up into my cheeks as I took my drinks and went in the opposite direction, toward Victoria. "The Lolitas are here!" I hissed in her ear as I gave her the water.

Her eyes grew wide and her head popped up. "Don't look," I

said. "Don't look. Just sort of casually glance toward Jonah—no, the other way—okay, yeah . . . a little more . . . see them?"

Victoria, to her credit, managed to stay on her feet. "Sweet mother of God," she whispered. "I've completely forgotten how to breathe."

I nodded in agreement, looking everywhere but at the band. Downstairs, I could see some kids spotting the band and whooping up to them, but I didn't dare look to see what the band did in response. It must've been good, though, because the whooping got louder. "I'm dying," I told Victoria. "Seriously. I can't feel my mouth."

She did the casual over-the-shoulder glance again. "I think they're coming over here."

"No!"

"Yes! Okay, Audrey, seriously? This is not a drill. This is the real thing. Don't screw up."

"Does passing out count as screwing up?"

"Without a doubt."

I looked past Victoria and saw that the band was, indeed, coming closer, although they were being stopped every five seconds by well-wishers and hand-shakers. Then one of them, the singer, glanced up at me, and we saw each other. I held his gaze for a fraction of a second and then looked back at my drink. "The lead singer just looked at me," I whispered to Victoria. It was getting really crowded upstairs, now that one of the bands had made an official appearance, and I had to lean in close so she could hear me.

"*So why aren't you looking back?*"

But I didn't answer because the band was coming closer and closer and then the lead singer was leaning on the railing next to me, laughing with the guitarist about something, and every single part of my skin was burning. If our arms accidentally touched, I might burst into flames. On my other side, Victoria was playing it cool, sipping at her water and watching the crowd down below, but if you looked closer, you could see her repeatedly tapping my ankle with her shoe, Victoria's Morse code for *Talk to him! Talk to him! Talk to him!*

Those three minutes when we stood next to each other were electrifying. It was so weird to be near someone that I knew but didn't *know*, and I suddenly understood why so many people kept looking at me, then looking away when I looked back. I know because I was doing the exact same thing to the Lolitas, and especially the guy standing right next to me.

My ankle was gonna be black and blue if I didn't act fast, so I was just about to open my mouth and say something stupid like "Great show!" or "I love your CD!" when some girl downstairs started climbing up the scaffolding on one side of the stage. "I'm no Plain Jane!" she was screaming, and let me tell you, she was no Sober Sarah, either.

"Oh, my God!" I said before I could stop myself.

And just like that, a British voice said in my ear, "Do you think she's gonna jump?"

"She should at least wait until the show's over," I replied before thinking, and then Victoria quit kicking me. "Fucking *finally*," I heard her whisper.

Drunk Girl was getting higher and higher and sections of the audience were cheering her on, including the Lolitas' lead singer. "Shake it, baby!" he was yelling, and then another chorus stage left started up with "Jump! Jump! Jump!" and she climbed higher.

"She's a little *too* good on that pole, don't you think?" the singer said again. "Like, maybe . . . ?"

"Wave a dollar bill and see what happens," I said. I had no idea I was so good at conversation when my mind was completely disassociated from the rest of my body. You learn something new every day, I guess.

"Ah, you'll have to loan me some," he said. "We haven't changed our money yet."

I felt like I shouldn't look at him, like he was the sun or something, but then he put out a hand and said, "Hi, I'm Simon. You're Audrey."

If I hadn't been hanging on to the railing, I probably would've toppled over. "H-How did you . . . ?"

He shrugged. His hair was all snarled and ratty and completely awesome, and his jeans looked like he had worn them during every show they had played. I wondered if they were his lucky pants, and then I realized I was thinking about his pants and my blush ran deeper into my face. Thank God it was so dark upstairs.

"Don't you know that word gets around?" Simon grinned. "'Audrey, Wait!' is a big fuckin' deal back home and then our manager said that you and your friend were up here dancing like banshees—"

Victoria had been waiting for her cue. "Hi, I'm Victoria, co-banshee," she said, reaching past me to shake his hand. No nerves for her. I wondered how she did it. I've been her best friend for eight years and I still don't quite understand how she works.

"Hi, I'm Simon, co-Lolita," he replied, and shook her hand. "And is this your fellow?"

Jonah, surprise surprise, saw his girlfriend and her best friend talking to the hottie opening act and decided that now would be a good time to make his way back to us. So introductions were passed around and we met Luc (bassist), Roger (drummer), and Charles (guitarist). I could feel the eyes of everyone else in the VIP area boring into our backs and all I had was one thought:

Thank you, Evan.

11

"I wanna always feel like part of this was mine. . . ."

—Jimmy Eat World, "A Praise Chorus"

WE ENDED UP watching the Plain Janes' set with the Lolitas, and halfway through the third song, when the lead singer was going spastic on the stage and looked like he was about to eat his microphone, Simon looked at me and smiled. "You should come backstage with us afterwards," he yelled into my ear. "There's gonna be a party but I'm not sure where yet."

"Okay!" I yelled back. I was already feeling pretty party-ready, since Simon was a pal and had let me finish his Jack-and-Coke for him. Most of the ice had already melted, but that was okay by me. It was also okay by me that I was able to drink from the same glass that he drank from. Next to me, Victoria and Jonah were laughing up a storm about something, and his arms were wrapped around her like ribbons on a present.

Everything felt *great*. Simon felt great standing next to me. He smelled even better, a combination of hair dye, his drummer's contraband joint that was passed back and forth between the band members, and somewhere way—*way*—down deep in the mix, soap. We weren't really talking that much, but every once in a while, I'd catch him looking at me or vice versa, and then we'd both smile and look back toward the stage.

The only real awkward moment was when, during their encore, the lead singer of the Plain Janes looked up toward our little VIP section and said with a laugh, "Here's our new favorite song," and then the band started to play the chorus of "Audrey, Wait!" and everyone started cheering on the floor and singing along. Everyone in the VIP area was looking at me, too, and I tried not to be weird about it.

Still. It *was* weird.

"If I had to guess," Simon said as the Plain Janes took a sharp left and veered into their final song, "I'd say you were blushing!"

"You'd be right," I said back. And then I started to blush more, since freaking Simon from the Lolitas (*ohmygodohmy-godohmygod*) had said that I was blushing.

This was, I decided, the best night ever. The rest of my life was gonna have to be amazingly wonderful, like I would have to cure cancer or save the rain forests or win a Nobel Prize, in order for it to ever surpass the greatness that was this night.

After the show, Jonah and Victoria and I followed the Lolitas down a small staircase into the crowded main backstage area, where someone had thrown a bunch of dark red curtains over the walls to make it seem less like a cinder-block cell and more rock-star-ish. "What's with the insta-décor?" Victoria said quietly to me as we surveyed the scenery.

"If Martha Stewart had a band, she would do it," I replied.

"Yes, because when I see red velvet, I think, '*RAWK!*'"

Apparently the party was happening backstage that night, since it was wall-to-wall people. Simon and his bandmates were laughing about something, and within the space of ten seconds, I saw a movie star, a famous record label guy, and that one actor who's on that one show, all sitting on the same couch. They looked bored, which kinda pissed me off. Were these the people that normally hung out backstage after shows? There should be a quiz, I thought, just to prove that you're actually into the music and not just there to see and be seen. Multiple choice, true/false, maybe even a little short answer. Definitely an essay question.

"Your arms look sooooo cute!"

There was a woman suddenly in front of me, so animated that she could have starred on Saturday morning television, and Victoria and I each took a step backwards. I personally don't like to stereotype women as dumb blondes because hello, I'm a blonde, and if anyone ever called me dumb, I'd act first and think later, but this woman, I'm sorry to say, was a dumb blonde. With dark roots. "Where did you get those cute arm-huggie things? They look soooo awesome!"

"Oh, um, they're just socks," I said as I tugged them up a little higher. "You know, it gets cold outside and there's nowhere to put a coat, so—"

"They are *adorable*, oh my God! I have to go get some!"

"Now leaving from track 3, the train to CrazyTown," Victoria said under her breath, and I gave her a poke in the ribs.

"You're lucky your arms are so skinny! My arms are soooo fat!" The woman's arms were the circumference of a twig.

"That's why I'm friends with her," Victoria jumped in. It was killing her to be quiet, I could tell. "Because of her skinny arms."

"*Would. You. Quit. It.*" I looked like an angry ventriloquist.

"Allll abbooooarrd," she whispered back.

"And you're Audrey, right?" Arm Woman hadn't even heard us. "I *looove* that song. 'Audrey, wait! Audrey, wait!'" She began bouncing around and singing like she was the only one in the room, sloshing her drink everywhere, and if people hadn't noticed that I was backstage, they sure did now. Even Record Label Guy and TV Actor Guy were looking in our direction.

I figured that the only way to stop her was to (a) trip her, (b) walk away, or (c) pretend she was on fire and tackle her to the ground for a quick Stop, Drop, & Roll, but luckily there was (d) none of the above, because Simon came back over and looked at Arm Woman, amused. She was still bouncing around and didn't even notice him. "I see you made a friend," he said. His voice sounded even hotter now that we didn't have to scream at each other to be heard over the music.

"It's a casual acquaintance," I said. "I'm not attached."

"Does this mean maybe you could come over here with me?" He held his hand out and gestured toward another part of the backstage area. "C'mon, these assholes are no fun."

My hero. Sigh. Swoon.

Victoria and Jonah and I followed Simon into the Lolitas' closet of a dressing room, which was filled with purple candles, tour cases, a table nearly collapsing with alcohol and water and sodas, and another table piled with candy, condiments, loaves of bread, and a tired-looking deli tray. The room was so crowded that no one could open or shut the door, and I found myself pressed up between Simon and the wall, holding another Jack-and-Coke. Victoria and Jonah had toppled over onto the arm of an old couch, where they were now perched precariously, giggling and helping themselves to cheese off the deli tray.

Meanwhile, the voice in my head was losing control. *Okay*, I thought. *Conversation. Gotta make conversation. Can't be a bump on a log. Don't look stupid. Dazzle him with wit and charm. Be natural. But be yourself. Talk about something. Anything. Current events, maybe? Is that boring? Depressing? Do I even know anything about current events? Will I sound stupid? Is he bored now? Does he look bored? GOOD LORD, WOMAN, TALK TO HIM.*

"There needs to be music," I blurted out. "A party with no music just doesn't sound right."

"So are you offering to DJ?" he asked.

Wit and charm went right out the window. "Oh, my God, that's my dream!" I squealed before I could stop myself. "You know how you always see pictures of DJs in New York and every-one's dancing and they've got the headphones on and all this music stacked up around them? That's like my perfect job!"

Simon grinned. "And if you were a DJ, would you play 'Audrey, Wait!?' That's what all the DJs are playing in New York clubs right now. You're the belle of the ball in Manhattan."

"Well, if everyone's already playing it, then I guess I'll have to be more original." But all I could think was, *playing in New York clubs?* This was a new one. Apparently my Do-Gooders message board rumor mill wasn't as up to date as I would have liked.

"You know," Simon continued, "if you DJ, then we can't talk. Or do anything else." He bent lower so he could speak into my ear. "Don't you know that DJs are always lonely at parties?"

A weird chill was going up my spine and down my arms. Conversation, I decided, was way overrated, and I was glad I hadn't taken the current-events route. "Just three songs," I told him, standing on my tiptoes so I didn't have to yell. Then I paused before saying quietly into his ear, "Just enough to get things started." *Holy crap, I'm doing it. Stand back, grasshopper, I am a flirting sensei and the world is my dojo.*

Apparently Simon thought so, too, because in five minutes, he had produced several of his bandmates' MP3 players and a pair of speakers, and I was kneeling on top of the band's dressing table in front of the mirror, scrolling through songs and frantically making a playlist. (I don't know whose player it was, and I prayed it wasn't Simon's, because somebody had way too many Barbra Streisand songs saved up.) Simon watched as I worked, resting his chin on my shoulder. Even his chin felt good. Not too round and not too pointy. I've never felt a hotter chin in my life.

It took a few minutes, and just as I finished, the musical gods decided to do me a huge favor. The dressing room had only gotten more crowded, so much so that all the smokers had to hold their cigarettes above their heads to avoid burning people. (I guess the Los Angeles smoking laws didn't apply to dressing rooms.) It soon became *the* place to be, because after the Plain Janes had showered, they appeared in the doorway and started squeezing into the room. I didn't see them, because I was too busy plugging in the MP3 player, but just as the Plain Janes appeared, fresh from their first show after drug arrests and breakup rumors and assorted dramas that only rock stars could experience, my playlist started and LL Cool J came blasting out of the gigantic speakers.

"Don't call it a comeback!"

The room went mental.

The Plain Janes thrust their arms into the air as if on cue, and the rest of us started cheering and clapping, and everyone who was standing was dancing, and everyone who was sitting started climbing up on whatever they were sitting on so they could dance, too. I could see Victoria and Jonah on the couch with at least five other people, all of them looking like they were surfing on the same board, they were so unsteady. I stood up on the dressing table because I wanted to dance, too, and Simon took hold of my hand and pulled himself up with me. He was, if I do say so, impressed. "Fucking fantastic!" he was saying. "That was bloody *brilliant!*"

And then he kissed me.

Mama said knock you out!

12 *"In the hands of a rock-and-roll band . . ."*

—Oasis, "Don't Look Back in Anger"

FOR THE NEXT HOUR OR SO, Simon and I kept to a tight schedule of making out, then talking a little, then making out again. I was so high on adrenaline and caffeine that I didn't even mind that everyone could see us, but after awhile, he pulled me behind one of the huge wardrobe cases so we could have some privacy.

Right then, though, privacy was the least of my concerns. After all, it had been six months since I broke up with Evan, and in that time, I had kissed no one. No. One. The closest I had gotten to any guy was with James under the counter and—

Hold the phone. Was I *insane?* Why was I thinking about James? Or Evan? Or the fucking *Scooper Dooper?* I was kissing Simon, lead singer from the Lolitas! More importantly, he was kissing me back! We were kissing each other! I immediately banished all other boys from my head and focused on the one in front of me.

"So," I said as we pulled apart to catch our breath. "Where's your next show?"

"San Diego, I think. Maybe Arizona. I don't even fucking know anymore." He grinned and began twirling a strand of my hair around his finger. "You have really sexy hair."

I love you, hair. I will never hate you again, not even when it's humid.

"Thanks," I said. "Yours isn't so bad, either."

"Yeah?" He leaned closer and kissed me fast. "What else do you think?"

If I told him what I was really thinking, he'd run screaming from the room. In my mind, I had already imagined myself flying across the Atlantic to visit him in London, having dinner together with our new friends Gwen and Gavin in some cute little restaurant before I went to work DJ'ing while my adoring rock star boyfriend wrote songs and won Grammys and made millions of dollars in royalties. However, I thought it best to keep that little fantasy to myself.

Just then, I saw Victoria across the room. She saw me at the same time and I realized that maybe I should check in with my best friend. "Um, can you just, um, wait here for a minute?" I said to Simon. "I'll be right back."

He pretended to pout. "How do I know you'll come back, though?"

My God, man, have you looked in a mirror lately? Trust me, I'll be back. "Two minutes," I told him. "Plus however long the wait in line is for the ladies' room."

That cracked him up. "You're such a trip!" he laughed. "Fuckin' *incredible.* Hurry up."

Victoria saw me separating myself from Simon and she left Jonah on the couch as we both pushed our way through the room. "It's like one big boa constrictor," she gasped as we both nearly fell out of the room and into the empty hallway.

"Bathroom," I said. "Now."

"Yeah, you think?"

We ran around the backstage area, showing our passes to every security guard who saw us, until we came across a room that just had a toilet and sink, and we scrambled into it as Victoria twisted the lock. We looked at each other for a second, then burst into our Happy Dance, the one that involved a lot of twisting and leaping and whooping around. "You're making out with Simon Lolita!" Victoria cried. "I saw you! Tell me everything!"

"He said I had sexy hair!"

"*Ohmygod!*" She jumped up and down. "What else, what else? Is he a good kisser? He looks like a good kisser!"

"I can't even feel my knees, he's so good!"

"Kneeless! That's so awesome! How's the tongue action?"

"Perfect! Not too much, not too little. What about me? Do I look like those fish on ice in the grocery store?"

"No, you look totally hot! Has he called you a bird yet?"

"A bird? What kind of bird?"

"I don't know. British guys always call women 'birds.'"

"No bird calls yet."

"Well, either way, you better remember every single word he says, because you're so telling me everything on the way home." Then she paused. "Do you think you'll get to go on his tour bus?"

The idea hadn't even occurred to me. I had skipped ahead by about five hundred steps and was already interior designing our London apartment. Wait, our London *flat*. "I don't know," I said. "I'm pretty happy behind the wardrobe case."

"How big do you think those bunks are, anyway? Big enough for two people?"

I laughed and we jumped around some more. Then we calmed down and I looked in the mirror. "How's my makeup?"

"Beautiful. That mascara is really holding up nicely. It's not even smudging."

"What about my lipstick?"

"You've got make-out lips. You don't need lipstick."

I turned back around to look at her. "Promise me you and Jonah won't leave without me? I don't want to end this night by having to hitchhike home."

She looked at me like I was an idiot. "Audrey. We're at a back-stage party with the Lolitas and the Plain Janes and about fifty other people whose pictures you have plastered all over your wall. There's free alcohol and cheese, and right now, Jonah's smoking hash smuggled in from Amsterdam. Trust me when I say this: We're not going *anywhere* without you."

13 *"Be my photo bitch and I'll make you rich . . ."*

—Belle & Sebastian, "Sukie in the Graveyard"

THE ONLY SLIGHTLY UNCOOL THING I had to do before going back to the party was text my parents to let them know I was okay. As parents go, they're pretty lenient with curfew stuff. The official deadline to be home is 2 A.M., but after midnight, I have to text them every half an hour so they know I'm alive and not being seduced by some roofie-dropping dirtbag. Victoria got wise and told her mom about my curfew, so our parents sat us down and gave us the whole "going out is a privilege not a right" speech, and now Victoria has the same curfew and rules, too.

I may have been busy making out with rock stars and impressing people with my mad DJ skillz, but I wasn't stupid enough to screw up my curfew. There were some kids at school who had to be home by ten on weekends, and the mere idea made my heart hurt.

Anyway, Victoria was half-right about her and Jonah staying at the party. The part she got wrong was the "we're not going *any - where*" part, since right after we got back to the room, and I found Simon, and we began making out without even a hello or a "hey, long time no see," the police arrived and declared the whole room to be a safety hazard. Their timing was pretty ironic, since Jimi Hendrix's "Fire" was playing, but also a relief, since every guitar player in the room—and there were many—was air-guitaring along with Jimi and making that horrible guitargasm face. Thank God Simon was a singer and I was spared the embarrassment of watching him do that.

"*Fuuuccckkk*," he groaned when he saw the firemen. "We gotta move this party back to the hotel." He looked down at me and grinned. "Come with us."

I glanced at the time on my phone. Twelve forty. It would take forty-five minutes to get home in order for me to walk in the door by 2 A.M., which left me with thirty-five minutes of Simon time. "I have to leave by one fifteen," I said.

"Oh, come on," he said, pushing up against me. "This is just the opening act tonight. The real party always happens at the hotel."

It was times like these that made me wish my parents were assholes. If they were, then I could just break the rules because I wouldn't care what they thought. But the truth is, I kind of *like* my parents. I didn't want them to worry about me or think that I was tied up in the trunk of some car. Or making out with rock stars at Sunset Strip hotels.

Damnit.

I tried to play coy. "I bet you say that to all the girls," I murmured, pulling him down so that my lips just touched his as I talked. "But I'm not like other girls." The Jack-and-Cokes had definitely made the flirting part of the night easier. Whoever had mixed them deserved a medal.

Simon said something that I didn't quite hear, and then he took my hand and, while the firemen kicked everyone out, he led me down the hall, back toward the stage, and then out a door and we were outside in a little courtyard, away from the fans who were camped out by the tour buses, away from firemen and Crazy Arm Woman and whoever else might interrupt us. All I could see were headlights cruising up and down the Strip, and the air smelled really good and salty from the late-night ocean fog that blew east and the sausage vendors that always set up camp after the shows. It was like our own private Emo Eden.

Once we were by ourselves, it got intense. More intense, in a way, than things had ever been with Evan. We had been each other's firsts and neither of us had seriously dated anyone before, so it was always a little awkward and fumbling. Not bad, but not mind-blowing. Simon, however, knew what he was doing. It was the kind of kissing where you had to remind yourself to breathe in order not to pass out and miss even a second of it.

After a few minutes, he put his hand under my shirt and began counting up my rib cage with his fingertips, and I wondered how far this was going to go. Or, more to the point, how far he expected *me* to go.

"Wait," I gasped. "Just . . . wait for a second. I need a minute."

We were both breathing hard, and he moved his hands so that they were on either side of my head, pressed against the wall. He laughed a little and brushed some hair out of my eyes. "Don't be scared, baby," he said. "Like you say, it's all good."

"I'm not scared."

"Liar."

"No, I just need a minute. Breathing is important to me, you know." I was trying to make a joke, but he was right. I was lying.

"Don't worry," he said. "You're not gonna suffocate." He ducked his head back down toward mine. "I won't let you."

We kissed for another minute, slower this time, but then we picked back up and when he put his hand up my shirt again, I didn't stop him. The air around us was filled with traffic sounds and crickets chirping and Simon moaning against my mouth, and I could feel myself starting to not care about anything except him, not parents or curfews or Victoria or anything else but how his hand felt on my skin.

"Come on, Euterpe," he suddenly whispered. "Inspire me."

The sentence hit me somewhere in the back of my head, and not because it sounded so bizarre. I had heard that name before. It was Greek. My dad always liked Greek mythology and used to tell me stories about gods and goddesses when I was a little kid. (My mother also had to talk him out of naming me Hera, which is a tale for another time.) But I remembered Euterpe. She was a Muse, one of the nine Muses.

"Wait, what?" I said, trying to pull away from him long enough to talk. "What'd you say?"

"I said, 'Inspire me.'"

"Before that part. What'd you call me?"

"Euterpe." He smiled against my mouth so that our teeth touched. "I said, 'Come on, Euterpe, inspire me.'"

The next time I broke off our kiss, I could tell he was getting a little annoyed. "What?" he said. "Now what?"

"It's just . . . do I inspire you? Like right now?" I was starting to get a bad tingly feeling in my toes.

"Well, yeah." He laughed a little and shook his hair out of his eyes. "That's what you do for everyone, right?"

"Um, not really," I said. I was trying to be cool about it, but my pounding heart was suddenly everywhere but in my chest.

"Oh, come on. I've heard 'Audrey, Wait!' It's like 'Sexy Sadie' for the Beatles, right?" Simon started singing into my ear. "*You came along to turn on everyone. . . .*" And just as he was about to move his hand even further up under my shirt, I remembered who Euterpe was: the Muse of Music.

And everything clicked together.

"Oh God," I said, and pulled away again. "Oh my God."

"What? You don't like the Beatles?"

"No, I love the Beatles, it's not—" I took a deep breath and looked at him, trying to see what he really wanted from me. "I'm not your muse. I'm not *anyone's* muse, all right?"

"You know about the Muses, baby?"

"Enough to know that I'm not one of them." The Jack-and-Cokes were long gone and I felt disgustingly sober. "It was just a fucking song, Simon. I didn't even write it."

"So help *me* write one," he said, and tried bending down to kiss me again. "We can be famous together. Let's help each other out. We can be—what's that word? Symbiotic. Use each other to survive."

"I know what symbiotic means," I snapped. (I didn't mention that it had been one of my favorite PSAT words last year, and that now he had totally ruined it.)

"Yeah, 'cause you're smart." Simon stroked the hair away from my face, but I pulled away. "So be smart now. You gotta strike while the iron's hot, right? You and me, we go on a few dates, make some press. The London papers will fuckin' eat it up. You'll be like the American Kate Moss."

I didn't even want to know who Simon thought he would be in

that twisted media fantasy. "So you only like me for—for the song? That's it?"

"Well, I mean, you're pretty hot, too. It's a win—win situation."

"Dude!" I said, and now I stepped away from him entirely. "In case you didn't get the memo, I'm only sixteen!"

I thought that would be my ace in the hole, the one thing to remind Simon that I was, in fact, a minor, and therefore as illegal as the cocaine the Lolitas' drummer had been snorting off the dressing table. But Simon just shrugged. "Well, that's all right," he said. "So's my girlfriend."

You know how you start laughing not because anything's funny, but because you're so mad and disappointed and crushed that it's all you can do? That's what I did, sort of laughing and wheezing and sighing all at the same time. Simon looked at me strangely and after a minute he said, "So is that a yes or a no?"

I shook my head. "It's the biggest no you've ever heard in your life, you fucking parasite."

He scuffed his shoe on the pavement and swore under his breath. "Fucking tease. No wonder he dumped you."

I just shook my head. "I dumped *him*. Try listening to the lyrics once in a while, Zeus."

He swore again and went back inside, slamming the door behind him. I stood by myself outside and looked at all the lights on the Strip and realized that despite all the lights and cars and stars, the street seemed so, so dark.

And then I wondered why I didn't hear crickets anymore.

I don't know why I told you any of this. After all, you know the whole story. You know that I wore cut-up tube socks on my arms.

You know that the Plain Janes played the chorus of "Audrey, Wait!" during their encore. You know that Simon and I spent the whole night making out, and that I got the party started with a great rap song and some serendipitous timing. You also know that the "crickets" weren't really crickets, but the Lolitas' tour manager crouched in the bushes with his camera phone.

And I know you've seen the video.

14 *"Sunshine, I wouldn't want to be in your shoes. . . ."*

—The Libertines, "Up the Bracket"

MY PHONE RANG at 8:32 the next morning. Victoria's ring. (Who else would be brave enough to call at that hour on a Saturday?)

At eight thirty-three, I threw a pillow at it.

At eight thirty-four it started up again.

At eight thirty-six I finally answered.

"Is the world ending?" I croaked. My tongue was thick in my mouth and my eyes were glued shut with leftover super-strength mascara. It had taken forever for me to fall asleep the night before, and now the last thing I wanted to do was wake up.

"It might be."

"Little green men?"

"No. Video on the Internet."

I forced my eyelashes apart. "Video of who and what?"

"You and Simon making out last night."

"What?"

By eight thirty-seven, I had crawled out of bed, stubbed my big toe on my desk chair, moved Bendomolena off my laptop, and logged in. "Send the link now," I begged Victoria.

"Already done. Check your IM." In the background, I could hear a car starting.

"Are you at Jonah's?" I asked her, a bit incredulous. Sure, Victoria's mom is Miss Civil Liberties and all that, but there was no way Victoria was allowed to spend the night at her boyfriend's house.

"Relax, I'm borrowing my mom's car. Jonah's probably still dead to the world."

"Where are you going?"

"I'm coming over to your house, you goober." She said it as though we had planned it for weeks.

"Right *now*?"

"Hello? I'm your best friend and this is a crisis. I'm on call 24/7, baby."

I was about to say, "Crisis?" when I clicked on the link and it took me to the Do-Gooders' message board, with a post entitled "OMG AUDREY AND SIMON LOLITA!!!!" It was only a link and I clicked on it, wondering how bad it could be.

Oh, it was bad.

The footage was grainy and a little orange (thank you, streetlights), but it was me and Simon making out in that private outdoor space. You could see us kissing and him gripping my hair, and then a small minute where I had pulled away before going back in again.

It was unmistakably us. I had spent the past six months looking at his picture on my wall—I would know him anywhere.

You could see my red boots and sock-covered arms.

And Simon's hand.

Under my shirt.

"Aud? Are you there?"

I swallowed hard. "Unfortunately."

"Don't worry, I'm on my way."

Bendomolena, disgruntled from being woken up so early, glared at me and then glanced at my picture on the computer screen. I swear to God, her little kitty eyebrows rose up in surprise. It was way too early to be judged by my cat, whose biggest accomplishment in life was rolling over. So I covered her eyes.

The drive home from the concert the night before had been torture. After Simon left me in the courtyard, I pulled myself together and then went to get Victoria and Jonah out of the party. "We have to go," I kept saying, and finally we managed to get out of there and back to the car. (I also think I signed two autographs in the parking lot, but I'm not sure.)

By the time Victoria turned left out of the parking lot, Jonah was passed out in the backseat and Victoria was sucking all the air out of the car with her enthusiasm. "That was amazing," she kept saying. "Best party *ever.* Fuck prom! Who needs to go to prom this year? We just hung out with the Plain Janes and the Lolitas!" Her eyes were shining so much that she could've used them for headlights. "Oh my God, Sharon Eggleston is gonna throw *up* when she hears about this! Promise me you won't tell her about it until I'm there, okay? I wanna see her face."

"Uh, Victoria? There's something—"

"So did you and Simon exchange email addresses? What about phone numbers? Are you gonna try to see him again before he—?"

"Look, something—"

"Check your text messages, I bet he's already written!"

There was only one way to stop her when she was on a roll.

"Vicky."

She stopped mid-ramble and looked over at me, one eyebrow raised. "Have you gone wrong?"

"Sorry," I said. And then I told her all about Simon. She was appropriately annoyed, then shocked, then outraged.

"He described you two as *symbiotic?*"

"Yep."

"What a poseur. I bet Mick Jagger never has to say 'symbiotic' to woo women."

By now, I had bitten off three fingernails and was working my way through a fourth. "Uh, I'm not really interested in how Mick Jagger woos women, Victoria."

"Well, someone should be, because I don't get it at all." She shivered a little. "So do you want me to turn the car around so we can go kick Simon where his balls would be if he had any? Because I will. I will turn this car around, so help me God."

By now she had made me smile. "He was a good kisser, though."

She *pffft!*'d the idea away. "Everyone has one good trait."

"He's not that good of a singer, either."

"*Please.* I didn't want to say anything, but he was *soooo* off-key the entire time. Dogs were howling outside, I swear."

"And didn't it look like Simon and the guitar player guy—what was his name?"

"Charles."

"Charles, thank you. Didn't it look like they were making lovey-dovey eyes at each other during their set?"

"It totally did! But it's all for the British press, you know. They love that shit."

"So it wasn't destined to work out, anyway." I shrugged. "I don't mix well with assholes, I guess."

"And that's what I like about you."

By the time I got home at 1:57 A.M., I was feeling a lot better, I was loving my best friend, and I actually felt bad for Simon for making such a big mistake.

Guess who felt stupid the next morning?

Victoria was at our house and in my room by 9 A.M. "Where are your parents?"

"I don't know. Farmers' market. Errand-running. Jogging. Whatever people do at this hour on a weekend. What did you bring?"

She produced some Styrofoam cups and a white bag. "I have coffee and breakfast burritos. Black and with extra salsa, just like you like."

"You're an angel sent from heaven," I sighed.

"Yeah, I get that a lot. And I also brought this." My angel from heaven was also wielding a huge hammer. "Guess what this is for."

"Um . . . you're going to help my dad with repairs around the house?"

"Ha. Funny. You should teach a class on how to be so funny."

"Are you going to brain me and put me out of my misery so I don't have to go to school on Monday?"

"Drink your coffee," she replied. "Caffeine will make you less suicidal. And this," she added, tossing the hammer on my bed, "is for smashing our Lolitas CDs."

I watched as the hammer thunked onto my pillows. "When I look up 'best friend' in the dictionary, there's a picture of you."

"I know." She batted her eyes seductively. "I went to Glamour

Shots just for the occasion."

So armed with Victoria, breakfast burritos, and glorious coffee, I braved the Internet once again. By the time my parents came home, Victoria and I had figured out that the video had originally been posted on YouTube, then to the Lolitas' message board, and then had gotten picked up by, well, everyone else. All the daily gossip sites had it, and the ones that didn't surely would by Monday morning. Some people had even made screencaps and posted those, so I could watch my humiliation and mistakes unfold frame by frame.

But it was the comments on the message boards that burned through the screen and into my skin.

"She's such a slut."

"OMG those arm things are FUG!"

"Awww, she's sooo pretty, I heart her!"

"I heard Simon has 5 STDs. That's why his last girlfriend left him."

"What an attention whore."

"Can we start calling her Courtney Love now?"

"A friend of mine was at the show last night and she said that Audrey was totally drunk and making out with everyone not just Simon but even the roadies too. Ew! Roadies!"

"Simon looks hot. He deserves better! Where can you get her arm warmers?"

"Your 15 minutes are up, Audrey. kthxbye."

By the time I had read two pages, I was done. "They're all crazy," I said, but my head felt fuzzy. "I mean, do they really think all this? About *me*? I'm a nice girl! I'm not a slut! I feed stray cats!" I was starting to become hysterical. "I'm the one who made my parents start recycling! I was practically the only person who joined Key Club for actual volunteer work, not just because it would look good on my college application!"

"Okay, hang on," Victoria interrupted. "First of all, if these people were cool, they wouldn't be home reading gossip sites on a Friday night."

"Oh. Well, um . . ." I shifted uncomfortably in my chair. "SometimesIdothattoo."

"Yes, but do you call people sluts on them?"

"Okay, point taken."

"See? They are not PLU."

"PLU?"

"People Like Us. I mean, I'm all for sharing our differences and all that, but we're cool girls. They"—she pointed at the computer screen—"are *crazy*. And they're hiding behind their fucking laptops or whatever. They're just jealous because they didn't get to make out with Simon."

"But . . . but . . . but they think I'm something I'm not!"

"Who cares? Have we not established that they're crazy?" She took a long drink from her coffee. "The way I see it, if crazy people hate you, you're ahead of the game."

"Audrey, are you actually *awake*?" I could hear my mom coming upstairs. The last thing I needed was for her to see photos of me making out in Hollywood. There wasn't enough coffee in the world for that conversation, so I slammed the laptop shut and, for reinforcement, threw Bendomolena on top of it. "I'm gonna buy you the best kitty condo ever," I promised her when she gave me a half-hearted swipe with her paw. "Just stay there."

"Stay there or you're gonna be a throw rug on my bedroom

floor," Victoria added under her breath. She takes a very no-nonsense approach with Bendy. They have an odd respect for one another, like two warriors engaged in battle.

"Wow," my mom said when she poked her head in the door. "You're both awake! Did the fire alarm go off?"

"Hi, Mrs. Cuttler," Victoria said. "Hope you don't mind that I came over. Audrey and I were just—"

If she said 'doing homework' or anything lame like that, we were dead.

"—getting an early start on this mosaic project we're doing."

I knew my cue. "Yeah, it's just some idea Victoria had. We have to smash up CDs."

"Well, be sure to do it outside."

"Is our daughter alive?" My dad came up behind my mom and grabbed at his heart. "My Lord, it's a miracle. I thought you were doomed to never see morning hours again."

I turned to Victoria. "Don't adjust your television. My dad's really that funny."

"I can see where you get it from," she shot back.

But I missed the jab because I was too busy looking at my parents' clothes, which were suspiciously . . . *athletic.* "Did you guys . . . do you go to *yoga?!*"

"For three weeks now." My mom flexed a bicep. "Check it out: I'm built."

"I did my first downward dog today," my dad added proudly, and Victoria made a weird strangled sound and then choked on her breakfast burrito.

"That . . . that's great, Dad. Really." I bit my cheek so hard that it hurt. "Way to go. Good personal growth and all that."

By the time they went back downstairs, Victoria and I both had tears in our eyes from trying not to laugh, and she ran across the room and buried her face in my pillow, muffling her howls of laughter. "Your *dad! Yoga!* Downward *dog!* Ahahahahah!"

I was laughing too hard to talk, but I joined her on the bed. "Are my parents PLU?" I asked after gasping for air and wiping my eyes.

"Oh God, I hope not." She sat up a little and raised up the hammer like a punk rock Thor. "So. Let's go wreak a little Saturday morning havoc."

15

*"Lying wide awake in the garden,
trying to get over your
stardom. . . ."*

—Pete Yorn, "Just Another"

TO SAY I THOUGHT ABOUT THE VIDEO for the rest of the day would be an understatement. It consumed me and made my stomach do contortion acts that belonged in Cirque du Soleil. Victoria and I smashed up the Lolitas' CDs ("C'mon!" she yelled from the side as I bludgeoned them into smithereens. "Put some muscle into it! Channel your inner Trent Reznor!"); then we found pictures of worthier rock stars to paste over the Lolitas on my wall collage, but nothing worked. By nighttime, all my finger-nails were nubs, and I had gone to work on my cuticles. I was a masochist from the wrists down.

The weird thing was, music wasn't fixing the problem. Normally, I could put on a well-chosen song or two and I'd feel better. But every time I tried to make a playlist, I thought of making the playlist at the backstage party. When I went through my CDs, my first instinct was to put on the Lolitas, but that CD was now at the bottom of a trash bag in a million pieces. And forget the radio. I couldn't risk hearing "Audrey, Wait!" come on again, lest my ears start to bleed in agony. It was playing all the time now, and not just on KROQ or KUXV or whatever radio station my parents pretended not to listen to. It was still moving up the Billboard charts—number fifteen, last time I checked—and it didn't seem to be stopping any time soon. I'd even heard my geometry teacher humming it in the hallway, but at least he'd had the good sense to look apologetic after he saw me.

So that night, I lay in bed in total silence, looking at the glow-in-the-dark stars on my ceiling. (I had spent a whole afternoon last year putting them up in the form of constellations, which Evan had called anal. "Just stick 'em wherever," he said. "You're gonna be sleeping anyway." Jerkface.) Bendomolena was asleep at the foot of my bed in her normal space—right between my ankles, so it was impossible to roll over without kicking her—and I could hear my dad watching TV downstairs. I couldn't understand how things stayed so normal with everyone else while inside, I felt like a tornado with no place to touch down.

My mom, however, is not an idiot. She knew something was up. "Audrey?" she poked her head in my door. "Are you asleep?"

"Yes."

"Somehow that answer doesn't surprise me." She opened the door a little bit more. "Are you feeling okay?"

"Yeah, why?"

"Because you're in bed at ten o'clock. And you didn't eat a lot of dinner. And your fingernails look like they lost a bet with your teeth."

"No, I'm fine."

"You sure?"

"Yeah."

"So I shouldn't be worried by your monosyllabic answers?"

"Not at all. See, there's three syllables right there."

Still, she came into the room and bent over the bed to kiss my forehead. "I love you, my crazy, music-obsessed daughter."

"Love you, too."

"You sure everything's all right?"

This is what I wanted to say: "No, everything's *not* all right, it's a mess, and I made out with a hot guy who turned out to be really mean and then pictures got posted online and girls think I'm a slut and the entire nation is singing about my love life and my best friend is totally in love with a great guy and they're going to get married and they'll leave me all alone and I'll be so depressed that I won't get into college and I'll end up being one of those creepy wrinkly old women who try to get backstage at hair-metal shows and hook up with roadies! So if you could just do that great Mom Thing you do where you fix everything and make it better, that would be perfect, okay? Is that good?"

But this, of course, is what I said: "Everything's fine."

It's the worst thing to be the best liar.

16

"To me my life, it just don't make any sense. . . ."

—The Strokes, "Barely Legal"

I HAD THOUGHT that Monday morning would be more of the same, just like after "Audrey, Wait!" premiered on the radio and everyone was all interested in me. I figured that people would be even more curious and Sharon Eggleston would flip her hair a few extra times and Tizzy would pop a blood vessel in her eye from sheer excitement and that sort of thing.

Ha.

By 10 A.M., I knew things were different. It was like people were *afraid* to talk to me, even people I had known since junior high. When I walked through the front door, there were clusters of people just watching me, staring like I was parting the Red Sea instead of going to first period.

Also, five different girls had homemade arm huggies on.

But what really sealed the weirdness deal was that Tizzy had suddenly gone shy. She was the first girl I saw with arm huggies, and of course, they were made from her dad's work socks and looked kind of wrong and wrinkly, but when I made eye contact with her, she got red and flustered.

This would not do at all. If anyone had the right to be all red and flustered, it was me, not Tizzy.

"Hey!" I said, running after her once class ended. I was going to ask her what was up, why no one was talking to me, but I got my answer without asking the question.

"Oh, hi," she said, and a huge goofy smile came over her face. "*Hi.*"

"Hi."

She couldn't hold it in any longer. It was like watching a rocket launch. "*Omigod, you made out with Simon Lolita!*" She grabbed my arm and began jumping up and down, pinching me with every syllable. "I saw the pictures online last night—my mom said I couldn't go online because I'm totally grounded right now, but she goes to bed so early so I snuck on the computer and Oh. My. God. I saw you and him kissing!"

Blastoff.

Beads of sweat were forming on her upper lip and her cheeks were crimson with excitement. "We've never had, like, a real celebrity at school before!" she continued. "Oh my God, I don't even know what to say! You're famous and you're, like, *talking* to *me!*"

"Tizzy, I'm not fam—"

"You are, though! Everyone's talking about you! *Everyone!* In the girls' bathroom this morning, everyone was saying that you're *sooo* lucky, and a couple of girls were all jealous, but don't worry, Aud, I told them that you totally deserve it and that Simon Lolita is lucky to have you and that you two are gonna be the cutest couple. Is it okay that I just called you Aud?"

"Tizzy." My head was spinning just watching her. "Breathe."

"Okay!"

"Try doing it right now."

"I am, I am!" She waggled her hands in front of her. "Is he coming to the winter formal with you?!"

It was all I could do to keep from shaking her. "*Tizzy*. We're not dating."

"But you made out with him!"

"I'm incredibly aware of that. But we're not dating. It was a one-time thing."

"Is he a good kisser?"

My brief hesitation was all she needed. "I *knew* it! I knew he would be! Sharon Eggleston was all, 'I bet he totally sucks,' but I was like, 'Nuh-uh, no way, he's *British*.'"

Sharon Eggleston. Fuck. She lived for this sort of popularity uprising, just so she could be the one to squash it. If our school ever performed a play about the French Revolution, she could play the guillotine.

I finally managed to disentangle myself from Tizzy, but only because I was going to be late to history, and when I walked in, Sharon had saved me a seat next to her. "Hi, Audrey!" she waved. "Over here!"

I was probably going to need someone to taste all my food from now on. Tizzy came to mind.

"Hi," I said, and I sat next to her only because someone else was in my normal seat.

"*So*. Tell me everything." She rested her chin in her hands and waited for story time.

"About what?"

"About what? About your fabulous weekend making out with Simon! What else is there?"

"Oh, that," I said, and laughed a little. "It was just this . . . thing."

"Thing?" she repeated. "C'mon, details—details, please."

Okay, now that pissed me off. Like Sharon Eggleston was my own personal diary or something. Like she hadn't spent months ogling my now ex-boyfriend from a distance and sending me creepy glances at me every chance she got. Like she wouldn't spread the details about Simon Lolita all over the entire campus w i t h i n fifteen minutes without even leaving her seat. Like I needed to give her another reason to hate me. Like we were even *friends*. "Well, I . . . I don't really like giving out details, Sharon. I mean, it's not a big deal."

Her eyes narrowed. The queen was not used to being refused by serfs. "Not a big deal?"

"No." I tried to smile a little. "You know, things happen, they pass. We're not dating, it was just one time. It's totally nothing."

"Nothing."

There was something in the way she said it that made goose bumps pop up on my arm. Somewhere, an executioner was sharpening his blade.

"That's right," I said, smiling wider. "Totally nothing. It's all good."

And then Mrs. Willis was yelling at us to turn around in our seats and pay attention for just once in our lives, and I became the most obedient student over. Sharon Eggleston's eyes, however, burned two hot holes into the side of my head for the rest of class.

By the end of the day, I was exhausted from not talking to people. Aside from Tizzy, with her verbal explosion, and Sharon, with her "friendly" conversation, the only people who actually talked to me were Victoria and Jonah. Actually, Jonah just wanted to know if I had a dollar for Del Taco, but still. It counts as talking.

And not that I was paying attention or anything, but James was not at school.

On Tuesday, Sharon and Natasha managed to corner me on my way past the library. "Oh, hi," I said, like I was greeting some really old relative who had tissues shoved up her sweater sleeves. "What's up?"

"Are you ignoring us?" Sharon said. She had her arms crossed in front of her, the way she always did to shove her boobs up and make them look bigger. Like she needed help with that.

"Ignoring you?" I repeated. "What are you talking about?" I knew exactly what she was talking about, though. And if I lived in Honesty Land, I would've been screaming, *Yes, I'm ignoring you, you twit! Get it through your impossibly shiny hair–covered head!* But that wasn't an option.

Yet.

She recrossed her arms and boosted her boobs even higher. "You know, Audrey," she began, "my friends and I have been really nice to you."

"Nice?"

"Yes, fucking *nice.* We invite you to lunch with us. When I first saw the pictures of you with Simon Lolita, I was worried about you. And then yesterday in history class, I *tried* to be a friend to you."

Victoria brought coffee and a hammer, I thought. *You just dug for details.* I really wished Victoria was here right now, too, because she would've said that without blinking. "Look, Sharon, things have just been really crazy lately and it's just that I haven't—"

"Is this how you treat friends, Audrey? By ignoring them?"

"Friends?" I said. "Sharon, you and I haven't been fr—"

But she wasn't even listening. "You know, Audrey, I could *ruin* you at this school."

I don't respond well to threats. (No surprise there.) "Oh, *really?*" I said in my fake friendly voice.

By now, she was so in my face that I could smell her vanilla lip gloss. "You always get everything you want, don't you? Or *every - one.* Evan, Simon fucking Lolita, and now James." Her teeth were clenched so tight that it hurt to look at her. "What makes *you* so fucking special?"

"James?" I sputtered. "Wait, wha—?"

"Hey, what are they doing over there?" Natasha, aka Darth Vader, was peering past Sharon and me, and we all turned to look at four girls who were standing about ten feet away, their camera phones flipped open, giggling excitedly as they took pictures of me and Sharon.

"Um, excuse me!" I yelled. "Could you maybe not do that right now? Or ever?"

"*New* friends of yours, Audrey?" Sharon sneered. "Are those the ones you *do* call back?"

But the girls kept clicking away, and then Natasha proved to be mildly useful when she said, "Do they go to this school?"

Because no sirree, they most certainly did not.

From across the campus, I could see Victoria and Jonah walk-ing together, their arms touching—hand-holding was one of the many things banned at our school, like guns and drugs and small animals—and Victoria saw me and her face changed when she saw the girls and their camera phones. I saw her mutter a string of expletives and then she untangled her arm from Jonah's and stormed over.

By the time she got to my side, I was already confronting the girls. "What are you fucking doing?" I demanded.

"Are you taking pictures of her without even *asking* her first?" Victoria said.

"Do you go here?" I added.

"You don't even *go* to this school, do you?!" Victoria screeched.

The girls looked somewhere between dumbstruck and giddy, like their adrenaline had frozen them into place. "Um, hi!" one of them said.

"Hi. What the hell?"

"You're Audrey, right?"

I threw my hands up in the air. "No, it's just a crazy coincidence. Yes, I'm Audrey! Why are you taking pictures of me?"

"Oh my God, it's really her," another girl said, covering her mouth and squealing a little. I knew this type of girl. She was a Teenie. The Teenies are the ones that always hang out by the tour buses after shows and scream, "I want to have your babies!" to the lead singers and only know the one popular song off the CD and totally humiliate the rest of us, who just want to say how much we love the music and how much it means to us. I hate those girls like I hate poison ivy and beets.

"Why are you taking pictures of me?" I said. "What are you doing here? How did you even figure out what school I go to?"

"Evan went here, right?" The third girl was pulling on her hair nervously. "We read it online and we're just really big fans of yours!"

"And his too! We loooovveee the Do-Gooders!" The second one was almost swallowing her own tongue in excitement.

But I was still stuck on the earlier statement. "Fans of *mine?*"

"Oh my God, totally!" The first girl regained her power of speech just in time. "I mean, the song is so amazingly awesome and then we saw that you're dating Simon from the Lolitas and just . . . gah!" Then she looked at my arms. "Where are your arm huggies?"

"How long did it take you to grow out your hair?"

"Is Simon coming to pick you up?"

"Did you and Evan really break up? Or are you still dating?"

"Will you take a picture with us?"

"Here!" The second girl thrust her camera at Victoria. "Will you take our picture? For our website?"

Victoria and I looked at each other. "Are you being Punk'd?" she asked me.

"You're being Punk'd?!" Now the girls were at the intersection of ecstatic and apoplectic.

"Excuse me, ladies!"

I looked over my shoulder and saw both our vice-principal and the school security guard running toward us, each of them with a walkie-talkie in his hands, Jonah not far behind. I also saw that a crowd had started gathering—but half of them were horny teenage guys hoping for a girl fight. Sharon Eggleston was standing to the side, arms crossed, looking bemused and annoyed. Not that she ever had another expression on her face.

"Okay, ladies, what's going on here?" Our vice-principal, Mr. Nielson, arrived, looking a little out of breath. The security guard arrived a second later, ready to kick ass and take names. It was understandable, considering that there was very little to do at our school besides catch kids sneaking off at lunch and smoking in the woods. This was going to be the highlight of his year, I could tell.

But back to the question at hand. It was a good one. What *was* going on? I decided to put it as plainly as I could. "These girls snuck onto campus and started taking pictures of me for their website."

"They're big fans of hers," I heard Sharon say behind me, and I didn't even have to turn around to know that Victoria was giving her a Look of Death.

Mr. Nielson turned to look at the girls, who were starting to realize their mistake. "Um, we just thought—" the first one began.

"What school do you girls go to?"

They got even smaller-looking. "Um, Kennedy?" The other public high school in our city.

"What kind of moron ditches school just to go to *another* school?" Victoria exploded. "At least you could go buy some CDs or go shopping or something!"

"Okay, Victoria," the security guard said. "That's enough." I could tell he kind of dug her, though, like he was thinking the same thing. I bet he was a total stoner in high school.

Mr. Nielson glanced at me briefly before turning to my fan club. "You three, follow me to my office. Audrey and Victoria, the bell's ringing in"—he glanced at his wristwatch—"thirty seconds, and I assume you have a class to go to. AS DO THE REST OF YOU!" he yelled to everyone else watching our little drama. "PLEASE FIND SOMETHING ELSE TO DO BESIDES BEING CASUAL OBSERVERS!" There was a rumor that Mr. Nielson had gone to Yale Drama School, a rumor I was starting to believe.

The girls looked back at me. Two of them had tears in their eyes. "Sorry, Audrey," the third one said. "We were just . . . *excited.*"

And then I felt really bad. I mean, I was a fan too. It had only been four days since my own personal rock star humiliation. But I had done it because I was excited too. I hadn't thought about cameras or consequences, and now look what had happened. I couldn't blame the Teenies, because sometimes I wasn't much different than them.

But at least when I ditched school, I didn't go to another one.

And to make my bad day worse, James was absent. Again. Two days in a row. Just an observation on my part. I'm a very observant person.

If you think Monday and Tuesday were exciting, though, wait until you hear about Wednesday.

Wednesday takes the cake.

Because that's when the magazines came out.

17

THE FIRST PICTURE I SAW of myself on Wednesday was scratched into the door of the second stall in the girls' bathroom. The bathroom that everyone used, of course. It was still early in the morning, not even 9 A.M. yet, and I went into the stall, closed the door, and lo and behold, someone had drawn a girl blowing a guy with the words AUDRY SUX DIK scrawled below it.

Victoria came in while I was washing my hands and she stopped short. "Don't use the second stall!"

"Too late." I pumped the soap dispenser extra hard. "You saw it?"

"Heard about it." Victoria disappeared into the stall so she could inspect it herself. "This doesn't even look like you!" she called out.

I rolled my eyes. "I don't think they were going for artistic integrity."

"And they misspelled your name!"

"I know! And for the love of all that is holy, how hard is it to spell 'dick'?" I shook my hands dry since we were out of paper towels.

"Geniuses, they are not." Victoria came back out and watched as I sent water flying everywhere; then she pulled some lip gloss out of her purse and started to apply it in the mirror.

"Hey," I told her. "Do you want more gloss? Some company sent a case of their new Kiss-Off lip gloss to the house yesterday. They're trying to get me to endorse it. They saw the Simon video, apparently."

Victoria's hand froze midway to her mouth. "People are sending you free cosmetics?" she screeched. "Oh my God, you're living my dream life. Are you gonna do it?"

I shook my head. "Hell no. They all taste gross and they come off in, like, thirty seconds."

"Who cares?" She was aghast. "If you endorse this, then you'll get *other* products, and then maybe you'll even get your own fragrance! I am totally coming over to get free lip gloss from you! Did they send mascara too?"

"No mascara yet. Maybe at the bottom of the box."

Victoria just shook her head. "Took you long enough to tell me," she muttered, trying not to move her mouth as she put on her own gloss. "That's why we have technology, Audrey, so friends can share exciting details about their lives with other friends. You're dropping the ball."

"I'll do better next time," I promised. "You'll be the first to know about the next product launch."

Victoria held the door open for me as we walked out. "Damn straight, I'm gonna know. I'm going to bribe your mailman to—"

Two girls suddenly walked up to me, holding a magazine and a Sharpie pen. "Um, Audrey, can you sign this?" I vaguely recognized them as freshmen. (Traveling in herds is one of their trademarks.) "Please?" They had the same starry-eyed look that the three girls from Kennedy had had the day before. I was becoming a pro at recognizing it.

Victoria immediately shoved her way in front of me and crossed her arms, ready to go off on them. Then she saw the magazine and her eyes widened. "Oh. My. God."

"What?" I looked over her shoulder and glanced down at the page.

A picture of me making out with Simon stared back. "Star Muse with Star Musician!" the bubbly pink headline read, and below, in smaller type, "Audrey Works Magic with British Guitarist!"

"Lemme see that," I said, and grabbed the magazine out of the girls' hands. There were four pictures at the top of the page, all of them screencaps from that damn video. Simon and I were locked together, one of my legs wrapped around his hip, his hands in my hair. In other words, they weren't Photoshopped. "Victoria?" I barely recognized my own voice.

"Do you need to sit down?" She was at my side in an instant. "Here, let's sit down. You're kind of pale."

"No, I don't need to sit down. I need a gun."

"No, you don't. You're very peaceful. You like fluffy animals and rainbows. No guns for you."

"Then a knife."

"Nothing with sharp edges. Here." She began steering me toward a low wall, leaving the freshmen girls behind us.

"Nunchuks, then."

"Oh, please. You'd knock yourself out cold before you hurt anyone else."

The magazine was starting to crinkle between my hands, and

I smoothed it out so I could read it better. "Do you think that this is everywhere?"

Victoria sat next to me and looked at the pictures like we had done online several days before. "Um, yes. It's a national magazine."

I groaned and covered my mouth. "Am I on the cover? If I'm on the cover . . ." I couldn't even imagine what I'd do.

Victoria pried the magazine out of my hands and glanced at the cover. "Celebrity Weight Loss Secrets!" she read. "Nope, not you, you're safe—oh. Wait a minute."

"What?"

"There's a small picture of you in the upper corner."

"With Simon?"

"Oh, yeah."

"I need a gun."

"We've talked about this."

"Oh my God! My *parents* are going to see this!" My legs were alternately hot and cold. "They're going to go the grocery store and buy apples and milk and they're gonna stand in the slowest check-out lane and look to their left and *wham*! It's me! Making out! With a guy!"

"Maybe you could offer to do all the shopping this week," Victoria suggested. "Or eat out a lot."

"My mother is gonna get a pedicure and read the article!" A horrible thought slammed into my head. "Is there an article? What does it say?"

"Okay, hold on, hold on. . . . . Here." She skimmed the page, nodding to herself. "Nothing bad. Nothing that we didn't already know. You're the new music muse, Simon plays in the Lolitas, et cetera." She kept reading. "It says here that Evan is currently on tour in Japan and had no comment through his spokesperson. Wow, Japan! Way to go, Ev."

"This is all his fault." I buried my face in my hands and rested my elbows on my knees.

"Hey . . . wait a minute." She was peering more intently at the magazine now, and then she shoved it under my nose. "Is that you in English class?"

I grabbed it from her so I could see for myself.

Oh. My. God. Yet. Again.

"That *is* you in English class!" Victoria crowed. "And you're sleeping!"

Sure enough, it was a grainy-and-obviously-captured-by-a-super-strong-camera-lens photo of me asleep in class, my head propped up on one hand as I dozed. (I honestly didn't remember falling asleep in class, but really, our teacher, Mrs. Himkin, has a voice like a white-noise machine, so it makes sense.)

And there was a very suspicious person in the background, smiling right at the camera. Sharon fucking Eggleston.

"That girl," Victoria fumed when I pointed out Sharon's cameo in the picture. "She's certifiable. How did she even know there were photographers taking pictures of you?"

"She spends her entire life posing," I pointed out. "It finally paid off."

Victoria just shook her head and continued reading the article. "'Audrey's a great girl, but I couldn't keep up with her,' says nine-teen-year-old bassist Simon, whose band the Lolitas is opening a string of dates for comeback kids the Plain Janes." She shook her head. "Wow, what an asshole. You really need to start dating math nerds."

"I need to join a convent."

"No, I changed my mind. What you need is a spokesperson."

I looked up just long enough to glare at her. "Not helping."

"Seriously, Aud, you do. You need someone to spin this, to tell your side of what happened. A good publicist would've kept this out of the press."

I glared at her.

"What?" she said. "I watch *E! True Hollywood Story* just like everyone else! These aren't industry secrets!"

The bell rang then and I took the magazine from her and stuffed it into my bag. "The fewer people who see this, the better."

Victoria watched, biting her lip. "Their circulation has to be, like, a million. Are you going to hide all of them?"

"*Not. Helping.*"

But of course there were already three copies of the magazine in my English class being passed around under the desks, and then four more in biology in the afternoon. Someone must have made a newsstand run during lunch, because while I tried to hide in the library, six different people came up to me with the magazine and ever-present Sharpie, saying, "Um, Audrey?" I signed because I didn't know what else to do.

For the first time in my life, I had absolutely no idea what else to do.

Someone did, though. During biology, an aide came up from the office and whispered something to our teacher, who then motioned to me. "Audrey?"

I went up, my face still flaming, my legs still rubbery, with—no surprise here—everyone watching me. "You're wanted up in the office," the teacher said quietly. "You can take your stuff with you."

"Oh." Was it possible to be expelled for being in a tabloid newspaper? I wondered. Would this be on my college transcripts? "Okay."

When I got to the office, the secretary motioned to a chair outside of the principal's door. "Go ahead and take a seat," she said. "He's in a meeting right now, he'll be out in a minute."

"Okay." It was becoming the easiest answer.

The chair was uncomfortable and hard, and I shifted a bunch of times before noticing that there was a copy of the magazine on the secretary's desk, buried between piles of paperwork. She saw me looking and gave me a half-apologetic smile. "My daughter's a fan," she said. "She loves the song. She's mad at me for not getting Evan's autograph when he went to school here."

I couldn't even try to be polite. "Fantastic."

And then out of the corner of my eye, I saw red hair.

James.

He was back!

He was standing in line at the front of the office, explaining something with a note in his hand, and he looked up just as I was beginning to stare. His eyes widened when he saw where I was sitting. "You? In trouble?" he mouthed.

I shrugged and waved back, trying to look both cute and innocent.

He walked over a few minutes later, once he was done at the front counter, and we both regarded each other. It was different to talk to him at school. There was no work to hide behind, no cones to scoop or sales to ring up. I didn't know what to do with my hands or arms. Fold them in my lap? Cross them? Play with my hair? Then I realized that James was doing the same thing, too. It was Awkward City for both of us.

"Hi," he finally said. "What'd you do?"

"I went to a concert on Friday night and made out with the lead singer from the Lolitas and their tour manager hid in the bushes and made a video of us and then sold it to the tabloids and now the principal wants to meet with me in his office." Like he wasn't going to find out in about three minutes, anyway.

James's eyes widened and he swallowed hard when I said "made out." "Oh," he said. "That's, um, yeah. That sucks."

"I know. Where have you been?" *Oh, God, I'm a moron.* "I mean, like, not that I was like, looking for you, but I was just . . . I saw that you weren't here for a couple of days and . . . I mean, I just noticed, that's all." *Jesus, Audrey, stop talking.*

He blushed crimson as I kept trying to explain myself. "I was sick," he said. "Food poisoning."

"Oh. Gross."

"Yeah." He shifted his bag awkwardly onto his back. "Are you still working this afternoon?"

"Yeah, I think so. Unless the paparazzi stop me from getting into the mall."

James smiled at my lame joke. How polite of him. "Cool."

"Cool."

"So I'll see you there."

"Okay."

But he didn't leave right away. "The Lolitas are way overrated," he finally said, almost as an afterthought. "They just don't know it yet."

I tried to say something in response, but there were too many words for me to sort out in my head. And by the time I got it together, James was already walking away. "See you later," he said with a wave.

I was about to say goodbye back, but then the principal's door opened and when he walked out to get me, I saw my parents sitting in his office, both of them wearing their work clothes.

Definitely a nine out of ten on the "oh, shit" scale.

"Audrey, why don't you come on in?" Mr. Rice was smiling, but it wasn't one of those friendly smiles.

I went in and sat down next to my dad, who gave my arm a squeeze and said, "Hey, kiddo," which was like the worst thing he could have done, since it made me totally want to start crying all over the place, but the day had been bad enough without me losing it in Mr. Rice's office. I vowed to keep it together until I was safe at home with my stereo, Bendomolena, and the saddest, most dramatic mix CD I could come up with. The Smiths were already going to figure in heavily, I could tell. *Sixteen, clumsy, and shy, that's the story of my life.* Word, Morrissey. Total word.

"So," Mr. Rice said as he sank back down, "there have been some developments recently, Audrey, and I've called your parents in so we could discuss the appropriate course of action in order to ensure the best educational experience for you."

If you don't speak Adult, allow me to translate that sentence: "You're fucking up and making us all look bad. Stop doing that so I can have an easier day at work."

But I just nodded and then glanced at the copies of the magazine on his desk. "I didn't know about those," I said quickly. "I just saw them today."

"Audrey." My mother leaned past my father to look at me. "No one's blaming you."

But my dad had other ideas.

"Are you sleeping in class?" he asked, jabbing a finger at the photo on page 67. "Because to the untrained eye, my dear, it looks like you're sleeping in class."

Cue the arched eyebrows from both parents. "Why are you sleeping in class?" my dad asked as my mom peered down at the magazine.

"Uh, Dad?" I said. "Here's a better question: Why are people *taking pictures* of me sleeping in class?!"

And then Mr. Rice interrupted so he could detail everything that had happened over the past several days: the video leaking online; girls sneaking onto campus to see me; all the kids who had been asking me for autographs or talking to me in the halls, making me late for class again and again; the graffiti in the bathroom stall. Let me tell you, you haven't yet plumbed the depths of embarrassment until your principal tells your parents about crude drawings of you performing sexual favors. *That* was a moment I could've lived the rest of my life without experiencing, and Mr. Rice can definitely expect to find my future therapy bills in his mailbox.

But then he kept talking, and it turned out there was more. Promoters were sending concert tickets to the school with my name on them, and the mailman was delivering twice as many letters because people were starting to send fan mail. And then, halfway through Mr. Rice's speech, his secretary knocked on the door and said, "These were just delivered for Audrey," and brought in a vase of a dozen pink roses.

"Wow," I said. My parents, who had been listening and nodding and saying, "Uh-hmm," and glancing at me like I was a ticking time bomb, looked like their heads were gonna explode when the roses made their appearance. I picked at my well-worn cuticles and tried to look like a model student. "So," Mr. Rice told them, "as you can see, we need to figure out a future plan going forward."

"Well, she still needs to go to school," my mother said. She was holding the vase with the roses and finally just set them on the floor. "That can't change, and homeschooling will *not* be an option." I could tell from her voice that she was going all Mama Bear on him, which made me feel a little better.

Mr. Rice nodded. "Well, for the time being, we were thinking about having her—"

I cracked. "I'm sitting right here, okay? You don't have to talk about me in the third person, I'm *sitting right here*. I can hear everything you're saying."

"Aud." My dad squeezed my arm again. "We're just trying to keep you safe, that's all."

"What I propose," Mr. Rice interrupted, "is that Audrey does her classwork here in the office every day. That way she can still participate in the educational experience but the disruption will be kept to a minimum."

I was horrified. "Like a zoo animal?" I said before I could stop myself. "This is supposed to *lower* my profile?"

Arm squeeze from Dad.

And in the end, that's what they agreed upon. Starting the next morning, my teachers would send my assignments up to the office and I would sit across from the secretary and do them. If I finished early, I could read. Joy.

I was shaking by the time my parents and I got to the parking lot. "This is social suicide!" I gasped. "It's inhumane! And it's sexist, too! If I were a guy, they'd be having a pep rally for me!"

"Get a grip, Susan B. Anthony," my mom said. "Let's just discuss this at home, okay?"

But the discussion at home was no better. "Look, Audrey," my dad said as he loosened his tie. He looked tired all of a sudden, and I felt kind of bad. "You could have mentioned this video to us. You could have *mentioned* that when you said were going to a concert, that 'going to a concert' meant kissing musicians backstage!"

Both my parents crossed their arms and looked at me. The Great Wall of Authority.

"I didn't do anything wrong! I just kissed a boy I liked!" I remembered the graffiti in the bathroom. "And that's *all* we did! I didn't know that his manager was going to take pictures and sell them!"

"You're sixteen years old!" my dad said. "A lot could have happened to you that night! You're lucky this is all it was!"

"*Lucky*? You call this luck?"

My mom inhaled through her nose. Total yoga breathing. "Audrey. There's a lot of attention on you right now. *A lot*," she repeated as the phone began to ring. "You live here: You know as well as we do that we've been getting calls for the past three days from every single news service in the country. And now we know why," she added to my dad, who nodded and grimaced. "Some things are going to have to change."

"Like what?" I asked. *Please don't say curfew, please don't say curfew.* . . .

"Like you not going out as much. Like you going to work and going to school—"

"And not sleeping in class," my dad added.

"—and then coming home," my mom finished.

"So now I'm grounded?!"

"No, not grounded, just staying out of the spotlight."

"Um, hello?" I knew I was starting to push my limits, but these were desperate times. "I never wanted to be in the spotlight, remember? *It* found *me*."

"Audrey, we're doing the best we can!" my dad interrupted. "You've kind of thrown us for a loop here! We read *What to Expect When You're Expecting*, all right? Believe me, this is *not* what we were expecting!"

"Yeah, I know, Dad, I wasn't expecting this, either! And at least you got a guidebook, y'know? Parents have, like, a million books telling them how to raise kids, but there's nothing telling me how to be a teenager! I'm doing the best I can too!"

My mother stepped in. "Everyone's on a time-out starting now."

For a minute, there was only silence as everything calmed down a little. I kicked my shoe on and off, and my dad took off his tie and sat down in a chair, still looking like a steamed lobster. "Better," my mother said. "Let's not become one of those *Jerry Springer* families, okay?"

I didn't have nails or cuticles left to bite. "Can I still call Victoria and IM her and stuff?"

"Of course." My mom sat down at the table and I followed her lead. "We're not trying to ruin your life, you know."

"Yeah. I know."

"Because if we ruin your life, then you're going to be one of those kids that lives in the den and never moves out, and your father and I have plans to retire someday. It's not in our best interest to ruin your life. We'd like to see Tahiti."

"Okay."

"Oh, c'mon, Audrey. I don't even get a laugh for that one? That was good, I thought."

I gave a tiny smile despite myself. "Can I go to work?"

"Absolutely," my dad said. "We're going to need every penny for the lawyer fees after I break this guy Simon's manager's neck."

"Um, can I go to work *now?*" I pointed at the clock. "I'm going to be late."

"Do you have a clean work shirt?"

"Maybe?"

Now it was my mom's turn to sigh. "Laundry. Tonight. Starring you."

18

"So if you're lonely, you know I'm here waiting for you. . . ."

—Franz Ferdinand, "Take Me Out"

THE SCOOPER DOOPER hadn't seen this much action since there was a power outage last summer and we had to get rid of all the ice cream in the freezer. (Normal people + free ice cream = anarchy. I almost had to put on riot gear.) Now, even though we were going into December, the crowds were getting bigger and steadier.

And they brought their cameras with them.

In the first hour of work, I had my picture taken with two babies, someone's rat terrier, four ten-year-old girls with braces, three guys who were dared by someone's older brother, and at least five girls around my age and their mothers. "We drove two hours to come here!" one mother said as she fanned herself with a copy of the magazine. "She"—she pointed to her daughter—"read on the Internet that you worked here and she was so excited to meet you! This is her birthday present!"

I looked to the girl, who was blushing. "Mom! Shut up!"

"Can we get a picture?"

"Um, sure, of course." I stood shoulder-to-shoulder next to the girl and smiled so wide that my face hurt.

We were both shaking from nerves when the flash went off.

And if that wasn't enough, these girls brought me gifts. Like, actual *gifts*. Arm huggies, stuffed animals, jingly balls for Bendomolena—someone must have leaked Bendomolena's name on a website or message board or something—nail polish, home-made vegan cookies, etc. One girl even brought in a picture she drew of me in her art class and it was actually good. "My mom," I told her, "is going to love this." (And she did. She ended up hav-ing it matted and framed and now it hangs in her office at work.)

James was in the background in probably half of the shots, his hair falling over his face as he scooped and wiped down the coun-ters and generally did all the work. In between photo ops, I crouched behind the counter and restocked the napkin holders, desperate to avoid all the people who kept walking past and star-ing. "So what happened?" James asked as I crammed a wad of nap-kins into a holder.

"With what?"

"Outside the principal's office."

"Oh, that."

"Are you suspend—oh, crap." He dropped a scoop of Root Beer Barrel on the floor and I passed him some napkins. "Thanks. Are you suspended?"

"No. But get this. I have to do all my schoolwork in the office. I'm not allowed in class anymore."

"Really?" James knelt down and tried to sop up the mess. "Is it like solitary confinement?"

"I don't know. I guess I'm disrupting everyone's learning process, or they're disturbing mine. Whatever."

"That's pretty stupid."

"Thank you!" For once, someone was on my side. "They might as well just start sewing scarlet letter *A*'s on all my shirts."

James smiled. His eyes got all crinkly in the corners when he really smiled. When he was doing his fake-customer smile, only his mouth moved. Like I said, I'm an observant person. "Or *F*s," he said.

"*F*s?"

"Y'know. For 'Famous'?"

"I'm not famous." I said it too quickly to be believable.

There was a pause for a minute. The napkins were slack in my hand. "I'm not famous," I said again. "At least . . . I don't want to be."

He nodded and cleared his throat. "Before work, I, uh, I went online and saw that video? The one with you and, um, that guy?"

Why did I feel like I had cheated? James and I weren't even dating, but it was like I had been caught.

"Do you like him?" James continued.

"You mean Simon?"

"Yeah. Simon."

It felt like there was a shimmery spiderweb thread between me and James, like if one of us did or said the wrong thing, it'd snap and melt away. My heart was ricocheting against my ribs and I pressed my hands against the cool metal of napkin holder. "At the time," I replied, "I thought I did. But he was—"

James looked up and his gaze was the kind that makes you understand how elliptical orbits occur, how one thing can pull you in so tight that you can't break away. My breath got shallow. "I don't like him," I whispered. "I didn't know him. It just happened. Sort of like an accident."

"Good." James didn't break eye contact. "'Cause I really hate him."

"Yeah. I hate him too."

"I know. But I hate him for kissing you."

Ding-dong! The automatic door chime told us we had customers.

Both James and I stood up so fast that I got a little dizzy from the head rush. His cheeks were flaming and I could feel the hotness in my own. The napkins were damp from being clenched so tight in my hand and there were beads of sweat on the back of my neck, almost like chills. I was either going to throw up or start dancing around—I wasn't sure which. What I needed was a time-stopper so I could figure things out. What did James mean by that? Did *he* want to kiss me? Would he have? Would our first kiss have b e e n surrounded by melting ice cream and recycled paper napkins? Were we saved by the bell? Was his heart beating as fast as mine? Did he want a time-stopper too?

"Hi, welcome to the Scooper Dooper!" James called out to our new customers, that fake smile returning with lightning speed. I had never heard him quite so boisterous. "Can we interest you in a free sample?"

But the customers who had interrupted us were no ordinary customers. They were our store's owner, Ron, and some guy in a suit who was beaming from ear to ear. Ron didn't really show up too much; owning this branch of the Scooper Dooper was just a retirement thing, a way to stay busy and make cash, but ever since he hired James, Employee Extraordinaire, he really didn't have to do much. He had the glowing orange look of someone who spent a lot of time on a boat and had never heard of SPF.

"Audrey!" he said when he saw me. "How are you? Our star employee!"

"Hi, Ron." I tried to do some deep breathing so I wouldn't

hyperventilate. "What's up?"

He looked like someone's proud grandparent. "Audrey, this is Mr. Farris." When I didn't say anything, Ron continued. "He's the regional sales manager for all the Scooper Doopers across the country. You know, *Mr. Farris?*"

I don't know about you, but if I ever became regional sales manager for the Scooper Dooper franchise, I'd try to pinpoint where my life went so wrong. Mr. Farris, on the other hand, seemed to have no problem with the fact that his business cards had ice cream cones printed on them. "*So* nice to meet you," he said as he pumped my arm up and down.

"And this is James." Ron introduced him the way you might introduce your batty, toothless great-uncle to your super-cool friends.

Mr. Farris barely acknowledged James before turning back to me. "Audrey, we've been hearing a lot about you lately at corporate headquarters."

"Oh?" *Oh?*

"Yes, sales have been up in this store nearly fifteen percent over the past four weeks, and I'd be lying if I said you had nothing to do with that."

I shrugged. "Well, I don't know about that, but—"

He cut me off with a grin. "*We* know about that. That's why we've designed a new ad campaign based around you!" He pulled out a glossy folder and flipped it open to show a bright pink press kit. "See this? This is just the beginning. We have plans for a national ad campaign, from Maine to Hawaii! How would you like to star in your very own commercial?" His eyes twinkled.

Mine, however, had gone flat. "I'd rather swim in battery acid."

"Excuse me?"

James choked and started coughing, which offered Ron a reason to jump in and no doubt save his year-end bonus. "Audrey! Such a kidder! Always joking!"

I could feel my brain starting to unravel like a ball of yarn and, in all honesty, it felt sort of good, like coming up for air after being underwater. "With razor blades," I continued. "I'd rather swim in battery acid *and* razor blades *and* spoiled milk—"

Ding-dong! Customers.

"Welcome to the Scooper Dooper!" James practically shouted across the store to our new customers. "Welcome to our very fine establishment! Would you like to try a free sample of anything? Anything at all! Just ask! Really, we don't mind! Try us!"

"Oh, I *will*," said a voice, and it was all I could do to keep from banging my head against the countertop.

Sharon Eggleston and Natasha sidled up to the glass display. "There's the star," Sharon said when she saw me. I was wearing a stained Scooper Dooper shirt with Chocolate Kiss smeared on the sleeve, and my face was still burning from both my encounters with James and Mr. Farris. Sharon had on (I hate to say it) a cute purple shirt and perfect jeans and perfect makeup. She had dressed up for the sacrifice, I could tell.

"Hi," I said to her, but only because my two bosses were standing six feet away. I swear, if I ever have to swim in battery acid and razor blades and spoiled milk, Sharon is *so* going to be my swimming buddy.

"Would you like to try a free sample?" James leaned past me toward Sharon and Natasha, the tiny plastic spoon already in his hand.

Sharon turned her full-beam smile on him and I burned inside.

"Yes," she said. "Absolutely. I would *love* to try any of your samples."

James could only sputter and probably would've died of embarrassment if Mr. Farris hadn't jumped in. "Audrey, why don't you help these young women?"

A mean Cruella smile drew Sharon's mouth up. "Audrey, is this your boss?"

I mentally drew a target on Sharon. "Yep."

Mr. Farris beamed with pride. "She's our best employee!"

She and Natasha exchanged knowing grins. "Oh, really? How convenient."

"Did—did you want a sample?" James was still trying his best to stammer out a full sentence.

"You can both help me," she announced, like we had won a prize. "But I just don't know what I want." She pressed a finger to her lips and pretended to think. "What do you suggest, Audrey? You're an expert at doing all sorts of things, aren't you? How about you try your hand at ice cream suggestions."

I thought back to the graffiti on the bathroom wall and said nothing.

"How's the strawberry?"

Everyone looked at me. "It's okay."

"Just okay?"

"It's great."

"What about Chocolate Kiss?"

"Great."

"Just great?"

"Great plus one."

"And French vanilla?"

And so on. We went through each individual flavor, and

Sharon and Natasha (will she *ever* breathe through her nose?!) sampled nine flavors each. James got each sample for them, and then Sharon ate each one in this really sexy way that no one in their right mind would do in public. "Mmm," she would say, making big flirty eyes at James the whole time. And then, "Umm . . . no, I don't think so," and she would hand me back her gross used sample spoon. "How about . . . ?"

And on. And on. And on.

By flavor number seven, some other customers had come in, but they wanted *me* to wait on them, not James, and Mr. Farris had tucked the shiny pink folder under his arm and was standing back, watching his profits grow with my humiliation. James was forced to get all the samples for Sharon and Natasha, and he kept dropping the sample spoons and fishing around for them on the floor, all knees and elbows and hipbones bumping against the cupboards.

And of course, after all that, Sharon got a small fat-free scoop of vanilla first on a cone, then in a cup; then she decided she wanted nuts on top, and it wasn't until after I poured the chopped almonds on that she said, "Oops, no, I meant the walnuts." I got the same thing for Natasha without even asking, and when she started to protest, I shoved it at her with as much control as I could muster. "It's yours now," I said through clenched teeth. "Try not to choke on it."

"Did you hear how mean she's being to me, James?" Sharon said in that stupid faux-pouty voice of hers. "How can you stand to work with someone else's castoff when she's such a bitch?"

"Thanks for coming by," James replied. "Watch your step on the way out the door. Wouldn't want you to trip and break your nose."

Wait a hot minute. Was he defending me?! He was defending

me! My heart leapt, then quickly sank back down once Sharon realized that the tide had turned and her latest boy-crush wanted to toss her out on her ass.

"This is just the beginning," Sharon hissed at me as she pushed her sunglasses higher up on her head. "You're fucking finished at our school."

"Yeah, way to pose in a paparazzi photo," I glared at her. "That doesn't look desperate at *all*, Sharon."

She glanced over at James, who was ringing up the sale. "I don't blame you for settling for her, James," she said to him. "You look like the kind of guy who shops secondhand for *everything*."

The adults in the room were already out of earshot, so I grabbed her change out of the register and shoved it into her hand. Then I leaned in and let my hair hide the side of my face. "Get. Out."

Sharon grinned at both of us, but something had changed in her eyes. There was no flirtiness now. It was war. "Thanks for the ice cream, Audrey!" she said. "I'll be back tomorrow!" She turned and walked out with Natasha a step behind, and I slammed the register shut so hard that it flew back open.

"I'm taking my break," I said to no one in particular, then yanked my hat off and went to the only place where it was quiet: the storage freezer.

All I did was pace for a minute, my brain racing. I wanted to call Victoria and tell her everything. I wanted to call my parents and tell them to come get me. I wanted to call Evan and tell him I would freaking marry him if it meant the song would never exist and I could go back to having a normal life. I didn't care anymore about VIP passes or free lip gloss or homemade gifts from fans. I just wanted to be normal, anonymous Audrey.

The day kept crashing over me like a wave and I sank down on a tub of Marmalade Madness and finally, finally started to cry.

The door opened a minute later. I didn't even have to look up to know who it was. "What, does someone want an autograph?" I snapped at James as I wiped my eyes. "A picture? A commercial? Or do they just want to harass me and threaten me with social extinction while sampling twenty billion flavors?"

James took several slow steps toward me, and when I didn't reach out and try to kill him, he sat down next to me and very, very carefully, put his arm around my shoulders. It felt like just a whisper of a touch, his arm was so thin and light, but when I started to cry harder, he moved closer and his arm grew heavier, pulling me back down to Earth. "This has been the worst day ever," I said through my tears. "I can't do this anymore."

"I know," James said, and even though he really had no clue, it was still a nice thing to say. He touched my hair again and again, barely stroking it, and I sniffled against his sleeve and tried to calm down. He was pretty cool about me crying all over him, too. Evan would always get really uncomfortable or say something stupid like, "Do you want me to go?" whenever I got upset. He certainly wouldn't have sat on a tub of ice cream in a huge walk-in freezer with me, that was for sure.

But James would. And did.

After a minute or so, I finally got it together and sat up, realizing that I was not having my best-looking moment. "I'm really sorry if I got snot on you," I said as I wiped at my face with my sleeve. "I'll pay for the dry cleaning."

He laughed and handed me a napkin from his pocket. "Don't worry about it." He had really nice teeth, not too perfect and not too wonky. Definitely a flosser.

"And I'm sorry that Sharon was a bitch to you."

"Well, she's a bitch. That's what they do. They're bitchy." He shrugged. "I don't really care about Sharon, anyway."

The freezer got quiet then, the sort of quiet that makes every thought in your head amplify ten times in volume. It was so cold that we could see our breath, tiny cloud puffs that came quickly. "What *do* you care about?" I asked. "If you don't care about Sharon."

"You," he whispered.

It was starting to feel warmer by the second, and the hairs on the back of my neck stood up. "Really?"

"Yeah."

"Oh."

"Audrey?"

"Yeah?" We were so close that our noses were almost touching.

"Do you think maybe you'd want to go out some time? I mean, with me?"

"Yes." The answer came so fast that I didn't even have time to think about it. "Yes."

"Okay."

"Okay."

"Audrey?"

"Yeah?"

"You . . . you have a pretty mouth." I could see him blushing, and I wondered if he had ever said something like that to a girl before. "You do. It's just like . . . yeah. It's perfect."

"James?"

"Yeah." His voice was really quiet, like he was trying not to breathe.

"Do you . . . ? Do you want to kiss me?" We were getting closer and closer, and then our noses touched once, twice, before our lips met.

I had my answer.

When we pulled apart, we were both gasping a little. "Wow," I said.

"Is that okay?" he asked quickly. "I didn't mean to—"

"No!" I said. "Don't apologize, it was fine. I mean, it was better than fine, but . . . yeah. Good executive decision. Two thumbs up."

He smiled, looking embarrassed. "We probably have to go back out there before Mr. Farris sends out a search party for you."

I had completely forgotten that I was supposed to be working. "Oh. Right." I tried to pat my hair down and smooth my shirt as we stood up, then realized that my knees were a little wobbly. Next to me, James put one hand on the freezer door and then, right before pulling it open, bent down and kissed me again, a quick impulse of a touch. "You ready?" he said.

I was still reeling from the second kiss, but I managed to nod before following him out into the fluorescent light of the back room. I had to squint against it, and then I went to the tiny employee bathroom to put water on my face while James went back to deal with customers and bosses.

In the bathroom mirror, I looked at my mouth. James thought it was perfect. Maybe it was. I smiled.

The girl in the mirror smiled back.

19

"Don't let them tell you that there's a right way to fall in love. . . ."

—Voxtrot, "Biggest Fan"

SO OF COURSE, the one time I really have to tell Victoria some-thing—kissage in the freezer with James, OMG!—I couldn't find her. She had been out with Jonah that night, so she didn't know anything about me and James, or about how I was now going to be forced to sit in the school office every day.

When I was driving to school, though, a phone call distracted me. My head was so in the clouds that I answered my phone with-out even looking at the caller ID, just assuming that it was Victoria because who else would dare call me at seven forty-five in the morning?

It was definitely not Victoria.

"Hello!" a voice said. "Is this *the* Audrey?"

"Um, sure," I replied. "Why not." *Who's this weirdo?* I thought.

"Audrey! This is Jim Jenkster! Agent extraordinaire! Honey, we are going to change your life starting today! Starting this very *minute!*"

"Jim Jenkster?" I repeated. Jim Jenkster was the tool who was always in the back of C-level celebrities' paparazzi photos, a slimy agent guy who had settled some sexual harassment lawsuits out of court. A real winner. But then again, anyone named Jim Jenkster is sort of set up to fail at life.

Still, I didn't believe he was calling me. "Jonah, is this you?" I asked. "It's ass o'clock in the morning—I didn't even think you were awake at this hour. Did Victoria put you up to this? Because if she's there I really, really, *really* need to talk to—"

"Oh, this is perfect already! That *voice*, your *vibe*! Honey, by the time all this is over, no one's going to remember the Do-Gooders, but everyone's gonna know who Audrey is!"

I sat in my car at the red light and openly gaped. This was so not Jonah. "Are you for real?" I said.

"As real as the sun in the sky! Or the UV rays in the tanning bed, heh heh!"

I started to laugh. I couldn't help it. "Why are you calling me?" I asked between giggles. "Because seriously, dude, I don't need an agent. Thanks, but go sell yourself to someone who's buying."

"I love it! Oh, darlin', I absolutely love it! You're so Audrey, Audrey!"

"No, I'm just Audrey."

"No, you're Audrey! Capital-*A* Audrey! Let me tell you what I'm thinking. We gotta start getting you to premieres, honey. That's the first thing. The red carpet plus you equals dynamiteness."

"Is that even a word?"

"Next, I've got a list of guys here. Hot ones. Hotties. All of them have pilots coming up for the spring. Big shows. Huge. We gotta get you seen with them."

I took a deep breath. This guy was truly unhinged. All that

tooth bleaching must have gone to his brain. "Look," I told him, "I'm not interested in dating TV actors. Or rock stars. Or anyone who has a publicist or frequents a red carpet. Okay? Later, alligator."

Then I hung up on Jim Jenkster. Agent extraordinaire.

And went to sit in the office.

By myself.

Sigh.

When Victoria walked past between first and second periods, she stopped short in the hallway. "What are you doing here?" she screeched, as three other students crashed into her. "Why aren't you going to class?"

"Because my parents got called into a meeting with the principal yesterday and they decided it'd be less of a distraction to the other students if I did independent study in the office." In light of the James kissing and that Jenkster nutcase, this news seemed a lot less exciting. "But look, Victoria, I have to tell you—"

"They *what*?!"

"Yeah, I know, it sucks, but listen—"

"Are they serious? What are you, like the panda exhibit from China that gets put on display at the local zoo? This is so unfair!"

"Yes, I know, panda exhibits are unfair, but—"

"You're *way* cuter than a panda, though. And pandas are pretty darn cute."

"Of course. But listen—"

"Fuck the pandas. Do you want me to call my mom?" Victoria craned her head to see if the assistant principal was in his office. "Because I can call my *mother*, the *lawyer*, and find out what sort of justification they have for *blatantly* violating your right to *free, public education* and—"

I grabbed her by her hoodie strings. "Victoria," I hissed. "We kissed."

That stopped her short. "Who kissed?"

"We did."

"*We* did?"

"No! James and me, in the freezer at work last night! God, why weren't you answering your phone last night? I have a million things to tell you! You're so out of the loop!"

"Back the truck up. You and James kissed? You? Kissed *James?*"

Now I was starting to blush. "Keep your voice down!" I told her. "People could be listening."

Victoria nodded wisely. "You're right. Magazines are probably paying people a lot of money for information on you."

Well. That was a new thought I didn't need. But Victoria interrupted me before I could think about that one. "Wait, so you kissed him? Or did he kiss you? That's very important."

"He kissed me." I glanced around, suddenly afraid of undercover spies. "And he asked me out. And he said I had a pretty mouth."

Victoria squealed with delight. "I *knew* it! I *knew* it! Oh, can I do the I-told-you-so dance? Please? I'm so good at it."

"Can it wait until lunch?"

"Barely!" She was wriggling all over. "I knew it! Oh my God, was it good?"

"Very."

"And you were in the freezer?"

I nodded. "I went in there because Sharon Eggleston got me all upset—"

"Sharon Eggleston was in the freezer with you?"

"No, just . . . okay, you know what? We need to talk at lunch. Somewhere private," I added as a group of students went by and pretty much stared at me the whole way.

"Okay, okay, but I want *mucho* details. Like, all of them. I want to know what his hair looked like when he kissed you and everything."

I couldn't help but smile. "It's very red. It hangs in his eyes."

She dug her fist into my arm. "Audrey has a *cru-ush. Agaaa-iiiin.*"

"Sshh!"

"Sorry, shutting up now."

"Okay, but get this," I told her. "There's even more. Guess who called me this morning?"

"Jim Jenkster," she replied without missing a beat.

I practically fell down from shock. "How did you know that?" I gasped. "Are you psychic? Oh my God, if you're psychic, we're gonna rule the world."

Victoria just shrugged. "He got my number from this sophomore that I tutored in algebra a billion years ago, so I gave him your number." She grinned. "Jenkster's a kick, huh?"

"You gave him my number?" I repeated. "Why? He's crazy! He made me feel slimy and we were only on the phone!

"Oh, come on, Aud. Tell me it wasn't hysterical talking to him. The guy's insanity personified. I thought you'd think it was funny."

Okay, she had a point. It was sort of funny. "If he leaks my number, I'm dead. You realize that, right?"

"And if you're dead, you won't be stuck in the office anymore. How long do you have to be in here?"

"I don't know. Until everything calms down, I guess?"

"Sucks."

"Yeah, thanks for the news flash."

"Do you want me and Jonah to try and spring you? He's really good at creating distractions."

"Please, no." I could only imagine what Jonah's idea of a distraction was. Probably something involving fireworks, mice, and a water gun. "I have enough distractions."

"Okay, but just say the word and we'll figure something out."

"Just think about everything you've ever seen in my closet and tell me what I should wear when James and I have our first date."

"Got it." Victoria's eyes were getting dreamy already, combing through my literal dirty laundry. "I'll come up with something, don't worry."

"No arm huggies."

"God, I *know*. Everyone's wearing them now. Jonah's little sister made her own from his socks. He was so pissed."

The bell rang and she glanced up at the ceiling. (Why does everyone do that when the bell rings? Have you ever noticed? It's like we expect the ceiling to come crashing down on our heads.) "Okay, going now, but yay! Yay for you and Jam—I mean, you-know-who!"

After she left, I was so lonely that it hurt.

Being in the office all day, I soon realized, was painfully boring. *Painfully. Boring.* But I did learn something. Without teachers or friends in class, I could get through the work a lot faster. By the early afternoon (and after I gave Victoria every single detail at our lunch of soup and coffee), I was done with all my schoolwork. Reading, homework, everything. I even did some sample SAT questions from this study guide my mom got for me. *That's* how desperate I was for entertainment.

It was becoming dire.

Between fifth and sixth periods, I heard a hissing over my shoulder and I glanced up to see James standing next to the low wall that separated the office from the hallway. And I know it's important to play it cool and all that, but I lit up when I saw him. I could feel it in my face. I couldn't help it. But it was okay, because he did, too.

God, we are such saps.

"Hi!" I said. "What's up?"

"Nothing much." He glanced around at my surroundings. "How's solitary?"

"So boring I'm about to gnaw off my own arm."

"Aren't you supposed to be doing, like, work?"

"Did it already. Call Mensa, I'm obviously a genius."

"Can they really make you sit in here all day, every day?"

"If they can make me wear gym shorts, they can make me do almost anything."

"Tell me about it. I've gotten used to admiring you from afar."

James was witty! Who knew? Okay, besides Victoria, I mean. And admiring from afar? I started thinking about all the unattractive things I'd ever done in front of him, like blowing my nose or sneezing during an allergy attack. "Well, maybe you can get some binoculars or send in some spies," I told him. "Make it like a cool Russian movie."

He grinned and looked around to see if anyone was listening. "Are you okay, though, really?"

"I'm fine. Has Sharon been around?"

"No, but I thought we didn't care about her. I *thought* we established that yesterday."

Boy howdy, did we establish that. But all I said was, "I also thought you promised me a date."

"Oh, um, yeah. That."

My heart did a swan dive into my toes. Why do guys do this? *Why?* You think they're gonna turn right and bam! They go left. "What?"

"No, it's just—"

"You don't want to go out anymore?"

"No, but I was thinking—"

"'Cause if you don't want to go, then we shouldn't go." *I'll just spend all my free time in the office plotting ways to ruin your life, creep.*

James stopped and took a breath. "You interrupt a lot, you know that?"

I shrugged. "I'm friends with Victoria. Our friendship would be one big monologue if I didn't interrupt."

"Good point."

"So you don't wanna go out?"

"No, I do, but . . ." He took another breath. "I just didn't want you to say yes because you felt like you had to. Like, when we were in the freezer and everything."

"James?"

"Yes?"

I glanced around to make sure no one was watching; then I put my index finger on his arm. "I'm already trying to figure out what to wear when we go out. Is that a good enough answer?"

His eyes widened. "So that's a yes?"

"Oh my God!" I finally said. "Yes! *¡Sí! Oui!* What language do you want it in?"

James started to crack up. "Do you know Swahili?"

"No, but I've got the time to learn."

We were getting closer and closer to each other and I had that nice dizzy feeling again. "You're twitterpated," Victoria had said at lunch. "You're going to wander into traffic if you think about him too much."

I think she might be right.

"*Ahem.*"

James and I both started and glanced at Connie, the secretary whose daughter was a fan of mine. She was typing at her computer and not looking at us, but she had one of those "you crazy kids" smirks on her face. "James? Don't you think you're going to be late?"

James went beet red and adjusted his bag on his shoulder. I saw a Sisters of Mercy pin on the strap. Be still my heart. "Okay, can I, um, call you later?" he said quickly. "I don't have your number."

I scribbled it down on a scrap of paper and pressed it into his hand. "Call. Or text. Or IM."

"How do you feel about carrier pigeons?"

I shuddered. "The equivalent of flying rats."

"Scratch the pigeons, then."

Connie was starting to clear her throat again, and if there's one thing I can't stand, it's phlegm, fake or otherwise. "Okay, talk to you later?"

"Yeah."

"And once again, yes."

"Okay." He grinned and then started to back away from the wall. Unfortunately, he tripped on his shoelace and almost did a faceplant on the linoleum, but he recovered nicely, and I watched him walk away from me. Again.

Connie was still smirking as I sat back down. "Um, Connie?"

"Yes?" *Typetypetypetype.*

"Do you think maybe you could, um, not tell anyone? About that? Or anything else you see me do in here?" It was weird to tell an adult what to do, but between Sharon Eggleston, our school's already-thriving gossip tree, and tabloid journalists, I figured I should protect myself.

"Honey, trust me, I see it all in here. I never say anything."

"Not even if someone—say, like a reporter—offers you a hundred dollars?"

She glanced up at me over her glasses. "Do I look like I'm for sale?"

"Um, no."

"Of course not." She went back to her typing. "But he's a nice boy."

I didn't say anything as I turned back to my SAT book, but I knew we were both smiling.

20 "When what you want is what you're getting . . ."
—Cartel, "A"

IT TOOK A WHILE before James and I could officially go out, mostly because my parents had me on lockdown and I wasn't sure how I was going to get them to let me out of the house. "Whatever you do," Victoria advised, "don't do the 'I'm the perfect daughter' routine. They'll know something's up."

"I already *am* the perfect daughter," I told her. I was standing in the bathroom, balanced on one leg as I tried to give myself a pedicure. Victoria and I had tried to go for mani-pedis earlier that week, but it was a disaster. It was crowded and we had to wait, and every girl and woman in there either stared at me or was reading a magazine that had my picture in it, and I lasted all of five minutes before I grabbed Victoria's elbow and we took our ragged cuticles and got the hell out of there.

"Besides," I added as I struggled to keep my balance, "this isn't like a punishment or something. I'm not grounded. They're just freaked out about everything. You know parents."

"They're so sheltered. Maybe if you invite James over so they could meet him?"

"Well, *yeah*. They're not gonna let me go without meeting the guy." I tucked the phone between my ear and shoulder so I could unscrew the nail polish, a bright red that I bought just for the name: Death at the Disco. Don't you love it?

I could hear Victoria typing in the background. "What are you doing?"

"Oh, just sending an email." She continued clacking away. "If I were you, I'd try to get your parents when they're down, like at the end of the day or something."

"When they're too tired to argue?"

"Exactly." *Clackclackclackclack.*

"What sort of manifesto are you typing, anyway?"

"If it works out, I'll tell you."

I glanced up. "No. Tell me now."

"Later."

"Now. Best friends don't have secrets."

"Later. And this isn't a secret, it's a surprise!"

I wanted to keep arguing, but I was too busy flailing and protesting and that's a bad combination when you're trying to paint your pinky toenail. I lost my balance and went flying down to the floor. "Owowowowow, oh fucking hell!" I said. Death at the Disco had spilled all over my bare legs. "Death at the Disco is everywhere!" I cried.

"Audrey? What just happened?" I could hear Victoria's tinny voice from the phone, which had rolled away and wedged itself under the door. "Disco what? Are you okay?"

I groaned and wondered if anything was sprained or broken or twisted. If I was forced to get a cast, I'd die. The last thing I needed was a ten-pound piece of plaster attached to my limbs. But maybe

I could do a collage on it or something, or maybe James and I could make it, like, our little project. Or maybe then my parents would feel so sorry for me that they wouldn't even blink twice when I asked to go out with James. Huh. Now that I thought about it, this cast thing was sounding better and better.

"Audrey!" I could hear my parents running up the stairs. "Are you all right? Where are you?"

"In here!" I called, then tried to arrange myself to look as pitiful as possible. "I'm mortally wounded."

"Mortally wounded people aren't sarcastic," my spoilsport dad said as they came into the bathroom. "What the heck did you do to yourself?"

"Is that blood?" My mom paled slightly. She's not good with blood. Remember my dad's dramatic and colorful Massive Blood Loss Incident of Halloween Three Years Ago? My mom almost turned it into the dramatic and colorful Massive Vomiting Incident of Halloween Three Years Ago.

I looked up at them from my spot on the floor. "Wow. You're both very tall from down here. And it's not blood, it's nail polish."

My dad bent down and picked up the bottle. "Death at the Disco," he read. "Well, isn't that ironic?"

"Don't you think?" I said before I could stop myself. *Damn you, Alanis Morrissette.*

Now my mom was squeezing my arms and legs. Those yoga classes had really built up her muscles. "Is anything broken?" she said. "Did you hit your head?"

"No, but . . ." I took a deep breath. "You know that guy James that I work with at the Scooper Dooper? Well, I used to think he was this huge dork, but he's not! Well, I mean, he kind of is, but he's also really sweet and soooo nice, and when I started crying he didn't even care that I got snot on him and now he wants to take me out on a date and that's so great because you guys would really like him and I want to go and he's also smart and funny. Oh, yeah, and college-bound, too." I wasn't sure about that last one, but I figured, statistically speaking, it was probably true.

My parents looked at me, dumbfounded. I blinked twice, then smiled. "Please?"

There was silence in the bathroom for a few seconds, then Victoria's static-y phone voice cut through it. "Smooth, Audrey. *Real* smooth."

My dad started shaking his head. "Audrey, are you ever going to be a normal teenager? Ever?"

I thought about it for several seconds. "Hopefully not. Is that the right answer?"

By the time I hung up with Victoria, got up off the floor with just some bruises and wounded pride, and used half a bottle of nail polish remover to clean up the bathroom ("It looks like someone staged a revolution in here," my mom said when she brought me more cotton balls), we were able to address "the James situation." My dad's words, not mine. As far as I was concerned, I had addressed "the James situation" last week in the freezer, and on every workday since then.

But my parents had other ideas.

"You can go out on three conditions," my mom said after I hobbled downstairs. "One, your father and I have to meet him first."

"You're going to love him!" I squealed. "He's so . . . so . . . well, he's kind of nerdy, but in that really cute Rivers-Cuomo-from-Weezer way."

"Oh, totally, I know," my dad said. "That's exactly what I thought when I met your mother."

"Am I being mocked?" my mom and I both asked at the same time.

"Number two," he continued as if we hadn't said anything, "you go on a normal date. No rooftop concerts in Los Angeles, none of those raves in San Diego or whatever they call them."

I actually drew back in my seat. "You think I'm a raver?" I said, incredulous. "Do I *look* like a tweaking raver?"

"Honey, I have no idea," my dad replied.

"What does 'tweaking' mean?" my mom asked me.

Whoops. Major tactical error. Never let on to your parents that you know more about drugs than they do. It will only end badly, possibly with you being forced into a private Catholic school and a plaid uniform, which is only attractive when worn ironically.

"I'm not a tweaking raver," I told them. "So don't worry about it."

"Okay, great to know, but either way, on this date, you do what normal teenagers do. Movies and hamburgers—"

"Veggie burgers, you mean."

"Veggie burgers. Slurpees. Whatever. No crowd surfing."

I sighed. "Crowd surfing sucks, Dad. All you ever do is get kicked in the head."

"Third rule," my mom continued. "You must call us every half-hour while you're gone. No exceptions. If your phone dies, you either beg, borrow, or steal someone else's, or you find a pay phone or come home to tell us you're okay."

"Cake."

"What?"

"Like, 'a piece of cake.' Consider it done." I was bouncing up and down in my seat, too excited to sit still. "Can I call James now and tell him? Or maybe I should call Victoria first and tell her?"

My dad laughed, shook his head, and took his glasses off so he could rub his eyes. "Audrey, my beloved only child," he sighed, "you're going to be the death of me."

21 "It takes more than a heartbeat to get me. . . ."

—The Sounds, "Much Too Long"

LATER THAT AFTERNOON, I called James. "Hey," I said. "Guess what?"

There was a pause. "Do I have to actually guess?"

"No, it'll take too long." I looked down at my bare toenails, which seemed to be the only body part that escaped the nail polish fiasco. "My parents said I can go out with you!"

"That's awesome! Are they making you bring a bodyguard?"

Downstairs, the doorbell rang. My mom was out and my dad was on a conference call in his office, so I climbed off my bed and went downstairs to answer. "No bodyguard," I told James. "Just a rabid Doberman."

James laughed, which was good, because when people don't get my sense of humor, things can go awry in a bad way. "Well, it'll be nice to have company in case things get boring."

"Hold on a second," I told James, then unlocked the front door. On our front porch stood two skinny guys, both of them looking excited and anxious.

"Hi?" I said. This was a first, I had to admit. Autograph-seekers had yet to show up at my front door, but thanks to Google Maps, it was inevitable.

"Hi," the first guy said, and then the next thing I knew, he was swooping in to kiss me while his buddy took a picture.

"Excuse me!" I spat, shoving him away with my free hand. Luckily I had managed to turn so that he only got the edge of my hair and not my mouth or any other part of my body attached to my face. "What the hell is your problem, dude?" I yelled. "My dad and an extremely insane cat are upstairs and they will fuck you up, I swear to God. Especially the cat. She's loyal."

"No, it's cool, I'm Milo, I'm the lead singer for this band, Frequency, and we just got signed and we're trying to get our first single out there and we thought that if you kissed us—"

I just shook my head. "You must be made of one hundred percent moron. Erase that photo." Then I put the phone back to my ear. "Hey, James? Can you hang on for just a second more? There's an issue."

"Yeah, sure. You okay?"

"Totally fine. I'm just . . ." How to explain this situation? I decided to go for the truth. "Some wannabe rock stars want me to kiss them so they'll get famous." Then I shot my bitchiest look at both guys, who were reluctantly erasing the photo and glaring at me.

"Is this a daily thing for you?"

"Not yet. Hopefully not ever."

"Did you kiss them?" he asked.

"Of course not!"

"Cool. I like your integrity."

"Yeah, I like it, too. I also like the fact that you just used 'integrity' correctly in a sentence." Then I turned back to the guys.

"Now scram, losers. And next time you kiss a girl, ask first. They're not all as nice as me."

By the time I slammed the door shut and got back to the phone, James was laughing. "Did you just tell them to *scram?*" he laughed.

"Yeah," I admitted.

"That's probably the dorkiest thing I've ever heard." He was still laughing.

I stomped back upstairs, still irritated by my run-in with the kissing bandits. "They were in a band called Frequency. Never buy their CD."

"I had no plans to do that."

"Cool. From the looks of them, they probably sound like Phish, anyway."

"So where were we before all that?"

"Um . . ." I thought back a minute, then laughed. "Well, you were glad I was bringing a Doberman on our date so that things wouldn't be boring. You might not believe this, James, but I'd enjoy a boring date."

"I can imagine."

"Oh, yeah. But my parents have some rules."

"Good. I love rules."

"Really?"

"Especially ones from parents of the girl that I want to go out with. Those are the best."

I giggled. *He's funny!* News like this had to be shared, so I started to sign on to IM, to message Victoria. It makes my parents crazy how I can do all of this at once, talk on the phone and email and IM. I'm just like, how can you *not?* I don't understand how they get anything done during the day.

"So what are the rules?"

"Well, first, they have to meet you." I logged in and watched my screen pop up. "Don't worry, though, that's easy. They just want to make sure you're not hideous or a pervert."

James gave a nervous little laugh. "Great. Can't wait."

"Trust me, if you can survive Sharon Eggleston, you can survive my parents. Second rule, we can't go to any concerts or anything on a rooftop, apparently."

"Do you normally go on rooftops?"

"No, my dad's just trying to cover all of his bases. He's paranoid. We're also not allowed to crowd surf while on our date."

"I hate crowd surfers. All they do is kick you in the head."

"I know, right? I tried to tell my dad that, but he wasn't getting it."

"I have to tell you, so far these rules sound pretty easy. I think I'm gonna win."

"Well, I also have to call them every half-hour, just so they know I haven't been killed in a fan stampede or something."

While I was talking to James, I found Victoria's screen name and IM'd her.

BlondeOnBlonde: hihihihihi guess what
GodSavetheQueen: hola chica
GodSavetheQueen: what
BlondeOnBlonde: James = funny!
GodSavetheQueen: haha funny
GodSavetheQueen: or
GodSavetheQueen: nervous tic funny
BlondeOnBlonde: haha funny

BlondeOnBlonde: obvs >: O
GodSavetheQueen: tee hee
GodSavetheQueen: now who's funny? lol
BlondeOnBlonde: not you

That's when my Instant Messenger exploded.

Suddenly I started getting messages from everywhere, and new IM windows were opening all over my screen. "Whoa," I said. "What the hell?"

"What?" James asked.

"I was IM'ing with Victoria and now . . ." I watched as the windows quickly filled my screen. "Holy crap, James, there's like a hundred message requests coming in. I can't even talk to Victoria anymore."

"Do you think someone gave out your IM name?"

"Maybe . . . ?" My computer was now frozen. "My computer's totally stopped. I can't even move the cursor." I hit a few buttons. Like I even knew what I was doing. "Fuck!"

"What's your IM name? I'll Google it."

"BlondeOnBlonde. No spaces."

"That's cute," he said. I could tell just by the way his voice went up that he was smiling. "I like that."

"What's yours?"

"BoysDontCry. No spaces. Or apostrophes."

I felt my heart flutter like a butterfly. "Is that your favorite Cure song?"

"Of course."

"Where do you stand on *Disintegration?*" This could be the thing that ended our relationship before it even officially began.

"Well, I think—oh. Wow."

"What?"

"I Googled your name and 'BlondeOnBlonde' and it took me to some message board?"

I sighed. "Is it the Do-Gooders' message board?"

"No, it looks like a fansite."

I winced. In the grand history of awkward moments, having your current crush on a fansite of your ex-boyfriend's band had to be up there. "Um, are they talking about me?"

"I think the whole page is about you. Hold on, I'm going to the message board." I could hear him clicking. "Yeah, someone leaked your IM. And your email address, too."

"My email?" I squeaked.

I could hear James clicking around. "These people know a lot about you. I should go on here and do some research before our first date."

I groaned. "Lies. All lies."

"Audrey!" James took on a mock-game-show-host voice. "Is it true that your favorite food is macaroni and cheese?"

"Um, I've never really thought about it. But . . . okay, sure. Why not? Yay for mac and cheese."

"It *should* be your favorite. Mac and cheese is awesome." He continued to boom in that fake voice. "Audrey, is your favorite color lilac?"

"Hardly. Pastels make me queasy."

"Me too. Where did they get all this info?"

I sighed. "Probably people at school. I heard that the tabloids are paying people for information about me, like where I eat and stuff." I knew this from sitting in the front office for the past week, where if I stayed quiet enough, I could hear bits and pieces of conversations from all the secretaries and parent volunteers. "I think the going rate is a thousand dollars cash if someone can produce pictures of me and Evan."

"That's crazy."

"Welcome to my life, James." I hit a couple more buttons on my keyboard, but my computer was good and frozen. "Damn, I really liked my IM name, too. It's gonna take me forever to think up a new one."

"Heyyy . . . do you have any pictures of you and Evan still?"

"Um . . ." This conversation was becoming a series of Awkward Moments. What was the right answer to that question? I felt like I was going to say the wrong thing no matter what. "Why?"

"Because then we could get Victoria to sell them and then we could take the money for our date and go all out."

I laughed. "What, expensive wine somewhere? Caviar?"

"I was thinking record shopping at RPM, actually."

"I love it when you talk like that. But I think most of the pictures got burned."

"How?"

"Me lighting them on fire in the bathroom sink."

"Oh."

"Sorry. But we can still go to RPM, right?"

"Well, I still have to meet your parents."

"And not let me crowd surf. And probably not stage dive, either."

"You know," James pointed out, "your dad didn't say anything about *sky* diving. Or *deep-sea* diving. So we still have a lot of options."

Oh God, I heart him *so much*.

22 *"You are everything I want 'cause you are everything I'm not. . . ."*

—Taking Back Sunday, "MakeDamnSure"

FIRST DATES ARE NEVER EASY. I mean, duh, that's a universal truth. But they can get a bit more complicated when your ex-boyfriend's song hits the Billboard Top 10 on the same day as your date with New Boy.

That's what happened to me. Because, you know, life's just awesome that way.

As it was, I was already a basket of nerves. I guess that's what happens when you spend day after day alone in the school office, pretending to care about Roman empires and geometry and whatever else I was supposed to care about during the day.

Anyway, on the Tuesday afternoon before my first date with James, the latest Billboard Hot 100 Singles chart was released. "Audrey, Wait!" had hit number ten. It was the fastest-rising song in chart history. The Lolitas' new song, "Hell on Earth," had surged forward, as well, but in England, it was at number nine, while the Do-Gooders were at number eight.

Throw the confetti.

I know all this because I was watching MTV2 with the sound

off while I was drying my hair on that Tuesday evening, and a little news blurb came up. I saw a picture of Evan's face juxtaposed next to a picture of Simon Lolita's, with my high school yearbook photo between them.

If you learn anything from me, learn this: Make sure you take the best yearbook photo you can. You never know where it'll turn up.

By the time I got the hair dryer turned off and the television sound turned up, I managed to catch the interviews with both of my exes. Talk about a surreal experience.

"I suppose we should call Audrey and thank her," Simon said with a wink to the camera. He was flanked by two of his bandmates, both of whom were smoking and nodding in agreement. He had that little smirk on his face that I had thought was sexy, b u t watching him now, it looked more like a paralyzed facial muscle and not nearly as attractive. Plus, he had bad teeth. God, how could I not have noticed that?! It must have been darker backstage than I thought.

"She's a special girl," Simon continued, lighting his own cigarette. Then as the lighter flame illuminated his face, "Very special. We should give her some royalties or something. Maybe write a song about her for our next album." Then he shared a secret grin with the viewing audience.

"Fuck your royalties and die," I said to the television as my wet hair dripped all over the floor. I hadn't even done my makeup yet and I was wearing old gym shorts and a T-shirt I got at a garage sale that said NEW HAMPSHIRE IS FOR LOVERS. "I hope you get food poisoning from tour catering," I added.

Then they cut to Evan and the Do-Gooders. The rest of the

band looked like deer in headlights, but Evan had practiced for these sorts of interviews for months. One hand to God, he used to TiVo MTV just so he could watch bands get interviewed and learn what *not* to do. At the time, I thought it was so hot that he was into his career while most other guys were getting high and playing endless rounds of Xbox.

Now, though? The words *control freak* and *egotistical maniac* came to mind.

"Audrey inspired the song, but I think we all agree that we wrote it," Evan was saying. "Or at least, *I* did. She got the ball rolling, but this is *our* band and *our* careers and hopefully after awhile, our fans will think of us without thinking about her."

For some reason, that made me even madder than Simon's comments. "You'd still be sitting around that loser's dorm room at UCLA if it wasn't for me!" I yelled. "You should buy me speakers for my car! Or a new iPod!"

But then Evan smiled that shy smile that always meant a snarky comment was on its way. Even at home, I saw it coming and winced. And sure enough, he grinned and said, "And I think some other bands should find their own girls."

Oh good Lord.

So of course our home phone was afire. By now, my whole family had stopped answering because of all the calls from the press. Even the calls from my fans, Simon's fans, and Evan's fans were getting out of control. If the president of the United States happened to call our house just to say hi, I doubt anyone would've answered for fear he would start asking questions about me. My mom and dad talked about changing our number, but we had had it for years and my dad was afraid that Grandma couldn't remember a new one. I pointed out that Grandma only called us on Christmas and Thanksgiving, but it made no difference.

I had even turned my cell off, which I was doing more and more lately. The number hadn't been officially leaked yet, but enough people had it so that I was getting more and more mysterious texts. One came in two nights ago that just said, "WHOREWHOREWHOREWHORE," and I sat there for a minute and stared at it for so long that it began to look like "OREOREOREOREOREOREO." Then I deleted it, switched off my phone, and went downstairs to see if we had any cookies.

I wasn't telling my parents any of this. They didn't even know that my email and IM address had been hacked. I signed into my email right after James and I discovered the address had been leaked online and sure enough, I had eighty-four new messages. It went up to 337 by the next morning. I read a couple and they were nice enough, mostly girls wanting to know what Evan was like, but it felt uneven, like a teeter-totter. They knew so much about me and I knew nothing about them. Why answer their questions and make it even more lopsided?

So now my ex-boyfriend and my three-hour fling were in a war of words on MTV and a war of songs on the music charts, and my *new* boyfriend was on his way to take me on our first official date.

And I was running late.

Yippee.

I was throwing laundry around with abandon when my mom came into my room. "I couldn't help but notice," she said, "that our phone has been blowing up."

I stopped mid-throw. "It's what?"

"Blowing up. Isn't that what you say?"

"Mom, please . . ." I sighed and tried to look patient. "You can't say things like that. It sounds weird. It offends my youthful ears."

"Okay, okay, it's been ringing off the hook."

"Thank you."

"Anyway, usually when our phone starts ringing like this, it's because . . ." She trailed off a bit. " . . . something's . . . happened . . . ?"

I went back to digging in my laundry basket. "Evan's song hit number ten on the charts today and he and Simon are trash-talking each other on MTV."

"Oh. Of course."

I glanced around at the mess on my floor. "Have you seen my white shirt?"

"Which one?"

"You know, the white shirt. The one that makes—" I stopped myself just in time from saying, *The one that makes my boobs look bigger.* "The one that makes me look taller," I finished.

"The crewneck with the short sleeves?"

"V-neck with three-quarter sleeves."

"Hanging up in the laundry room downstairs."

I hurried past her, found the shirt, and yanked it off the hanger. I wasn't used to doing so much laundry. It was just natural to assume that everything I wanted to wear was dirty. But now I was being vilified in the press and online for wearing arm huggies the night I met Simon. "Sooo last year!" one magazine screeched at me, giving me their "What Were They Thinking?" award, and since I pride myself on having at least some fashion sense, I decided that wouldn't happen again. Regardless, the pictures of me wearing the arm huggies were everywhere, so now everyone hated them, just on principle. "This is all Audrey's fault," one message-boarder raged. "She totally ruined them and she needs to go."

All this over *arm huggies*. I mean, really.

"So when you say trash-talking . . ." my mom continued as she followed me. "Were they talking about you?"

"Not really," I fibbed. "Just about each other. Do you know if Dad has any argyle socks?"

"Probably. Are you going to wear them on your arms?"

See what I mean? "Arm huggies are so over, Mom."

"Of course." She gave me a wink and leaned against the doorway. "So how are you?"

Are you kidding me? I wanted to scream. *You want to do the mother-daughter thing now? NOW?!*

"I'm fine. I'm late." I went down the hall, combed through my dad's sock drawer, found the argyles, and yanked them onto my feet. Again, my mom followed me.

"Because your father and I were thinking that maybe you should take it easy. Maybe you should quit at the Scooper Dooper."

That caught my attention real quick. "Now you want me to quit the Scooper Dooper?" I cried.

"Not quit, but maybe a leave of absence?"

My parents had immediately vetoed the endorsement deal, to my immense pleasure, but this was going beyond. "How am I going to pay for gas? Or get new speakers?"

"Well, maybe we could—"

We were interrupted when the doorbell rang.

"Shit!" I cried. "Sorry, Mom. Shoot! It's him! He's early! I'm late! I'm not wearing any eyeliner yet! He won't even be able to see my eyes if I'm not wearing eyeliner!"

"Relax, your dad will keep him occupied."

I froze. "Mom. He *cannot* be alone with Dad. I'll die. I'll never even get to go on my date with James because I'll be dead and you'll have to put me in a casket without any eyeliner on because I'll be so dead that I won't even care."

My mom opened her mouth to say something, but Victoria's voice floated up the stairs as my dad answered the door. "Is she home?" I heard her ask.

"Oh, thank God," I sighed. "I'm upstairs! Please come save me!"

She ran up the stairs two at a time and burst into my room. "Guess what! Great news! Hi, Mrs. Cuttler!"

"Hi, Victoria." She grinned. "I'll be downstairs, Audrey, in case you need to be resuscitated."

Victoria waited until my mom was on the stairs. "Great! Fucking! News! What would be the best thing that could ever happen?"

"If after I died, I was reincarnated as Meg White?"

"Okay, the second-best thing."

"If my parents acted totally normal in front of James and didn't humiliate me and send me screaming for the hills?"

"Audrey! Just play along, okay?"

I started searching in my jewelry box for my tiny knife-blade charm necklace. "Okay, sorry. Best news ever! Hit it!"

She took a deep breath. "Okay, now, don't be mad."

I looked up. "The best news in the world usually doesn't start with 'don't be mad.'"

"I know, I know, but . . . okay, you know how everyone's always trying to get information about you from everyone at school?"

"Ha!" I held up the necklace, triumphant. "Put this on me?"

She came around as I held up my hair and looked in the mirror. "So last week," she began, but I cut her off.

"Victoria, I'm sorry, but I don't have time, okay? James is gonna be here in like, thirty seconds, and I haven't done makeup or anything."

"You already look beautiful."

I eyed her in the mirror as she clicked the clasp into place. "Don't do that."

"Do what?"

"Be all nicey-nice so I'll listen to you. It won't work. And where are my shoes?" I leaned over the banister. "Mooooom! Where are my shoes?"

"I'm not the shoe fairy!" she yelled back.

"But if you were?"

"By the garage door!"

I peeked back at my bedside clock. "Crap! Five fifty-three!"

"What's the big deal?" Victoria said. "You still have seven minutes. I can tell you so much in seven minutes!"

"I don't doubt that."

She followed me into the bathroom as I began to draw on eyeliner. "But seriously, you need to hear this."

"You know what I've already heard?" I tried to keep my face extra still as I drew. "James and Simon verbally bitch-slapping each other on MTV today."

"Yeah, old news. I got a text alert about it."

"From who?"

"MTV. I'm on all of the alerts now. Any time your name is mentioned in the news, I know about it."

I sighed. "Great. Hand me the eyelash curler?"

She did. "Okay, so you know how your family isn't talking to any agents or publicists or anything?"

"Very aware, thanks." It was hard to talk without blinking.

"Well, the other day, I got this email from this producer and he was like, 'We hear you're Audrey's best friend,' and I'm all, 'What about it?' and he's all, 'We want to talk to her.' So I started talking to them." Victoria took a deep breath and leaned against the door-jamb. "I'm talking to a lot of them. It's like with the lip gloss, y'know? There's a lot more than just lip gloss out there, Aud. Lip gloss is like the tip of the iceberg, and it's all there for the taking. And this way you don't have to be involved."

"How benevolent," I said, letting the irritation creep into my voice. "And when you talk to these leeches, what do you talk about?"

"Selling your soul. It's a seller's market, Aud. We should do it now."

"Not funny." I released my eyelashes, then looked at Victoria's watch. "Shit. Can I hear about your little group discussions later? Please?"

"Well, when? Because I'm kind of on a time crunch right now."

I zoomed back into my room, threw everything into my super-cute red patent leather purse, then went back to add a second coat of mascara. "Me too. James is gonna be here in five minutes."

"I think this is more important."

I almost stabbed myself in the eye with the mascara wand. "This from the girl who's been trying to set me up with James for the past three months? And did you bring that one lip gloss?"

"Yeah."

"Can I borrow?"

"You have a whole box of gloss just waiting for you! And it was free!"

"Yeah, but yours is better. C'mon, I'll love you forever."

"You'll love me even more once I tell you the good news." She began digging around in her bag and produced the gloss. "Don't lose it. It's my favorite and I have no money to buy more."

"No worries."

Victoria glanced out the bedroom window. "Does James drive a black Toyota?"

My heart picked up the pace. "Yes! Is he here? Oh, God, please don't say yes!"

She was oddly quiet.

"Victoria! Is it him?"

"You said not to say yes!"

"This is a really bad time to go all literal on me!" I smeared on the lip gloss, grabbed my bag, and flew down the stairs, Victoria close behind.

"Mom! I think he's here!"

"Let the roasting begin!" my dad yelled back.

"Dad!"

"Audrey!"

"Look, Aud, okay, I'm just gonna say it!" Victoria just cannot be stopped. I don't even know why I bother to try. "This is big!"

I ran past the garage door and didn't see my shoes. "Mom! They're not there!"

"What's not where?"

"My shoes! By the garage door!"

"Which shoes?"

I was ready to rip all my hair out.

"Remember that email I was sending last week?" Victoria kept going. "The one I was writing when you faceplanted while painting your toenails?"

"It's a painful memory on many levels, but yes, I remember. Where are my freaking shoes?!"

"Okay, it was just to confirm the following two words!" Victoria said as I rushed toward the hall closet. "Reality! Show!"

The doorbell rang and I pulled open the closet door and found my beat-up black Converse, the ones that Victoria had drawn silver hearts on during a particularly mind-numbing English class. "Who put them in the closet?" I cried.

And then the words *reality show* finally registered in my brain.

"Wait a minute!" I turned to Victoria. "What reality show? I'm not doing a reality show!" I cried as I yanked the closet door open wider.

Then there was a muffled *flump!* sound followed by a "Yeeeeeooooowwwwllll . . . !"

I froze. "Bendomolena?" I slowly peeked around and saw my cat standing there, looking like she had been hit in the face with a closet door. Which, of course, she just had. "Oh, Bendy! Oh, your cute little face! I'm so sorry!"

"Meeeeoooowwwwwlllll!" I guess my cat inherited my dramatic gene, because she was really milking this one. Of course, I *did* just smash her.

I dropped my shoes and bent down to pick her up. "Lift with your knees," both Victoria and my dad warned at the same time, then exchanged grins.

"I think your date is here, Audrey," my dad said. "I'll let him in."

Uh-oh. I cut him off and held Bendomolena up in front of him as my mom walked past, ever the rescuer. "Look at her nose!" I cried. "Does it look redder than normal? Do you think I broke it?"

My dad raised an eyebrow. "She's a cat, Audrey. Her nose is already red."

"No, it's normally pink! I think I hurt her!"

"Hi, James, come on in," my mom was saying, and I looked past my dad and Victoria to see him standing in our entryway. He was taller than both my parents, but then again, neither of them are Amazons.

"Come on in, James," my dad said. "Welcome to the circus."

James gave me a nervous wave. "Hi, Audrey. Hi, Mr. Cuttler." He shook hands with my dad like he was pulling the pin out of a grenade.

"Hi," I said to him. "I think I just broke my cat's face."

"That's a cat?"

Victoria grinned. "I've been saying that for years."

"So," my dad said to James. "You work at the ice cream store with Audrey. How's it going?"

"Uh, just fine, sir."

I guess my mom could see my eyeballs starting to bulge, because she expertly stepped in and said, "Audrey speaks very highly of you, James."

And then I guess Victoria saw my eyeballs practically fall out of my head at my mom's idea of conversation, because *she* stepped in to run her own brand of interference. "Isn't that the biggest cat you've ever seen? I think she's world-record material."

"What's her name?" James asked.

"Bendomolena," I told him. "Does her face look broken?"

"Um, no. Just kinda cranky, maybe?"

"I just smashed her face with the door. By accident, I swear."

James gingerly patted her head. "Good thing she's got all the extra padding."

After everything calmed down and they all convinced me that Bendy didn't have a concussion or brain damage, Victoria left ("Audrey! We're talking tomorrow about . . . that *thing*! That we talked about today!" she yelled before going out the door), and it was just me and my mom and James.

And my dad. Who never fails to disappoint.

"So," he said to James as we stood in the entryway. "Do you plan on writing a song about my daughter?"

"Oh, my God, Dad," I sighed. "He's not a musician."

My dad looked to James for confirmation.

"I can't play a single instrument," he agreed. "I can't even snap my fingers."

"And do you plan on doing anything that will make her even more famous?

"Um, no? I mean—" James stopped to clear his throat. "No, sir. Not at all."

"You're not gonna sell pictures of her to tabloids?"

James blushed and I knew he was thinking about how we had been joking about that very thing earlier. "No, sir. Never."

"You're not in with the paparazzi?"

James was blushing so bad that his ears were red. "No, sir."

"Okay. Dad? You've met him. Mom, you've met him." I had to step in before James's head exploded with embarrassment. "And James, you've met my parents. Can we go now? Please? Before Dad tries to get a DNA sample?"

My mom smiled. "Home by midnight."

"I know, I know." I half-guided, half-shoved James toward the door. "And call every half an hour," I added before she could remind me.

"You have money?" my dad asked James.

"Yes, sir."

"You don't need to borrow any from my daughter?" Evan had always been borrowing ten and twenty dollars at a time from me, which drove my dad crazy. Come to think of it, it drove me crazy as well.

"No, sir, not at all."

"Bye, Mom. Bye, Dad." I gave them both a look. "We have to go now."

"'Bye, have fun!" My mom waved. And then, because she couldn't resist, "Try not to attract too much attention!"

By the time we were in James's car, I was exhausted. "I? Am so sorry," I told him. "Really. They're just overprotective right now."

"No, it's okay." He was fastening his seat belt and looking relieved. "How do you think I did?"

"Well, I'm in your car, so I'd say fine." I smiled as he kept shoving his hair out of his face. "Although I did lose count of how many times you called my dad 'sir.'"

James started to laugh. "He's your dad! What was I supposed to do? I was trying to make a good impression!"

I had never really heard James laugh before. It was an unusual one, the kind that you hear and it makes you laugh too, even if you don't know what's so funny. "No, it was cute," I told him. "I'm only teasing. Sort of."

"Yeah, I kinda guessed." He was looking at me oddly. "Hey.

You're not wearing those arm things of yours."

I fastened my seat belt. "C'mon, dude, those are so over. And I won the worst-dressed award for wearing them, so yeah. Don't expect to see them again."

"Okay. You hungry?"

"Starving."

"Then let's go."

So we went.

23 *"Reoccurring episodes with each and every kiss. . . ."*

—New Found Glory, "All Downhill From Here"

ASIDE FROM THAT whole meet-the-parents-and-Victoria-and-the-cat-with-the-smashed-face scenario, my first date with James was definitely becoming one of the Top 5 Moments of My Whole Life. From the car to the restaurant, James held my hand the whole way. Some guys just have a knack for hand-holding, have y o u noticed? They're not all limp or sweaty-palmed, and it doesn't feel like they're leading you around like a little kid.

We went to this twenty-four-hour diner by the beach, and the air was cool and salty, like I could put my tongue out and taste it. And then I found out the restaurant he had picked had a jukebox, and James's cool factor jumped up five thousand points. Three songs for a dollar? A bargain at twice the price.

"So if you did get your own TV show," James mused over veggie burgers and french fries, "could I guest star?"

"You better," I said as I dipped a fry in ketchup. "You can be the wacky neighbor who lives next door. Every show has one."

"Audrey, which part of me sounds wacky to you?"

"Well, it doesn't even matter, 'cause there's no way I'm doing it.

What would they film? Me sitting in the office, doing SAT questions? Ooh, so scintillating. Stand back, *Real World*! Audrey has arrived!"

In fact, everything was going so well that I felt it was okay to ask James a question that had been bothering me for awhile. "So," I said as I bit into a deliciously floppy french fry. "Can I ask you something?"

"Uh-oh."

"No, it's not bad! I promise!"

"I'll decide if that's true." He sipped at his Coke and raised his eyebrows at me as if to say, "Go ahead."

So I did. "What took you so long?"

He choked mid-sip and came up sputtering. "What?"

I handed him a napkin. "I mean, when I first started working at the Scooper Dooper, you wouldn't even talk to me. Remember when I asked you what music you liked?"

James gave me a small smile as he wiped his mouth. "Butter pecan," he murmured.

"Exactly!" I cried, smacking the tabletop for emphasis. "That's all you said. 'I think we need more butter pecan.' What was up with *that?*"

James sighed. "I kicked myself for days afterward."

"And you never talked to me, either, unless it was about sugar cones or reorders. Why?"

"Well, um, Audrey, you're kind of . . . um, intimidating? Kind of?"

I drew back. "Intimidating?"

"No, not in a bad way, just like . . ." He set his napkin down and leaned forward. I could tell he was choosing his words carefully. "You've just got all this, like, light around you. You're always talking or dancing or flipping the radio stations around. And you talk really fast, too. And I'm not really like that, and I didn't know what to do. So then I just sounded stupid every time I opened my mouth." He took another sip of Coke. "And then there was the fact that you had this cool musician boyfriend."

I smiled. "Oh, yeah. Him."

"Yeah. Him."

I couldn't resist. "That is so cute."

"Oh, jeez." He balled up his napkin and ducked his head so I wouldn't see him blush.

"Don't hide! It's cute that you were jealous! So when did you know you liked me?"

James sat back up and thought a minute. "I'll tell you if you tell me."

"Fair enough."

"On your first day, right after I told you that we weren't allowed to change the radio station? You changed it five minutes later and you knew all the words to all the songs for the entire shift. And then you did that little dance every time a song you liked came on. That was pretty cute."

"That's the happy dance," I told him. "I do it a lot." Had he liked me for that long? I thought about all the times I had left work early to go meet Evan, or to go to one of his shows, leaving James behind to close by himself. It made me feel a little sick to think of it, like I had done something wrong without even knowing it.

"Okay, so when did you like me?" James asked.

I didn't even have to think about it. "When the song first came on the radio and I broke the ice cream scoop, and you said, 'Scoop now, think later.'"

James's eyes widened. "*That?* That's what did it for you? I thought it was gonna be the mix CD!"

"Oh, that was the second moment," I assured him.

"It took me, like, two days to make that for you. It was like a piece of my soul I was giving to you, and if you didn't like a song, you were going to hate me."

I nodded. "I've been there. I obsess over mixes all the time. If there's one bad song on there, it kills the whole thing."

"So did you like it?"

"I *loved* it. I played it all the time. I still do."

"Really?"

"I swear."

We would've kept smiling at each other like two hopeless dopes if I hadn't realized the time. "Oh, half an hour in," I said. "Gotta report back to the generals."

"Yeah, you do that. I don't want your dad to come after us."

I waved the thought away as I called home. "If anything, he'll just fuck with your head."

"How reassuring. Thank you, Audrey."

"Anytime."

"Hello?"

"Hi, Mom, it's me. I'm alive and sober. But there's still time for things to get exciting."

"Ha. Are you having a nice time?"

"Um, yes." I rolled my eyes at James. "Can I go, please? Now that I've proven I'm unharmed?"

"Okay. Thanks for sticking to the deal, sweetie."

"No prob, Bob." I hung up as fast as I could. "Sorry about that."

I was about to say more, but then "Audrey, Wait!" came

blasting out of the jukebox at full volume, and for some reason, James and I both drew back from each other. "Sorry," I said to him again. "Sorry, it's only three minutes and forty-nine seconds. It'll be over soon."

James shrugged. "I don't care. Be right back." Then he stood up and made his way through the crowd over to the jukebox, digging a crumpled dollar bill out of his super-skinny jeans. I watched him go and saw a booth of people from our school, giggling and looking over at me. They were the ones who had picked the song, I knew it. So I examined my hair for split ends and picked at my veggie burger and waited for James to return.

James came back just before the song ended. "Okay, just had to balance out the music selection," he said. He moved a lock of red hair out of his eyes. "I hope you like it."

"If it's not The Song, then I'm going to love it," I assured him. "Trust me."

The song finally ended and the next one came on. Some familiar jangly guitar notes were strummed, and then, "*I need someone, a person to talk to. Someone who'd care to love, could it be you?*"

The Violent Femmes. "Kiss Off." Perfection. Sheer ultimate perfection. "Seriously, James," I started to say, but I was smiling too hard to speak. Plus my throat felt a little scratchy, like when you get overwhelmed with emotion and can't really talk.

"*You can all just kiss off into the air! Behind my back I can see that stare!*"

James was mouthing the words, nodding his head in time to the beat. When he saw me getting all emotional, he grinned and leaned forward. "Just so you know, it's gonna play three times in a row."

Looking back, it was absolutely the worst thing we could have done, attracting attention to ourselves, two music geeks singing along with a song for the whole restaurant to see. But it was just so much fun, and I was sitting with this awesome guy who obsessed over mix CDs he made for me and picked the perfect song at the perfect time. And he didn't care about any of the other bullshit, like MTV or magazines or random boys trying to kiss me or the fact that while we were on our first date, we listened to a song written about me by my ex-boyfriend. I liked James and James liked me and we both knew it and if you think about it, that's like a miracle. A real true miracle. Everyone says that babies are miracles, and don't get me wrong, I love cute little pudgy babies, but if you think about it, me having a baby right now would not be a miracle. *At all.* But finding someone that gets me? That's the real work. That's where the miracles are.

And that made everything else less important.

"Do you want to go to RPM?" James asked after the song played for the second time. "It's new music Tuesday, you know."

"Oh, believe me, I know. Sure, let's go."

We were halfway to the record store and I was scrolling through James's MP3 player, playing parts of songs before finding one I liked better, when he suddenly made a left-hand turn. "Where are you going?" I asked. "You have to go straight." (I'm kind of a nightmare backseat driver. Jonah can tell stories about me that would make you cry.)

"Yeah, I know, but . . ." He kept looking in the rearview mirror and when he got to the next intersection, he made another left. "They say . . . that you're supposed . . ."

Now I was trying to look in the rearview mirror too. "What's going on back there?"

"I think . . . we're being followed?"

"By who? If it's Sharon Eggleston, I'm gonna rip her throat out and hand it back to her. You can help, if you want."

"I don't think it's Sharon." He started to make his third left-hand turn. "If you think you're being followed in a car, you should make four left-hand turns."

I glanced at him. "How do you know that?"

"I read it in this cheesy spy novel once."

I suddenly imagined James as this super-cute spy, which distracted me from the problem at hand. "It's pretty cool that you know that," I told him.

"I think it's true, too. I mean, the four-left-turns part."

Now I was trying to see out of the side mirror. "Is it just one car?"

"Um, no."

"How many?" I could barely see a thing.

"I think . . . three? Maybe only two? And they might have cameras?"

I looked at him. He looked at me.

James spoke first. "So," he said casually as he made his fourth left. "Have you ever outrun the paparazzi before?"

24

"You can't be close enough unless I'm feeling your heartbeat. . . ."
—hellogoodbye, "All of Your Love"

JAMES MADE IT to the parking lot of RPM Records and slowly parked the car in a spot close to the front door. "Okay," I said. "I've seen this on TV plenty of times. We can't run, because then they'll chase us."

"Right," James said. We were about ten seconds away from having them trap us in the car with their cameras and we were both clumsily yanking our seat belts off and reaching for the car door handles.

"And don't go all Naomi Campbell and try to hit them," I continued. "They'll sue you and you'd have to work at the Scooper Dooper for the rest of your life to pay the legal fees."

"You sound like you've done this before."

"No, I've just seen it on TV." I grabbed my bag and started to open the door. "If all else fails," I told James, "lie down and play dead."

"Don't run, don't punch them, play dead. Got it. Let's go."

James and I must have looked like two crazy aerobicizers as we made our way through the parking lot, not running but walking as fast as our legs would carry us. Still, that didn't stop the photographers from trying to get our attention.

"Audrey, who's your new guy?"

"Make out with him yet, Audrey?"

"What's the name of his band?"

"Audrey, over here!"

"Is this your first date?"

"Audrey, have you talked to Evan yet?"

"What do you think of Evan's success, Audrey?"

"Any comment about the Do-Gooders and the Lolitas, Audrey?"

By the time James and I made it to the front door of RPM Records, I could barely see. The camera flashes popped and popped until it looked like the world was filled with exploding stars, and if James hadn't half-shoved me into the store, I don't think I would've been able to see the front door.

Once my vision cleared, I realized that the entire store was staring at us. Well, us or the photographers, who were still taking pictures through the windows. Even the super-cool employees looked a little surprised. "Wow," one of them said. He was wearing black square-framed emo glasses and pushed them back up on his nose. "Audrey. *Cool.*"

Now, I've been shopping at RPM since I bought my first Strokes record, but never has any employee there known my name, said hello, or shown any sign of recognition. So in a night of firsts, this was another one to add to the list. "Hi," I said. "There's kind of a problem in your parking lot."

It ended up that the night manager had to come downstairs and, as James put it, "regulate those paparazzi bitches." I know James said that to make me smile, and it did, but it was so hard to relax when everyone at the store kept stealing glances at me. We went to the import section first and I started flipping through the A's, but I could hear the tiny *clickclickclick* sound of camera phones going off. Every time I looked up, though, they were nowhere to be seen. And then Mr. Emo Glasses came over and said, "Are you finding everything all right?" and I heard *clickclickclick* again and I knew it was only a matter of time before pictures of me and him wound up on the Internet. Maybe he already knew that.

Meanwhile, no matter how much regulating the manager did on those paparazzi bitches, he couldn't stop more from waiting in front of the store. I could see them outside the door, cameras in hand, waiting for me and James to step outside again. "I'm fine," I told Mr. Emo Glasses, then went down the aisle to where James was flipping through the *L*'s. "Hey," I said. "Find anything?"

"Not really." He released the stack of CDs so that they flopped back into the bins and then looked at me. "But I'm not really paying attention."

"Yeah. Me neither." Then I paused. Cue the awkward conversation. "You know your picture's gonna be everywhere tomorrow morning, right?"

James went crimson. "*My* picture?"

"Well, yeah. That's why they're freaking out. They know we're on a date."

"Oh. Oh, wow. Um . . ." James glanced over my head toward the hysteria just outside the door. "That is, um . . . weird. Definitely weird."

"Still want to be the wacky next-door neighbor on my reality show?"

"Well, hell, for this sort of inconvenience I want a pay raise and a promotion to 'love interest.' What's that clicking noise?"

"Someone's camera phone."

"Great."

"Let's just go upstairs and look in the clearance bins," I told him. "No one's ever up there, it's just crap CDs that they can't even sell for a buck."

So we hurried upstairs, where I was right—it was empty save for an employee who was reading a magazine behind the information desk. Obviously no one had filled him in on the brouhaha downstairs, because he didn't seem remotely interested in me or James. (Side note: How awesome is the word *brouhaha*? I hereby resolve to use it more often.)

"Better," James sighed once we had made our escape. "Much, much better."

We walked the aisles together, holding hands as he browsed one side and I browsed the other. But then it started getting more and more populated, and by the time we were halfway through the section, it was as crowded upstairs as it had been downstairs. The previously oblivious employee now looked annoyed. "I think," I whispered to James, "if we went into the bathroom, fifty people would suddenly have to pee."

By the time we were done shopping, James had found an old Smashing Pumpkins import and I had the newest CD from Qwerty, this wacky new band that consisted of three Canadian siblings and no drummer. "No drummer, right?" James said when he saw my CD.

"You've heard of them?"

"My brother saw them open for Doomsday Scenario last year."

"Your brother saw Doomsday Scenario?" I was beside myself. "Why didn't you go? And why didn't you take *me?*"

James sighed heavily. "It was an eighteen-plus show."

"I hate when that happens! Do you know how many good shows I've missed because of that?"

"Probably as many as me. But my brother said that Qwerty were better than Doomsday."

"Not *even* possible."

"He swears to it."

We were walking downstairs while talking, which is probably why we didn't notice the commotion at first, but when we got to the base of the stairs, screams erupted from outside.

Like, *screams.*

The flashes from the previous paparazzi shots were nothing compared to this time. There must have been at least thirty of them, and the exploding stars from before had become one big giant supernova of *flash!click*! I could also see girls outside, and some of them had on shirts that read IT'S ALL GOOD! and TEAM AUDREY. (Which, as the girl who was never going to be captain of anything sports-related, *ever*, was kind of gratifying for a minute.)

"Whoa," James said under his breath and he let go of my hand, which fell heavy and slack against my leg. Both of us were just staring, and then we looked at each other, because it was painfully obvious that there was no way in hell we were going to get through those doors and back to his car. Not unless we wanted to be torn apart like turkeys on Thanksgiving.

Everyone was calling my name, their voices barely muffled through the glass doors, and the store's security guard was standing in front of the doors with his arms folded. The store manager was standing next to him, and when he saw James and me, he came rushing over and began shoving us back upstairs. "Get away from the windows! Here, into the office," he said as we both turned and ran up the stairs with him. "Don't worry—the police are on their way to get you out of here safely."

"The police?" I squeaked. "Really?"

"Really," he said. "Don't worry, this happened to us when we did a signing with those *High School Musical* kids. We're well-trained in crowd control."

"Your dad," James said under his breath, "is going to kill me."

"No, he's not," I promised. "This isn't your fault."

"Okay, in here," the manager said, shuffling the two of us into a bare-bones windowless room that had stacks and stacks of CDs and promo stuff and rolled-up posters lying everywhere. The life of a record store manager was starting to seem better and better, I had to admit. Free CDs being mailed to you every day? Bands showing up to do signings and in-store performances? Being able to listen to music at work? Sign me up, please.

But at the time, it was just super scary. I was trying not to freak out, and I could tell James was trying to do the same, even though his cheeks were flushed and he kept shoving his hair behind his ears.

"Audrey, can I get you anything?" the manager said. When I shook my head, he turned to James. "James?"

"No thank—wait. How do you know my name?"

"The press outside seemed to know who you were."

"How do *they* know my name?" Now James was starting to look alarmed.

"Whoever saw us at the restaurant and called them, told

them," I sighed. The pieces were far too easy to string together.

"Oh, man." James sat back in his chair, his legs akimbo. "Oh, man. *Shit*."

Cue my guilt complex.

"I am so sorry," I kept saying to him after the manager went back downstairs. "I am so sorry. I am so, *so* sorry."

"No, wait, why are you apologizing?" James wheeled his chair over to mine so we could sit next to each other.

"Because I did this to you, and now everyone's gonna start calling your house and your picture's going to be everywhere and—"

"But it's not your fault, right? I mean, you didn't do any of this, did you?"

I looked at my hands in my lap. "I shouldn't have dated you right now. This isn't okay. It's not fair to you or your family or just—"

James ran a hand through his hair and sighed heavily. "Okay, Audrey, look—"

"I like that, by the way."

"Like what?"

"When you say my name. 'Cause sometimes people just say 'Aud,' which sounds like 'odd.'"

"Well, 'odd' is a good word for you, I have to admit. But seriously, Audrey"—we both smiled when he said my name again—"this isn't your fault. And I'd rather be dating you and being chased by paparazzi than not."

"Really?"

"Swear to God."

"'Cause there's probably going to be a lot of that. At least for the time being."

"Do I still get to drive like James Bond? 'Cause that was pretty cool."

"That *was* cool." I grinned. "You and your four-left-turns thing."

"Thanks. I try."

"And it was hot, too, you pretending to be all spylike."

"Really?"

"Really. If it wouldn't have endangered our lives, I would've totally made out with you right then."

James's blush went up into his ears. "Oh, yeah?" His voice sounded a little higher than normal.

"Yeah." I rolled my wheelie chair closer to his. "Wanna reenact the scene?"

If kissing Simon had been like a wildfire, kissing James was something smaller and stronger. It was birthday and prayer candles, ones made for good thoughts and strong hopes and wishes and promises. I needed some of those right now.

"You know," James said after we broke apart, "I'm really looking forward to the day when we aren't kissing in storage freezers or weird offices."

"By the looks of things," I told him, "those days are far, far away."

25 *"Swallowing panic in the face of its force . . ."*

—Joanna Newsom, "Peach, Plum, Pear"

THE SECOND PHONE CALL I made to my parents that evening was a bit more eventful than the first one. "Um, Mom?" I said, and I guess my voice sounded all funny, because she got it.

"Uh-oh."

"Um, yeah. The paparazzi? They followed me and James from the restaurant? And now we're kinda trapped at the record store."

"Trapped?"

"By the paparazzi. And some fans. But it's okay, because the police are on their way—"

"The police?"

"The police!" My dad suddenly piped up in the background.

"Audrey, we're on our way," my mom said, and then she hung up before I could tell her to leave Dad at home. And not that I wanted my parents to show up on James's and my first date, but it was sort of a relief to think that people who were really good at being in charge would be showing up soon.

After my mom and dad got there and realized that James and I were okay and not damaged or anything, my dad went berserk.

"Do you mean to tell me," he was screaming at some police officer just outside the office, "that my sixteen-year-old daughter cannot even go on a simple date without being harassed in such a manner?"

I looked at James.

He looked at me.

My mom looked at me.

James looked at my mom.

My mom looked at James.

I looked at my mom.

"I am a taxpayer!" my dad continued. I had heard those words so many times before, but usually it was being muttered at the TV or a newspaper, not yelled at the police. "And I expect my daughter to have the same rights as any other teenager in this town and—"

"Sir, I understand your frustration, but right now, your daughter is not a normal teenager and—"

"Not normal?" I said.

"Not normal?!" my dad yelled. "She is as normal as the rest of them!"

"Well, when you put it that way . . ." I said, thinking of all the people at our school that I would never want to be like.

"Not now, Aud." My mom was rubbing her head in that headachey way.

"Sorry, but Mom, can you please go stop Dad? Before someone clubs him over the head?"

It turned out to be the worst advice I could have given her, because she went out to calm my dad down, but then she got sucked into the argument, and pretty soon it was the police versus my parents. I could hear the officer trying to placate them, but I knew it was useless. "He's doing it all wrong," I told James. "Believe me, when they're tag-teaming, they're unstoppable."

"They sound pretty mad," James said. He had paled considerably when my dad started yelling, and even more so when my mom jumped in.

"They met at a political rally at Berkeley," I sighed. "Social justice is kind of their gig."

"Oh."

"Still want to date me?"

"Still think your dad isn't going to kill me?"

"Yes."

"Then yes." James was quiet for a minute. "Are you sure he's not going to kill me?"

"Social *justice*, remember?"

But then the yelling started up again and James and I both sighed and flopped back in our chairs. "I'm dead," he moaned.

It ended up that the police officers had to go outside and tell everyone to "STAND BACK! STAND BACK, PLEASE!" before we could leave the store. When we walked out, flashbulbs went off yet again and my mom kept trying to hold her sweater over my head, but all that managed to do was suffocate me with synthetic fibers and cause me to step on the back of James's slip-on Vans, which promptly slipped off. I really wanted to hold his hand, just so I could know he was there and so he would know I was there, but no way could we do that, not with all the cameras. And besides, there were some autograph seekers, pushing covers of last week's magazine toward me, trying to get me to sign the article about me and Simon. I brushed past all of them and their Sharpie pens and followed everyone to the parking lot.

"Head down, feet forward," one of the officers said as we shuffled into the lot.

It was the best advice I heard that night.

26 "By protecting my heart truly, I got lost in the sounds. . . ."

—Regina Spektor, "Fidelity"

THE NEXT MORNING brought nothing but crankiness and misplaced anger, which aren't the best feelings to have after a first date. I slept for shit that night, with paparazzi and camera flashes hiding in my head, popping out every time I closed my eyes. Judging from how my parents looked the next morning, they slept about as well as I did.

"Do you want something to eat?" my mom asked me. "Maybe eggs or something?" I could tell she felt bad for me, since our family has always had a DIY attitude toward breakfast. I've been putting cereal in the bowl myself since I was three years old and figured out how to climb up the pantry shelves. Eggs might as well have been a foreign custom, as far as eating them for breakfast was concerned.

"I'll eat on the way to school," I told her. The weather outside was gray and cloudy, totally mopey weather, and I grabbed the entire box of Cheerios and a banana. "Look in the paper tomorrow for pictures of me eating straight out of the box," I told her. "I'm sure those will be super flattering."

"Honey, you can't let this—"

"Mom." I stopped in my tracks and turned around. "I do not. Want to talk. About this."

She took a deep breath and I could tell she was deciding whether or not to push the subject. "Okay," she finally said. "Have a good day at school."

"Which part? The part where I get to be stuck in the office with no one to talk to all day? I'm sure that'll be especially swell. Or maybe when everyone starts asking about me and James and trying to get information to give reporters. That could be a real highlight."

And then I left before I could tell that I had hurt her feelings.

I'm sure I looked sort of insane, clomping into school with a box of Cheerios tucked under my arm, my hair flying everywhere, and puffy bags under my eyes. There was a new banner spanning the ceiling of the main hallway, right toward my locker, and I craned my head back to read it. AUDREY, WAIT! IS AT #10! it read. LET'S MAKE IT #1! GO, DO-GOODERS!

"Hey, superstar," someone said to me, and I gave them the finger without even looking to see who had said it.

"Yo, Aud, I'm kidding. Wait up, I'm totally kidding!"

I glanced over my shoulder and saw Jonah jogging to catch up with me. "I swear, I'm only kidding," he said again as soon as he was close enough. "Don't kill me."

"Oh, God, sorry," I sighed. "I'm just in the crappiest of crappy moods, Jonah."

"Yeah, I heard about your date last night."

"From who?"

"Victoria. Who else?"

"But I haven't even talked to her about it yet!"

"She saw the pictures online."

"Is she here?"

"Yeah, she's somewhere." Jonah looked around the hallway. "She'll find you, I'm sure. She's all excited about some reality show thing? I don't really know what the hell she's talking about."

"Consider yourself lucky."

"Are you gonna be on a reality show?"

"Would you watch if I was?"

"I'd TiVo that shit, for sure." He nudged my shoulder. "So where's your new guy?"

"Probably hiding somewhere to avoid me." Despite all of James's reassurances the night before, I still thought that our first date had been too Dickensian with its "it was the best of times, it was the worst of times" dramatics. And, to be honest, that was not the sort of excitement I had been going for. I was hoping for ice cream freezer excitement, if you get my drift. Or even just a conversation where we weren't interrupted by a camera.

"Well, any guy that hides to avoid you, you just tell me and I'll straighten that fool out." Jonah punched his fist into his open palm, then grinned. When Jonah smiles like that, you can't help but smile back, especially because we both knew that he would never actually hit someone. He won't even kill spiders. (Unlike Victoria, who whacks the hell out of them with a folded-up magazine.)

"Thanks, Jonah," I told him. "You're a pal."

"No worries."

"Want some Cheerios?" I held out the box to him.

He peered into it. "Where are the marshmallows?"

"No marshmallows. Just fiber and heart-healthy goodness and the taste that kids love." I shook the box at him.

Jonah wrinkled his nose. "Dude, kids love the taste of marsh-mallows."

I shrugged. "More for me, then."

Right before the first bell rang, I got a text from Victoria. "Bathroom 9:30," she wrote, and I sent an "OK" back. This had become our preferred on-the-sly method for talking during school, since we didn't have any classes together and there was no way we were going to wait until after school. So much could happen between eight fifteen and two o'clock! Was I really supposed to wait to talk to her?

I brought the box of Cheerios with me to our meeting.

"Uh, nice breakfast," she said. She was standing in front of the bathroom mirror, pulling product through her tiny spikes of hair.

"Just for that, you can't have any," I said as I opened each one of the stall doors, checking to see if they were occupied. "Good, no one's here. We can talk. Did you see that lame banner?"

"Yeah, I know. The pep squad is, like, doing phone drives to request the song on radio across the country. The Do-Gooders are the most famous thing to come out of school, besides you."

"Great."

She turned around to face me. Her cheeks were bright pink with excitement. "Anyway, Aud. This. Is. *Amazing*."

It wasn't the response I was expecting. "Excuse me?"

"You got media swamped at RPM Records! Did they give you any free stuff? Or a shopping spree? Or a gift card? Can you at least get a discount? Can your friends get a discount?"

"What are you talking about?"

"You brought them so much publicity!" she squealed. "Tell me they at least gave you some promo stuff."

I could feel the beginning of a massive headache. "No, I just wanted to get the hell out of there."

"Well, maybe when you do the reality show, they can film some scenes—"

"I'm not doing a reality show, Victoria. First off, you don't even make any money doing them." I was about to continue my list of why-nots when I glanced in the mirror and saw my undereye circles. "Do you have any eye cream?" I asked Victoria. "I've got full-on luggage."

She produced a small pot of cream and handed it to me. "You don't make money from the show directly, but then everyone will see you and then the advertisers—say, RPM Records—"

"All right!" I interrupted. "You know what? Can we just not talk about this right now? Can we maybe talk about something more important, like the fact that my first date with James got interrupted by a million photographers, five police officers, two *way* overenthusiastic RPM employees, and let's not forget my parents, who got into a shouting match with the five police officers? Do you think *maybe* we could discuss that! Because I'd like to, if that's okay with you!"

Victoria looked a little taken aback. I'm not a yeller, but when I hit my limit, I hit my fucking limit. "All right," she said after a few beats. "Let's talk. Don't hold back."

I ignored her sarcastic shrink talk. "James hates me!" I wailed.

"Did he actually say that?"

"No, but—"

"Oh, then, by all means, accuse him of it. He's done absolutely nothing to prove himself trustworthy or faithful to you."

Now it was my turn to be quiet for a few seconds. "I know," I finally admitted as I dabbed on some eye cream, then handed her back the jar. "Want some Cheerios? Your boyfriend hated them."

"Yeah, I know. He'll only eat cereal with marshmallows. Even then, he just goes through and picks out all the marshmallows. Fucking nasty." She reached into the box and pulled out a handful. "So when are you seeing James again?"

"We're meeting in the library at lunch."

"Ooh, sexy rendezvous choice. The dusty books, all the hidden desire, the uncracked spines—"

I gave her an odd look. "The fact that no one ever goes in there."

"Yeah, there's that, too." She glanced at her watch. "You better get back to your classroom."

I suddenly didn't want to leave her. Even though she was pushy and more opinionated that a Supreme Court justice, she was my friend. She was familiar. She was Victoria. "Can't you fake sick or something and come up to visit me?" I said, trying to sound lonely and pitiful.

"And fuck up my GPA? I've already sacrificed the Perfect Attendance Award."

"I don't know if getting chicken pox counts as a 'sacrifice.'"

"Still." She fixed her hair one last time, then patted my shoulder. "Come on. Buck up. There are twenty thousand girls who would give their left eye to be you right now. It could be worse."

"Oh, so now I'm not grateful enough that I've had my life interrupted?" That slow-burning rage was starting back up again.

Victoria sighed and held the door open. "Come on," she said. "Let's go back to your crazy life. Don't forget your Cheerios."

By the time I met James in the Animals & Wildlife section of our school library, I had motored my way through half the box and felt like I was wearing one big Cheerio around my waist. I suppose that, *technically*, no eating was allowed during school hours, but Connie the secretary wasn't saying anything. She probably knew about my date last night with James, thanks to her daughter, and besides, she and I had formed a sort of silent partnership. She let me eat cereal out of the box and disappear to the bathroom for minutes at a time, and I didn't say anything when she pretended to have a headache and snuck out to get her hair done.

"Here," I said when I saw James in the library. "Please. Take the Cheerios. I'm going to explode."

He smiled and took the box. "So my brother has started calling me 'King Stud,'" he replied. "I don't think it's a compliment."

"Can I just apologize one more time?"

"Sure, let's round it up to an even million," he replied.

I was about to say more, but then he kissed me, and for a brief minute, everything was all right. "Hi," he said softly after we broke apart.

"Hi," I sighed. "I missed you."

"The King Stud missed you, too." I could tell that he was enjoying this new nickname.

"Uh, this third-person thing isn't going to work for me, King Stud," I told him. "And neither is the 'King Stud' part."

"Okay, all right, I'm over it." He hung onto my elbows and took a step back. "Wow. You look exhausted."

"Yeah, well, this fluorescent lighting isn't exactly a girl's best friend."

"Did you sleep at all last night?"

"No. Did you?"

"Nope. I was kind of hopped up on adrenaline."

"I know what you mean."

"I figured you might." He shoved my hair out of my face and I let him. "Are your parents still having coronaries?"

"No, they're calm. At least for right now. Who knows, though? One more magazine, one more phone call from US Weekly? They could snap. It won't be pretty." I glanced around in either direction before pulling him further down the aisle. "But seriously. They might make me stop working at the Scooper Dooper."

"Really?" James looked stricken.

"Really. I think last night was the final straw. I think the house might go to full-on lockdown. For me, anyway. I'll be lucky if I see daylight again before New Year's." I was still pulling him further into the aisle's recesses. "Look at me, I'm already so fucking paranoid. In two weeks, I'll probably be putting combination locks on the refrigerator. Just wait."

"Work is going to blow so hard if you're not there." He sort of looked like a kicked puppy, all defenseless and sad. It was terrible.

"Well, they didn't say that I had to quit yet," I pointed out. "Maybe they won't make me leave."

But then neither of us said anything, and both James and I knew it was only a matter of time before I was officially jobless. We weren't idiots. We were both there when our first date ended with a police escort. "Sucks," he finally sighed. "Sucks, sucks, sucks."

"Wanna come over after school?" I asked after a minute, trying to think of ways to make both of us feel better. "You should take advantage of the offer before I get locked in the garage, you know."

He grinned. "Are you gonna show me your collage wall?"

"Maaaayybe. Will you rent movies before you come over?"

"Maaaayybe. What do you want?"

"Something really bloody and violent, with jaw-dropping thrills and chills." I waited until his face showed the appropriate level of shock. "Ha! I kid! Your pick."

James raised an eyebrow. "Okay, in my limited dating experience," he said, "and we are talking *limited* dating experience, girls tell you to pick the movie, but they don't mean it. They're just testing you."

"That's the kind of shit that girls like Sharon Eggleston pull," I told him, then watched as the grin slid off his face. "What? Is she behind me with a butcher knife or something?"

"No, but . . ." He sighed heavily. "Okay, you have to promise that you're not going to freak out or anything."

"I'm not gonna freak out." I was crossing my fingers behind my back, though. "What is it?"

"I heard this girl talking today in my history class—the one who's always hanging out with Sharon and was there that day at the Scooper Dooper?"

"Natasha," I told him. "The mouth breather."

"Yeah, that one. Anyway, she was saying to some other girls that Sharon was the one who called the paparazzi and told them that we were at the diner last night. And that they paid her two hundred and fifty dollars, cash, for the info."

"And you promised," he added quickly, "that you wouldn't freak out."

"Freaking out is too mild a reaction!" I cried, then remembered we were in a library. "She's scummier than the bottom of a pond! She's like—God, I can't even think of anything as disgusting as Sharon! Not only did she get to ruin our date, but she made money doing it! Gah!"

James leaned forward a little. "Okay, breathe," he said. "And did she really ruin it? 'Cause it was sort of fun. At least until your parents showed up."

I took a deep breath and realized he had a point. While Sharon had been sitting around at home and making secret phone calls with Natasha, I was the one on a date. I'd take that over two hundred and fifty dollars any day. "It *was* fun," I admitted. "But I still hate her."

"Cool." He grinned and waited until I smiled back. "So what movies am I bringing over?"

"Any movie. I mean it, I'm open to anything."

"What if it has animated bunnies?"

"*Love* animated bunnies!"

He smirked. "Somehow you don't strike me as the animated-bunny type."

"And what makes you so presumptuous?" I wrapped my arms around his waist and put my chin right against his sternum, craning my head to look up at him. "Hmmm?"

"I think it might be that knife charm on your necklace last night."

Something inside me burned bright when he said that. A hell of a lot of people had seen me last night, but only one person had noticed the tiny details. Only one person had been close enough to see what really mattered. And that person was still standing with me now.

27 "Ten days of perfect tunes, the colors red and blue . . ."

—The Knife, "Heartbeats"

THAT AFTERNOON, after James came over and we motored our way through a bag of red Twizzlers and DVDs of *The Nightmare Before Christmas* and *The Notebook* ("Two thumbs up on the picks," I told him when he held up the movies and waited to see my reaction. "See, no judgment whatsoever!"), we went upstairs to see my collage wall. My mom was downstairs, so we had to leave the door open, but I was perfectly happy to just lie with him on my bed, nothing else. With Evan, we were always talking about *him*. Even when we were cuddling, he would talk nonstop about the band, his songs, who wasn't speaking to whom, and on and on. One time, I even nodded off mid-rant, too tired to care about chord changes or song bridges. There was never any time to be silent.

With James, though, there was no way I was falling asleep. It felt like every nerve ending was buzzing with happiness, and even though I was all warm and content, I burned with adrenaline. Or it might have been sugar from the Twizzlers, but that's not very romantic.

"Your turn," he told me, handing me a penny from my change jar. We had come up with our own game, which involved us throwing pennies at my collage wall. After it bounced off a picture, we listened to a song from that band. So far we had gotten through the new single from Doomsday Scenario; Scenic Panic, a local band who'd gotten a one-page write-up in a U.K. magazine two weeks earlier; and two songs in a row from AFI, since theirs was one of the bigger posters on my wall.

I took the penny from him and launched it straight into Björk's forehead. "And *that's* for wearing a swan dress," I said as I scrolled through her songs before clicking on "All is Full of Love." "Prepare yourself for something mushy and sappy," I told James.

"She wore a swan?"

"To the Oscars. Long story." I curled back up against him and watched as Bendomolena stalked into the room, swished her tail twice, and stalked out again. "See that? She's staking her territory. She's jealous of you."

"She should be. With this bod, this hair . . ." He reached up and tugged on an unruly lock of red hair. "There's a lot to envy."

I grinned and pressed my face into the zipper of his hoodie. "Ouch." I readjusted myself.

"Did you just give yourself grill face?"

"None of your beeswax. And I happen to like your hair."

"What about my bod?"

I lifted my head just long enough to give him a look. "I can't call it your 'bod,'" I told him. "Not without laughing so hard that I pee my pants."

"No King Stud, no 'bod.'" He sighed loudly. "You've left me with nothing. I'm a shell of a man."

"No, you have me," I told him, setting my head back down on his chest.

We were both quiet as his hand tangled in my hair, as I listened to his heart thud in my ear. "I can hear your heartbeat," I said after a minute. "Good news: You're alive."

"Audrey?"

"Hmm?"

"I really like you."

"I know. I like you, too."

"No, I know you know. And I know you like me, too. I just . . ." He paused for a minute and then smoothed my hair that he had just snarled up. "I just want you to know that, okay? I don't want you to be scared that I can't handle this. I mean, you know, whatever *this* is." He waved his hand to indicate the general insanity that had taken over my life.

His heart was beating even louder now, and I closed my eyes and tried to calm my pulse down to match his. "I'm not scared of that," I murmured, and I wasn't. "That doesn't scare me."

"What *does* scare you?"

I thought for a minute, tapping my index finger against my bottom lip. "Sock puppets."

"Excuse me?"

"They're horrifying."

I could hear his breath hitch in his rib cage. "Audrey, they're just socks."

"Yeah, I know. *But they talk.*"

Another pause. "You know sock puppets aren't real, right?"

"No, but think about it." I sat up a little so I could see his face. "How creepy is it that some guy took an old sock . . . *and gave it eyes?* Actually, all puppets in general are scary. And ventriloquist dummies. Oh, God, ventriloquist dummies!" I shivered. "Can I change my answer to ventriloquist dummies?"

James blinked. "You're crazy."

"No, I'm just self-aware."

"So no puppet theater at your next birthday party. Got it."

"No balloon animals, either. They're creepy, too. Especially when they pop."

James rolled his eyes. "You're the most *self-aware* person I've ever met."

We were both trying hard not to smile, but I gave out first and fell into giggles. (It should be noted that I'm not a giggler. My laugh is rather honky. I believe "angry duck" is the way Victoria described it once, just before I tried to disembowel her.)

"You're sure you're ready for whatever happens?" I asked him after I recovered. "Really and truly?"

"Bring it on."

"Yeah," I agreed as I dropped my head back against his chest. "Bring it on."

28 *"This fame thing, I don't get it. . . ."*

—R.E.M., "E-Bow the Letter"

OF COURSE, when you say, "Bring it on," it sounds cool and tough at the time. (It should also be noted here that *Bring It On* is an awesome movie and made me want to be a cheerleader for about five seconds, before I realized that me + cartwheels = death). But people definitely brought it. Good Lord, did they bring it.

The press, of course, had caught on to the fact that the red-headed guy that I'd gone on a date with was the same guy who worked with me, and now pictures of James at work were on almost every website out there, taken by twenty million camera phones. (If you want to know what it's like to be famous, get a thousand people to aim their camera phones at you and start clicking. That's fame in a nutshell.) And Sharon Eggleston, who would probably eat dirt and bugs on live TV just for the chance to be famous, figured this out and decided to start hanging around the Scooper Dooper to be in the photos.

Not that anyone gave a shit about her, though.

Instead, the latest gossip was who was going to be cast in the video. When the Do-Gooders went to film their acoustic set for

AOL (the one that got a gazillion hits when it went online, I'm sure you saw it), they did an interview where they talked about who was being cast in the upcoming video. (Okay, I watched the interview online just like everyone else. I admit it.) "We don't know yet," Evan said. He was drinking tea, which surprised me. Evan hates tea—he says it tastes like piss. "Maybe we'll cast Audrey herself, who knows?"

"Hell to the no," was my response.

But to the press, that sort of open-ended answer gave them all they needed to start speculating on who was going to be in the video. "Starlets Fight for 'Audrey, Wait!'" one magazine screamed. James and I thumbed through the magazine together, reading our favorite parts out loud. By the fourth paragraph, I was in shock. "According to a source, 'All the girls are after this part,'" I read out loud to James while he rooted through the Teddy Grahams box to find a whole teddy. "'The label is tight-lipped, but rumors are spreading that Ashlee, Lindsay, and several other starlets are all in the running. Even Audrey herself has requested to star.'"

"Who's their source?" James giggled. "Sharon Eggleston? Is that their source?"

"Oh my God," I gasped. "They think I'm like *those* girls! They think I run around and crash my car and forget to wear underwear." I sank into the kitchen chair and stared at James. "I'm having a life crisis. Pass me the Teddy Grahams."

He handed over the box. "All that's left are little paws and legs at the bottom of the box," he said. "It's a massacre."

"Are you gonna leave me for Paris if she gets cast in the video?"

"Yes," he said seriously. "I'm glad we can finally talk about it. She's the kind of girl I've waited for all my life."

"Do you think she'll have you?"

"Of course she will." He popped a few more Teddy Graham limbs in his mouth. "I'm dating a celebrity, haven't you heard? I'm right up her alley."

Christmas shopping became completely out of the question. I thought I would try going to some little out-of-the-way shops two cities over and try to blend in with all the shoppers, but a couple of paparazzi ran across the middle of a busy intersection when they saw me going into Winkin' and Blinkin', this cool electronics gadget store. Unfortunately, when they ran across said intersection, it was against the light and they ended up causing a lot of honking and swearing, as well as two fender benders.

While all this was going on, the owner of Winkin' and Blinkin' kept asking me to sign something—"anything!"—that he could put in the window, like I was an actual working celebrity. "No, it's okay, it's okay," I kept saying with this stupid embarrassed grin plastered on my face while I watched the carnage ensue outside. When I finally managed to leave the store, I had to stuff my dad's gift into my purse so no one would take pictures of it and ruin the surprise, but then it fell out just before I got into my car and sure enough, the photographers saw what it was; some stupid entertainment newswire picked up on it and ran the story in some holiday shopping guide; and suddenly everyone in the free world *had* to have this universal remote control, and they *had* to buy it from Winkin' and Blinkin'.

Victoria added the store to her list of Places Where We Could Get Free Things.

In twenty minutes, I had indirectly caused two car accidents and created the most popular Christmas gift for adults. I was like the elf from hell. An anti-elf. But the worst part was that I had to give my dad his gift early, since everyone knew what it was. He kind of broke my heart, too, because he kept trying to act surprised as he unwrapped it, even though we both knew he wasn't.

Then a couple Saturdays before school let out for Christmas break, I was all set to do volunteer gift-wrapping at the mall, as per my responsibilities as Key Club secretary. (Don't be fooled by the impressive title.) It was a long day, but Victoria would always volunteer, too, and Jonah would dress up as Santa and usually everyone would get really caffeinated and hyper and be rolling on the ground with laughter by the time the day was over. But the plans got changed when Mrs. Marchette, the teacher in charge of organizing the volunteer gift-wrapping, came up to me in the office and said, "Audrey, I think this year it might be better if you help coordinate the volunteers." In other words, "Don't show up to gift-wrap, because you'll cause a stampede and the Scotch tape will fly."

"I've been banned from volunteering!" I moaned to James on the phone. He, Victoria, and my parents were the only ones who had my cell number, because someone—and if you're reading this, I *will* find you, oh yes, I will—hacked into my phone and got the number and posted it online, so I had to change it for a third time. Greatness.

"You weren't *banned*," James started to say, but I was in no mood to be consoled.

"Banned from volunteer work! Do you know how bad that is? Like, if you break the law and they sentence you to community service, you're allowed to volunteer! Criminals are better than me."

"Not all of them," he said.

"Don't even try to make me laugh."

"Okay."

But on the volunteer Saturday, James showed up at my door. He and his brother, Pierce, had worked out this system for coming over where James would duck down in the backseat of Pierce's car; then Pierce would drive him over to my place and deposit him as close to the front door as possible. The paparazzi hadn't caught onto it yet, but only because the local Neighborhood Watch had started calling the police every time they saw a photographer on our street. (My parents sent all the neighbors bottles of champagne to say thank you.)

"Hi," James said after my mom let him in. I had heard the bell, but door answering was another thing on my 'No Can Do' list. We had been surprised too many times by fans of mine and Evan's. But now James was standing in the doorway to my room, loaded down with gifts, wrapping paper, scissors, and curling ribbon. My mom was standing behind him, mouthing, "I like him!"

"I need a volunteer," James explained. "I'm a really bad wrapper." He crossed his arms and made the Westside sign, only he did it upside down so it looked like an *M* instead of a *W*. "And rapper, too, come to think of it."

It can take a long time to wrap gifts when you have to kiss your boyfriend every five seconds for being so wonderful.

Don't even get me started on how many concerts I was missing. At first, Victoria and I had started keeping a list, just for fun, but it stopped being funny after I missed Scenic Panic's Third Annual Save-a-Turkey Thanksgiving benefit concert. I loved that show, I loved that band, and I knew that everyone else would be there. James went with Victoria and Jonah, and they all called me and held up their cell phones so I could hear it, but whatever. It wasn't the same. I wanted to dance and save a turkey, too.

Then the L.A. radio station that was now playing "Audrey, Wait!" on heavy rotation announced the lineup for their holiday show, and I was bereft. Doomsday Scenario were playing, amongst many, many other bands that I either hadn't seen live or loved seeing live. I was sort of thinking about going, but then they announced their special guest.

The Do-Gooders.

"You're going," Victoria said. "You and me. We're so going."

"Are you high?" I asked her, then sipped at the hot apple cider she had brought me from Starbucks. "I'm not going to that."

"Too late. I already got tickets."

"You what? They haven't even gone on sale yet."

Victoria grinned. "I happen to know some people who know some people."

"Who do you know?"

"You, doofus!" She punched my shoulder. "I just emailed the promoter and told them that Audrey from 'Audrey, Wait!' wanted to go to the show, and it was done."

"You what?" All of a sudden, I felt sort of dizzy.

"Seriously, Audrey—what do you want? Shoes, hats, bags, Earl jeans? All we have to do is make a phone call." She laughed delightedly. "Isn't it ridiculous? I mean, if you have to deal with Sharon Eggleston and paparazzi and that freaking nutball girl Tizzy, you might as well get some cool stuff, too. You could use a break, y'know?"

I was speechless. Well, not really, but you know what I mean. "Victoria!" I cried. "This is insane!"

She giggled. "I know, right?"

"No, I mean—forget it. I'm not going. Remember what happened last time I went to a concert where people knew who I was? Let me refresh your memory. I ended up starring in the third-most-popular video on YouTube!"

"Look, this time, just don't make out with any musicians and you'll be fine."

I sighed heavily. "Everyone's gonna recognize me, and then they're gonna realize that Evan and I are in the same building, and then they'll take *pictures* and *Photoshop* them and—"

"Don't be so dramatic. Look, it's not for a while, so just breathe, calm down. Ask your dad for some yoga tips or something." She snickered under her breath.

"Evan. Is going. To be there!"

"Relax—you probably won't even see him." She swirled the last of her cider in her cup. "So what are you gonna wear?"

"A paper bag over my head."

"You'll probably start another trend if you do that."

"I'm not going."

"Yes, you are." She patted my knee. "I can be very convincing."

I sighed. I didn't want to fight with my best friend. Especially not now, when I needed her more than ever. So instead I just poked her in the shoulder. "Traitor."

She grinned. "Dude, Doomsday Scenario. They're gonna tear the place up."

"*Big* traitor."

She eyed me carefully. "What can we do to cheer you up, Gloomy Gus?"

"For starters, don't call me Gloomy Gus."

"We could go try on really expensive shoes and make all the salespeople really mad at us?"

"No. That's depressing. I always want the shoes when we're done."

"Yeah, I know." She sipped again. "We could go to the MAC store and look at all the hot guys wearing eyeliner and ask them for application tips."

"Um, perhaps you haven't met my boyfriend yet."

"Oh, like I'm single? Just think of it as artistic appreciation. They'd probably even give you all of the limited edition holiday makeup for free, just 'cause you're Audrey."

I sighed. "I think I might change my name."

"New Year's resolution?"

"Survival instinct." I sipped at the apple cider and got a mouthful of warm whipped cream. "Thanks for the cider, Victoria."

She was about to reply, but the doorbell rang, followed by a loud, off-key chorus of "Jingle Bells" coming from outside. "Oh, for the love of Baby Jesus!" I heard my dad shout. Victoria craned her neck to look out of my room toward the front door. "What's going on?"

"Carolers," I told her. "You can't swing a dead cat without hitting one of them. They've been arriving by the truckload."

"Did this happen to you guys last year?"

"Nope." I rolled my eyes. "Shocking, I know."

Victoria just shook her head and opened her mouth to comment when the caroling suddenly went awry. "You said your piece and now I've got to say mine! I had you and you strung me on the *liiiiiinnnnneeeeee!*"

We looked at each other.

"Are they singing in harmony?" Victoria finally asked. "It doesn't sound half-bad."

"Just make them go away," I moaned.

Victoria patted my knee. "Think of it this way. They're serenading you."

"Bah humbug."

She grinned. "That's the spirit!"

29 "Then we'll turn it up and we'll play a little faster!"

—The Academy Is . . ., "Slow Down"

VICTORIA AND I had the same conversation for the rest of the week leading up to the concert. It went something like this:

"What time should we leave for the concert?"

"I'm not going."

"Traffic probably won't be too bad, since it's on a Saturday. Wanna say five o'clock?"

"I'm not going."

"You're right, four is better."

"I'm not going."

"Four it is!"

Do you see what I have to put up with?

The day of the show, Victoria was honking outside at three fifty-five. This struck me as odd for two reasons.

1. Victoria is usually late.

2. She doesn't have a car.

So I immediately went outside to see who was honking and I found my best friend sitting in a brand-new convertible BMW. She was wearing heart-shaped sunglasses that matched the car's cherry-red exterior and a look that said, *I am so obviously cooler than you.*

"What did you do?" I cried.

She looked at my lazy-day jeans and ratted hoodie. "You're wearing that?"

"Let's focus on the car right now," I said. "Where did you get this? Did your mom win the lottery?!"

She grinned. "Remember that reality show?"

I immediately began looking for cameramen hiding in the trees. "If they're filming right now, Victoria, I swear to God—"

"Relax, Captain Paranoid. No one's filming. But I told them you were still thinking about whether or not to do the show and they thought you needed a little persuading." She patted the car's cream interior. "Nice persuasion, huh? We're supposed to be using it to 'scout locations,' but whatever."

"They sent a BMW?!"

"I'm telling you, Audrey, you would not *believe* the shit they send celebrities."

"This is blackmail."

"No, it's America. Let freedom ring. Now go get changed or we're gonna miss the first bands."

"I'm not going, I already told you."

Victoria held up her MP3 player. "Would you like to hear the sound system in the car?"

I bit my lip. "Yes, but no."

She immediately cued up a song and I heard some of my favorite guitar notes ever. "*Your lipstick, his collar, don't bother, angel! I know exactly what goes on!*" Victoria knew that I loved Taking Back Sunday and that I had listened to "Cute Without the 'E' (Cut from the Team)" on repeat for three days straight last summer.

"That's not fair," I said. "You're using one of my favorite songs against me. You're cheating."

Victoria just smiled and turned the radio up.

"When everything you'll get is everything you wanted, Princess!"

Oh my God, the stereo system in that car was sent from the heavens. I could feel my resolve weakening with every note.

"Five minutes," Victoria said. "Go put on something decent. No paper bags allowed."

My parents were out for the evening, so there was no need for a debate with them. It only took me four minutes to change into decent jeans, a white tank top, and a dark green cardigan that was so worn at the wrists that I could poke my thumbs through the holes. "Very Kurt Cobain on *Unplugged*," Victoria said as I climbed into the car. "I like it."

"Less talk, more music," I replied. "I can't believe I'm doing this."

"Less talk, more music," she repeated back to me. "Turn it up."

30

"The center of the earth is the end of the world. . . ."

—Green Day, "Jesus of Suburbia"

I WAS SO SEDUCED by the car that I had temporary memory loss and forgot that we were heading toward a concert where I knew I'd be spotted. But then Victoria followed the signs off the 101 toward the arena and artist parking and when we got out of the car, my knees were literally shaking. "Victoria?" I said, but she was too busy trying to figure out where will-call was, and so I just followed her because I didn't want to be by myself.

I wasn't by myself, though—I was surrounded by a bunch of people who all kept stealing glances at me. Victoria got our backstage passes and I hung mine around my neck and tugged on it nervously. "C'mon," she said, pulling at my arm. "Let's go see if they've got food."

"If I eat, I'm going to throw up," I told her.

"Stop being so dramatic," she replied. "You've already been backstage before. You're a seasoned professional."

Backstage felt really hot and crowded and small, even thought it was huge. There were probably a billion people back there and I kept seeing people I recognized, people whose pictures were col-laged onto my bedroom wall. Victoria was trying to play it cool, I could tell, but every so often, she would turn to me and grin. "Isn't this fucking amazing?" she whispered at one point.

"Do you think Evan's here yet?"

"Dunno. This is so much better than the Lolitas' backstage."

My stomach flipped. Granted, at that concert, I'd sort of sealed my notoriety, but at least we had danced and Jonah had been there and it had all been new and exciting. Here, everyone was jaded. No one seemed to be having a good time and I wondered how many people were there for the show and how many people were there to just be seen.

And I wondered which category I was in.

"I'm gonna go get a Diet Coke," Victoria said, and before I could quietly beg her not to leave, she had disappeared down the hall. I took a deep breath and leaned against the cool cinder-block wall, trying to look invisible.

"Hey, you're that girl!"

I glanced up, praying that whoever it was was talking about some other girl, and I saw the guitarist from Doomsday Scenario looking right at me and grinning.

I was so going to throw up that it wasn't even funny.

"You're Audrey!"

"No, I—" I started to say, but then he was standing next to me and honest to God, I think I was a foot taller than him. And I'm not that tall. "Hi," I squeaked. "I like your band."

"Awesome song," he was saying. "So fucking awesome." He was looking up at me and I felt like some huge awkward giant. "Did you write it?"

"Um, no, no, I just—"

"Fucked the singer. Yeah, welcome to the business." He

grinned. "So. Got any hot friends? We're writing our second album in Burbank and right now it's just a bunch of bros in the studio. We need *inspiration*."

I realized that he and I had different definitions for "inspiration."

"Excuse me," I said, then backed away from him and stumbled down the hall. I heard someone else say my name and I ignored them before realizing it was Victoria. "Hey," she said excitedly. "Were you talking to the guy from Doomsday Scenario?!"

"Sort of," I replied. "He's gross."

"Really?" She glanced at him over my shoulder. "Is he a dirty old man?"

"Yep." I could feel my stomach flipping again. "Victoria, I mean, I know that this is supposed to be fun, but—"

"You're not having fun," she sighed.

I shook my head. "Everyone's looking at me and I don't want to see Evan or the Do-Gooders and I just want to leave."

She looked at me for a long minute. "You really want to go?"

"More than anything in the entire world."

Victoria sighed and toyed with the backstage pass around her neck. I felt like the worst friend in the world, but I couldn't feel like this anymore. If it kept up, I'd be so mentally scarred that I'd never be able to go to another concert again. "I'll make it up to you, I swear," I told her. "But it's . . . it's not fun like it was last time."

She glanced around and saw that, in fact, the whole hallway population was watching us talking out of the corner of their eye. "Okay," she sighed. "Let's go."

We didn't talk the whole car ride home.

The stereo was so loud, we probably couldn't have heard each other, anyway.

31 *"Oh, I think I smell a rat!"*
—The White Stripes, "I Think I Smell a Rat"

ONE OF THE FEW BENEFITS of spending all my time in the school office was that I didn't have to deal with Sharon Eggleston every minute of every class. In fact, I hadn't seen much of her, which made me nervous. It's important to always have your enemy in your sight. Who knows what could be going on behind your back?

I found out the last day of school before Christmas break.

I was walking across the campus after lunch, coming back from the Spanish department, where I had to hand in my final exam. Since I couldn't sit in the regular class, all of my teachers had given my finals to the office, and Connie the secretary (I should really try to learn her last name) watched over me as I took them. And for once in my life, they weren't bad. I had had nothing to do but study in school and study at home, so the ironic thing is that my GPA was the highest it's ever been. My parents were positively gleeful. "Your social alienation is the best thing that's ever happened to you!" my mom crowed.

It's nice to know whose side they're on.

I had hoped that maybe I would be let out of the office long enough to go to one of the sugar-spun holiday parties that all of my classes would be having. I had heard that they were watching *How the Grinch Stole Christmas* in geometry. I used to make my parents call me Cindy Lou Who when I was a little kid because I loved that cartoon so much, so I really wanted to watch with everyone else.

No way, José.

Instead, I was stuck playing solitaire on Connie's computer and reading the copies of *Vogue* that she stowed in her bottom desk drawer. Totally fucking depressing.

But it got worse after lunch.

Like I said, I'd just handed in my surprisingly easy Spanish final essay and was heading back toward the office when I saw her and him.

By her, I mean Sharon Eggleston.

And by him, I mean James.

They were standing by his locker and she was way too close to him, almost like she was his jacket. *That's* how close she was. She was saying something and laughing, and James was doing that nervous smile that he used to do with me before we knew that we liked each other.

Uh-uh. No way. Not on my watch.

I marched over so fast that I was breathless by the time I got there. James saw me coming and he started to frantically wave with a huge smile on his face. "Audrey," I could see him telling Sharon, and she threw a look over her shoulder at me before standing away from my boyfriend.

"HI!" James said as he stepped away from Sharon and started

to wrap an arm around my shoulder. But as he stepped away from her, I stepped away from him.

"What the hell?" I said. "What the hell? What the hell? What the hell?"

Sharon calmly straightened her sweater. "Aud, relax. Jealousy is so unattractive."

"So is boyfriend stealing!"

"*Boyfriend* stealing?" James repeated. His eyes grew wide. "Audrey, no. Nuh-uh. No way in *hell*."

I got as close to Sharon as I dared without catching whatever creepy sexually transmitted disease she probably had. "You? Don't talk to him. Ever again. You're a fucking leech!"

"Audrey—" James was pulling at my shoulder, but I kept shrugging him off, too irate.

"You didn't get Evan," I yelled at her, "and you sure as hell aren't gonna get James, either! Just stay away! Get your own damn love life!"

Sharon just smiled serenely at me, like she was the fucking Mona Lisa. "Audrey," she said in the same voice that people use when they talk to little kids, "why so defensive? Hmmm?"

"I'm not defensive!" I yelled, which of course sounded *completely* defensive. What can I say? I was furious and tired and had eaten way too many candy canes that day to be rational. "You're delusional! He's my boyfriend, not yours!"

"Then how come you never go out with him?" She smiled a thin, terrible smile. "If you love him so much, how come no one knows it?"

I would've kept on threatening her life and such, but James wrapped an arm around my waist and began carrying me away from the scene. "Put me down!" I struggled, but he waited until we were around the corner and far away from Sharon before setting me back on my feet.

"What are you *doing?*" I huffed as I shoved my hair out of my eyes. "What the fuck was that?"

"I could ask you the same question!" he snapped back. It was the first time he had ever been snappy with me, and the two of us stood staring at each other, both panting and flushed.

"You were talking to Sharon Eggleston!" I finally told him.

"So you're automatically just gonna jump to the conclusion that I'm cheating on you? With *Sharon fucking Eggleston?!*"

I paused. "No, it's just . . . she's . . . she's a really bad person, okay? She tried to steal Evan a long time ago, back when we first started dating."

"Well, I'm not him." James's jaw was flexing and tightening and I could see the hurt in his eyes. "In case you haven't picked up on the thirty thousand differences between me and Evan, let me give you one more: I'm not gonna date Sharon Eggleston."

"So why was she all pressed up against you, then? And why were you doing that nervous smile?" I wasn't done being mad about that part.

"Because she made me nervous!" he cried. "And I was at my locker and I turned around and she was right there! I didn't know what to do! She's a girl—I can't just threaten to bitch-slap her like *you* can, you know!"

It's hard to have an eye-to-eye argument with someone who's nearly a foot taller than you. "I didn't threaten to bitch-slap her!" I told him. "You stopped me before I could!"

"Yeah, feel free to thank me anytime for that, by the way! Jesus, you girls and your fucking *drama!*" James tightened the strap on his bag and pulled it across his chest, then ran a hand through his tangled hair. It was always tangled. I loved that about him. Sharon Eggleston would only make him comb his hair. That's the kind of girl she was.

"Look," he said. "I have to go. I'm already late for calc. Can we just figure this out later?"

I nodded. "Yeah. Go. Fine."

"I'll call you."

"Fine."

"Yeah, fine."

I watched him walk away down the hall, his messenger bag slapping against his legs with each step. I could still smell Sharon Eggleston's perfume in the air, even though I was all alone.

Back at the office, I went right up to the front desk and pawed through the basket of Christmas candy, pulling out three more candy canes before going back to Connie's desk to sit and stew. I wondered if James was right, if Sharon was running around outside trying to get news of the fight into the next issue of whatever magazine would pay her the most money. I already knew James was right about one thing: I had played into her drama plan, hook line and sinker.

The office Christmas tree was next to Connie's desk and I stared at it for the rest of the afternoon, my eyes misting over several times. I felt like one of the ornaments, transparent and fragile, dangling on the edge, with only a thin silver wire to keep me from shattering all over the ground.

32 *"There are angels in your angles. . . ."*
—The Decemberists, "Of Angels and Angles"

I CALLED JAMES when I got home. "Can you come over?" I said after he picked up. I considered it a good sign that he still answered after seeing my caller ID. "Please?"

"I think Pierce is working." James's voice wasn't quite flat, but it wasn't the voice of someone super eager to hear from me, either.

"Well, what time does he get home?"

"I think five? I'll text him and call you back."

Pierce, it turned out, got off at four thirty, and James was at my house by five. I would've gone to his house in a heartbeat, but I was too paranoid that the paparazzi would show up and infest his cul-de-sac.

The pictures of him and me after our first date had made it into last week's *People*, accompanied by a blurb that read, "Who's arm in arm with rock's favorite siren? Audrey Cuttler leaves RPM Records with her unidentified new date, rumored to be a musician." Which was a total lie, of course. James and I both had our heads down in the photo and he was way behind me. "You can see my shoe!" my mom said when she saw the photo, and sure enough, her dirty white sneaker was in the corner. James's mom had apparently sent a copy to his grandparents in Oregon. "She used to send copies of report cards and, like, Little League photos," James had sighed when he found out.

But all of that was out of my head now. All I wanted to do was apologize to him and make it right, make it like it was before.

So of course I answered the door wearing a ring made of aluminum foil around my head.

"What is that?" James said after he had rushed inside and Pierce squealed out of our driveway. He tapped at my makeshift arts-and-crafts project with one finger. "Are you trying to attract aliens?"

"No, they've probably already heard of me. But this," I added as I gestured to my head, "is my halo."

"Your what?"

"My halo. You might have noticed that it was missing earlier today. But good news! I found it! And it was sitting next to a big apology for you."

I could tell he was trying not to laugh, which was exactly what I wanted him to do. "A big apology?" he asked. "Or a huge one?"

"Gigantic. Elephantine."

"Elephan—what?"

"PSAT word. But don't interrupt me!" I sidled up to him and wrapped my arms around his waist, pressing my face against the cold denim of his jacket. "I'm sorry," I told him. "I was crazy. I was DramaGirl."

After a second, his arms went around me. "Yeah, you were pretty aggro."

"Well, I hate Sharon Eggleston, but I also ate seven candy

canes today," I told him by way of explanation.

"Did you save any for me?"

I reached into my pocket and pulled out a mini candy cane, one that I had in fact been saving just for him. "Here," I said, and tucked it into the top of his hoodie so that it peeked out over the zipper. He promptly pulled it out, ripped the wrapper off, and popped it into his mouth. "There would have been more," I told him, "but I got hungry."

"S'okay. This one's fine."

We stood together for a minute, breathing so our chests went up and down at the same time. "Audrey," he finally said, "don't let Sharon create all this, okay? Just . . . don't play into it. Please."

"I know. Did I mention I'm sorry?"

"Yeah, you did. And I am, too. I shouldn't have carried you down the hall like that."

"No, you probably should have. I was about to rip Sharon's eyeballs out. And it was very King Stud of you."

"Really?" I could tell that he was smiling. "Can I tell Pierce you said that?"

"No, because then he'll tell someone and then they'll tell someone and it'll be online and in the gossip columns by Christmas Eve."

"Okay. And I swear that I'm not in any way attracted to Sharon Eggleston. At all. Ever. She's too . . . just too. Too *too.* And she probably doesn't collect concert ticket stubs."

"Or wristbands from waiting in line to get on the floor at shows," I agreed. "And she probably has all of Creed's CDs."

I could hear the rumble of James's laugh against my ear, and I tightened my arms around his waist. "I'm sorry," I told him again.

He patted my halo, then lifted it off my head and placed it on his own. "What do you think? Too much? Does it clash with my outfit?"

"I think it goes perfectly with dirty jeans."

He grinned and bent down to kiss me, a perfect peppermint moment. "I love you with or without your halo, Audrey."

Waitaminute.

He loves me? He *loves* me? He? Loves *me*?

HE LOVES ME! JAMES SAID HE LOVES ME!

This needed confirmation.

"Uh, not to make this awkward or very, very embarrassing, but did you just say you loved me?" I twisted my hands in the bottom of his sweater, our lips about two inches apart.

"Well, yeah, I mean . . . yeah, I do. I always kinda *did*."

"I love you, too," I told him, and I felt like I was going a million miles an hour and standing still all at the same time. "I do. You're amazing. I'm so glad I started working at the Scooper Dooper, because it was so worth it."

"Even after we had that power outage last summer?"

"Even then." I stood on my tiptoes to kiss him again. "Can we not ever fight again?"

"Done." He barely interrupted the kiss long enough to talk, and that's how Bendomolena found us, standing in the darkened entryway, a shared tinfoil halo looping our hearts together.

33

"Sometimes I think that I'm bigger than the sound. . . ."

—Yeah Yeah Yeahs, "Cheated Hearts"

AFTER CHRISTMAS, my parents finally killed my job at the Scooper Dooper. If someone had told me three months ago that I'd be upset to leave the Scooper Dooper, I would've told them to check their head. But now that meant extra hours away from James (and that back freezer).

"You see James all the time," my mom pointed out when I protested. "You've got the SATs coming up."

"They're five months away!"

"You need to focus more on your schoolwork."

"Mom, my grades are awesome. And sad as it is to believe, work is like the only time I can get out of the house! What am I gonna do for money?"

"Your father and I will give you an allowance." She was busy in her office, paying bills or some other scary adult thing, and not looking at me. If my mom doesn't look at me while I'm trying to negotiate, forget it. There's no way I'm winning.

But there was always my dad.

"And don't ask Dad, either," she added. My mother, the mind

reader. "We both agree that this is the right thing. You've got people lining up halfway down the mall to take pictures of you through the glass door, Aud. They had to bring in extra security. That's not safe."

"Mom, have you watched the news lately? High school isn't all that safe, either."

"This is not a discussion."

The day after that disaster, "Audrey, Wait!" hit number one on the Billboard Hot 100.

"Ho. Ly. Crap." Victoria got the notice as we were walking to history (for her) and geometry (for me). She scrolled furiously through the messages on her phone with a weird half-smile on her face. "Aud. *Aud.*" She tugged on my arm. "The song is number one."

"Gee, great. Wait a minute, let me put on my excited face."

"Oh my God, this is incredible. This is huge. Do you realize how *huge* this is?"

I glanced at her as we turned the corner, where the pep squad was frantically changing the "Audrey, Wait!" countdown banner. 'AUDREY, WAIT!' IS AT #1! it read now.

"Are you kidding?" I asked no one in particular. "You're kidding me, right."

Victoria didn't even bother to respond. "The Lolitas haven't even cracked the Top Five," she reported. "Take that, Simon."

"Oh, God. Please, let's not bring him up, okay?"

"I'm just saying. . . ."

But I tuned her out. Her enthusiasm was so annoying that I wanted to smother her with a couch cushion. (Okay, not really like that, but you know what I mean, right?) Whose side was she on?

It was like all of this was so *great* and she was so *happy* and it made me want to gag. Excited Victoria and Hermit Audrey were not exactly peanut butter and jelly. It was going to get ugly, and even though I could see the fight coming, there was no way I could stop it.

The ugly came a week later.

34

"So here we are at the last broadcast. . . ."

—The Doves, "The Last Broadcast"

I WILL RIGHT NOW SAY that half of the fight between Victoria and me was my fault. I was woefully undercaffeinated (and then way overcaffeinated, as you'll see), irritated by how much homework I had, and exhausted after staying up all night texting with James and then having Bendomolena sleep on my head. I was irrational and cranky and just *meh*.

That being said, Victoria totally started it.

It was the day that the video for "Audrey, Wait!" was about to premiere and Victoria was coming home with me to watch it. "I don't even wanna see it," I told her as we walked to my car in the parking lot after school.

"Oh, whatever," she scoffed. "You're gonna see it eventually. You might as well see it with me."

"It already leaked online," I told her. "Can't you just watch it there?"

"No, 'cause my monitor sucks and your family has high-definition TV."

"The better to see my traitorous ex-boyfriend."

"You sound like a bitter old woman."

I bit my tongue at that point. I was tired of hearing how I was being unreasonable, especially from someone who could still go wherever she wanted with *her* boyfriend. "James is gonna come over later to study," I told her.

"Study. Ha. Is that what you're calling it now?"

"Yes, because we actually are *studying*. I'm tutoring him in English and he's tutoring me in geometry." I started the car with more oomph than it needed. "It's practically the only thing we're allowed to do together."

"Well, you know," Victoria said in her very-innocent-but-not-so-much way, "*Teen Vogue* wanted to do a photo shoot with you and James on a date, but you turned them down."

The white noise in my head got a little louder. "That's not exactly the sort of date I want with him. You're missing the whole privacy thing."

She *pfft*'d the idea away. "Privacy is overrated."

I glanced out my window and saw three girls looking at me from two cars over. "That's easy to say, " I told Victoria, "when you still have a private life."

At my house, I popped open a Diet Coke while Victoria dove for the remote control. "Want anything?" I asked her.

"No!" she called back. "Hurry up, it's coming on! Are you TiVoing this?"

I grabbed another Diet Coke, sensing that I would need more energy before the afternoon was over, and fell onto our couch with what I hoped was the right amount of nonchalance.

Because as much as I wouldn't admit this to Victoria, I did kind of want to see the video. As mad as I was at Evan, as mad as

I was at all of the Do-Gooders just for existing, I *knew* them. I knew how hard they had worked. I had sat through band practices, equipment load-ins, horrible shows that once left Evan teary-eyed with frustration. I had watched them upload songs to the band's MySpace page (the one no one ever friended), watched them painstakingly address, stamp, and mail CDs to every single A&R guy in North America. None of their success was unearned, but Evan didn't have to use our breakup to get it.

In typical MTV tease fashion, the video premiered at nearly the end of the hour. "Oh, come *oooonnn!*" Victoria screamed at one point as another block of commercials started. "Babies are being born! I'm getting older! Play the damn thing already!"

I sipped from the second Diet Coke. The caffeine was starting to hit me with its familiar zippy feeling, and I could feel all my nerve endings dancing around. Perhaps two Diet Cokes in less than an hour had been a bad idea. "You know," I told her, "maybe the video will suck so bad that it'll never get played again and the Do-Gooders will crash into obscurity."

She threw me a glance over her shoulder. "If memory serves, you thought no one would ever hear The Song again, either."

I considered lobbing my Diet Coke at her head, but I didn't want to waste it. I'd probably need the rest of that caffeine by the time the video was over.

By the time it started, Victoria was like a nervous puppy, wriggling everywhere and setting me on edge. "Here it comes!" she said, slapping at my knee.

"Ow."

"Aren't you excited?"

"Ow. Thrilled."

The VJ introduced the video while dozens of girls screamed in the background, and then it started. The scene opened on what looked like a mirror image of Evan's bedroom, with a girl coming up the stairs toward it. It was Caitlin McGregor, the girl who was in that movie last summer and then got busted for pot and sent to rehab. She had long blond hair and a black bag that looked just like *my* black bag slung over her shoulder.

And she was wearing arm huggies.

"You are fucking kidding me," I said. Victoria had stopped jumping around and was trying to figure out why I looked so murderous.

"You said your piece and now I've got to say mine! I had you and you strung me on the *liiiiiinnnnneeeeee!*"

The scene cut to Evan and the band playing in a backyard, where they looked really styled. The camera zoomed in on Evan, his face all scrunched up in make-believe agony as he screamed-sang the words. "We said we loved and it was a lie! I touched your hair and watched you die! You crucified my heart, took every part and hung them out to *drrrrryyyyyyy!*"

And then they cut back to Caitlin, going into Evan's room while Evan sat at his desk. I knew this scene, I knew exactly what would happen, and I knew this because I had already lived through it.

Not only had Evan written a song about our breakup, but he'd made a video about it, too.

"This! Is! Our! Break! Up!" I yelled at Victoria. "Look at this! This is exactly what happened! And Caitlin fucking McGregor is playing me!"

"What's wrong with Caitlin?"

"She went to rehab!"

"People are human, Audrey."

"She went *three times*! Is that what people think of me?"

I glared at Victoria, then back at the TV. Caitlin and Evan were having this faux-dramatic conversation, in which Evan kept making puppy dog eyes. "This is the lamest video ever," I announced.

"It's kind of a cool angle," she said as the camera followed behind "Audrey's" head and toward Evan. He looked sweet and loving, the obvious Good Boyfriend to my Evil Girlfriend doppelganger. (PSAT word.)

"Look at this!" I gasped, pointing at our TV. "Look! This is exactly how it happened!"

"Caitlin doesn't even look like you, Aud. Relax."

"She's wearing arm huggies! This is slander! Or . . . something equally bad and illegal!"

Victoria glanced at the video, where the girl was sitting on Evan's bed, looking aloof and bored, like she would break up with him every day. "Hey, wait a minute," I told Victoria. "I didn't look that bitchy!"

"Don't you own that shirt?" she replied.

I squinted at the television. "Audrey" was wearing a white T-shirt that had the shoulder seams held together with safety pins. "That's the shirt I was wearing when I broke up with him!" I gasped. "Oh my God! That's the exact same shirt! I made that shirt myself! Are you *serious*, Evan? You couldn't even remember our anniversary, but you remembered the shirt I wore when we broke up?"

"It's a memorable shirt," Victoria pointed out.

We watched the video in shocked silence. Well, *I* was shocked into silence. Victoria was too busy noticing camera angles or whatever held her attention while I was defamed in front of a national audience.

Again.

The video started to wind down as "Audrey" walked down the stairs while Evan stood in the doorway, lip-synching the words and trying his best to look wounded. And when Fake Audrey walked out the front door, there was a redheaded boy waiting for her in a car at the curb. He looked at Audrey conspiratorially, kissed her, and the two of them zoomed off.

I literally did not breathe for thirty seconds, I was so mad.

By the time it was over, I was pacing the living room, ready to throw the remote control through the window. "Are they touring right now?" I screeched at Victoria. "Because if they are, I'm flying to whatever nightmare tourist-trap town he's currently in and I'm going to beat the crap out of him. And not just Evan. That asshole director, too. And MTV."

Victoria sat on the couch and watched as I flew around the room in a fit. "Aud—"

"You know what! I've had it! This is it! My dad has a lawyer and I'm gonna sue Evan! I'm suing the record label, I'm suing the band, I'm even gonna sue that stupid pothead manager of theirs!"

"Don't you think you're overreacting?"

"Are you kidding?" I yelled. "I'm at Defcon 5 here! It's not over-reacting until someone loses an eye!" That caffeine was certainly effective.

"Aud, seriously, you need to calm the fuck down."

"Okay, first of all," I told her, "telling someone to calm down is the absolute worst way to get them to calm down. And second, are you kidding? Calm *down*?! After going through hell for the past three months? Calm down after being stalked by photographers? Calm down after my new boyfriend sees this video? What a great idea. Calm down. Why don't I just take a little nap? That'll solve everything. Or better yet, you know what? Fuck it, I'm going to Disneyland."

Victoria's eyes were starting to spark. They often did that, but rarely at me. "When are you gonna realize that you're not an average girl anymore?" she said. "Is that gonna kick in anytime soon, or are you just gonna keep your head in the sand?"

I was amazed. I mean, Victoria could do and say some amazing things, but that one really took the cake. "I *am* an average girl!" I started to yell back, but she cut me off by pointing at the television, where my likeness was busy ripping out Evan's heart.

"No, you're not!" Victoria shouted back. We were standing six inches apart now, and even though I'm taller than her, it felt like she was bigger. "Look at this!" she yelled. "Look at you! This is not average, this is not normal! Jesus, Audrey, you're awesome! Half of the free world loves you! And you're blowing it!"

"Excuse me!" I yelled back. Across the room, Bendomolena was hiding underneath an armchair. I could see her tail swell up, the way it always did whenever she got scared. "Whose side are you on, anyway?! Mine or theirs?"

"What are you talking about?!"

"You know what I'm talking about! 'Audrey, call RPM Records so we can go shopping! Audrey, do a reality show so I can get a bunch of free stuff! Hey, Audrey, wanna go backstage? All you have to do is tell them who you are!' It's all you talk about anymore—it's all you seem interested in!"

"You're mad because I like having fun?!" she screamed back. Victoria's not really a screamer, but when she goes for it, she can make the heavens quake. "I'm trying to help you get through this because I'm a good fucking friend, but no! You just want to sulk and stay home and feel sorry for yourself!"

"Then what about that stupid car?" I yelled. "How was that helping *me*, exactly? It's like you're my friend only because of the free stuff!"

Oh my God, if Victoria could have, I think she would've punched a hole in our living room wall. "They sent that car because they wanted to," she fumed. "Jesus, Audrey, when did you forget how to fucking enjoy yourself? Six months ago, you would've been all over that! We would have been going to concerts every single night! So sue me if I'm not sitting around in a dark hole somewhere, sulking about how much my life sucks because I'm famous! Just because you're not having fun, Audrey, doesn't mean the rest of us can't!"

"Every time I go outside, someone takes a picture! They hide in the bushes! Last week I had to go buy moisturizer and this week I read about it in three different magazines!"

"Who fucking cares?"

"*I* care, Victoria! Or does that not matter anymore? Does my opinion not even count?"

"Oh, no, it definitely counts. In fact, that's all that counts!"

"What the fuck does that mean?"

"News flash, Aud! You're all you talk about anymore, and even then, all you do is complain! You're a fucking whiner!"

"I'm not a whiner, I just—"

Victoria was reaching for her bag and yanking on the pink-and-red-striped ballet slippers that I loaned her ten dollars for two years ago. "You are so fucking ungrateful," she swore as she worked. "I swear to God, you get opportunities thrown at you just for breaking up with your boyfriend, and all you do is complain and whine and mope. Well, excuse me for trying to make sure that the world knows how awesome my best friend is! Excuse me for wanting people to get to know you so they won't say shitty things about you anymore! Maybe what everyone's saying at school is true! Maybe you really are just becoming stuck-up!"

"They are not saying that," I said. Tears were in my eyes and blurring my vision so bad that it looked like two furious Victorias were in front of me.

"They are," she shot back. "But you know what I think is so fucking funny? You're turning into the guy you broke up with! It's all about you, all the time, and you don't care about anything else."

I felt like she had slapped me. No one's ever slapped me before, but it couldn't hurt as much as what she had just said.

"You don't talk to anyone!" Victoria continued as she slung her bag over her shoulder. "You never ask me how I'm doing, or how Jonah is! Every time we're together, you don't want to do anything! All you do is hang out with James and you probably spend most of your time with him complaining, too!"

"Just get out!" I told her. "Go home! Call Jonah to come and get you!"

"I'm fucking walking," she spat. Her eyes were shiny and wet, too. "And I really liked that video!"

I stormed over and yanked open the front door, refusing to look at her as she walked out. As soon as she was gone, I slammed it shut and stalked upstairs to my room, where I slammed my bedroom door two times in a row just because it felt good. Then I went to my computer, ready to put together the angriest mix CD I've ever made in my life, something with lots of screaming and rage. But just then the cordless phone rang and I snatched it up and answered it without even glancing at the caller ID. It was Victoria, I knew it. She and I had never fought like this before and there was no way it could last more than five minutes. She'd apologize and then we'd do all of our girly crying and hug and it would be okay.

It had to be okay.

"Victoria?" I answered. My voice was shaking as bad as my hands.

"Um, Audrey?"

I frowned. So not Victoria. "Yeah?"

"Aud, it's me."

It took three seconds for me to place the voice, but when I did, it was like I had never stopped hearing it.

"Oh," I said. "Evan. Hi."

35

"'I'm sorry' won't cut it for the rest of your life. . . ."

—Valencia, "Away We Go"

I HAD FANTASIZED for months about what I would say to Evan if we got a chance to talk again. I had planned the perfect sentence, the perfect words, the perfect half-annoyed, half-bored voice to say that sentence in.

So of course, he finally calls and what happens?

I sneeze.

Loudly.

"Bless you," he said.

"Thanks," I replied. "So what the *fuck* were you thinking?"

"Okay," he sighed. "Look, I'm not calling to fight with you, Aud, all right?"

"Fine, we don't have to fight. We never *did* fight, in case you forgot. I just want you to answer that question. What were you thinking?"

"I was mad, okay? I was mad at you that night. I didn't think that all of this was gonna happen because of that one song!"

"Do you even know what's happened to me?" I demanded. "Do you even know what's been going on?"

"Um, people tell me things. I don't know, we've been on tour in Japan and—"

"Well, I've been on tour in hell! I have to spend all day at school in the office because otherwise too many people ask me for autographs. Bendomolena's a nervous wreck because so many carolers, aka fans in disguise, rang the doorbell during Christmas. I think every third person on the Internet has called me a slut or hacked into my phone—"

"Yeah, I tried to email you but it just bounced—"

"I've got the paparazzi all up in my face every time I step outside! And that *video*! I just saw it! Victoria and I just got into a huge fight because of that stupid—"

"You and Victoria had a fight?"

I was momentarily derailed. "Yeah," I admitted.

"Wow. You guys never fight."

"Yeah, well, things are different right now." I picked at the split ends in my hair. "She wants me to do more interviews and I don't want to." I sighed heavily and let my hair fall back down. "God, Evan, why'd you do this?"

"Aud, I'm sorry, okay? I am. I'm really sorry. I didn't know that it would get so crazy. But my life's insane, too, you know. I haven't been home since September."

"Liar. You just played the holiday concert."

"No, I mean, like *home* home. I saw my mom for like ten minutes that night."

"Oh, please. Like Justin said to Britney, cry me a river."

"Aud? Do you really think you're the only one whose life got turned all fuckin' upside down?"

Well. That comment shut me up for a minute, long enough

for Evan to keep talking. "I mean, it's been so awesome, everything that's happened, and I'm grateful and all, but sometimes . . . I'm just tired. It's not the same. It's different."

"Different like how?" Try as I might, I couldn't help but feel a teensy bit sympathetic, if only because he sounded so tired.

"I don't know. Just . . . different."

Good Lord. Sentences like that one were Reason Number Twenty-four that we broke up in the first place. "Good insight, Evan. It's all clear now."

He laughed, that weird little giggle of his. "I miss you calling me on my shit, you know that?"

"I miss calling you on your shit, too."

"Yeah," he sighed. Then there was a pause before he asked, "Are you really dating that guy from the Scooper Dooper? Or is that just a rumor?"

"Oh, do you mean that guy that you totally just humiliated in your video? That guy? James?"

"Yeah, James. You're really dating him? 'Cause I saw this picture in *People* on the plane back from Osaka and—"

"*Everyone* saw that picture. And yes. We're dating."

"Do you love him?"

"Evan," I said carefully, "with all due respect, that's none of your business."

"Right. Okay. Sorry." His voice was heavy and I wondered how bad I should feel for him.

There was silence between us for a minute and I rubbed my forehead, suddenly exhausted. It wasn't even four thirty yet. "God, Ev," I sighed. "It's been almost eight months. It's been over four since the song came out. Why are you calling *now*? What do you want?"

"I want you to come to New York."

I don't know what answer I was expecting, but it certainly wasn't that. "Excuse me?"

"I want you to come to New York. We're doing a live set at MTV and I want you to be there."

"No way. Absolutely not. You are out of your mi—"

"It's in front of an audience, two hundred people, in-studio, live on-camera interviews, three songs performed by the band." He was reading the information off a piece of paper, I could tell. "They want to interview you, too."

"No."

"They'll fly you out, Audrey. Cars to and from the hotel. Security if you need it. But they really, really want you to come."

"Why?" I was beyond skeptical.

"Well, I mean . . . if we make up on camera, it'll be huge for ratings. That's basically what they said."

"Who's 'they'? The Big Bad MTV Executives?"

"No, it's . . . well, it's everyone. And me too. I'd like it if you were there."

"For the ratings?"

"No! No, just . . . it'd be nice to see a familiar face, you know?"

I did know. I remembered not wanting Victoria to leave the bathroom the day after my first date with James, just wanting to see something that was comfortable. Just thinking about Victoria put a lump in my throat, and I had to swallow hard.

"Aud?"

"I'm here."

"So . . . ? What do you think?"

"I don't know."

Holy shit. Was that really what I just said? What was I thinking? I had spent months trying to avoid the cameras and now I wasn't sure if I wanted to go face them willingly?

But it was live TV. On live TV, I couldn't be misquoted. I could speak for myself without a reporter twisting my words, or worse, making up words entirely. For the first time, people could see who I really was, that I wasn't a terrible girlfriend or a cheating slut or whatever else they were calling me.

For the first time since I heard "Audrey, Wait!" there appeared to be a glimmer of hope.

"Aud?" he said again. "You there?"

"No, I'm just . . . I'm thinking, Evan. I have to think, okay?" But my mind had gone past thinking and was way into overdrive. "When do they want to do this?"

"It's happening this Saturday."

"*This* Saturday?"

"Yeah. And your mom or dad has to come with you, since you're not eighteen yet."

"Can I tell you tomorrow?"

"Yeah, I think so." I could hear someone talking in the background, and then Evan covered the phone with his hand and said something like, "She says she'll tell us tomorrow." Then he came back. "Yeah, tomorrow's okay."

"Who was that?"

"Uh, Susan? She's our press agent from the label."

"Is she the same press agent who set me up with that *L.A. Weekly* interview? If I come out there, I want to meet her first."

"Uh, sure, okay. Aud?"

"Yeah?"

"I . . . I miss you. Not like, you know, not like I want to start dating again 'cause I know you're with James and everything, but . . . I just miss all of us fools hanging out."

I rested my head against the cool edge of my desk and struggled not to cry. Between this and Victoria, I wasn't ready to be nostalgic. "I miss you too," I whispered. "I'm sorry that I hurt you. I'm not sorry we broke up, but I'm sorry I hurt you."

"I'm sorry too. I know I did a bunch of shit wrong."

I wiped quickly at a tear and laughed a little. "Do you realize this is the most in-depth conversation we've ever had?"

"Yeah, I know, right?" Evan laughed too. "Ironic."

"Way ironic." I dabbed at my eyes one last time. "Okay. I have to go. I'll call you tomorrow, but what number?"

"This one. Here, just in case it came up weird on your phone." He read off the digits and I scribbled them onto a Hello Kitty notepad. "I really hope you come, Aud," he said. "I'm psyched to see you again."

"Yeah," I said with noticeably less enthusiasm. "Psyched. Me, too."

36 *"Perhaps, at last, the song you sing will have meaning. . . ."*

—Guided by Voices, "Fair Touching"

I DIDN'T KNOW WHAT TO DO. I absolutely did not know what to do. And worse, I had no one to talk to about it, either. Victoria and I still hadn't talked, and I was half too scared and half too mad to call and tell her. It was the longest we had not talked since she got laryngitis in the seventh grade.

I had IM'd with James that night, but I didn't tell him about my fight with Victoria or Evan's proposal, either. He was too mad about the video.

BoysDontCry: worst
BoysDontCry: video
BoysDontCry: ever
JustaGirl: I know
JustaGirl: sorry
BoysDontCry: pierce tivo'd it
BoysDontCry: I want 2 kill him
JustaGirl: evan or pierce?
BoysDontCry: both

BoysDontCry: how r u?
JustaGirl: : /
BoysDontCry: not me im >: (
JustaGirl: got 2 go, dinner
JustaGirl: talk l8r? <333

But the truth was, I wasn't hungry and I hadn't been sum-moned to eat downstairs. I just needed more time to figure out things in my head before I talked to James about it, especially now that his likeness was going to be in heavy rotation on every music channel, not to mention every single fan website and blog.

I tried going to bed early that night, thinking that a good night's sleep would clear my head and fix the problem and when I woke up, I would magically know what to do.

So when the clock hit midnight and I had tossed and turned for the eleven millionth time and all the sheets had come untucked, I chucked that plan out the window.

Even without all the hubbub, though, I wouldn't have been able to sleep, thanks to Bendomolena's snoring. She can really get loud if she falls asleep on her back, and Victoria and I once spent a whole Saturday trying to mic her so I could make her snore my new ringtone. It never worked, but it had been fun.

Fuck this, I thought. *I'm getting up.*

I wasn't the only one who couldn't sleep, it turned out. My dad was downstairs watching the History Channel (or, as I like to call it, the War Channel) and eating some sort of cookie. "Mom's gonna kill you if she sees you," I said when I saw him.

He didn't look too threatened. "I thought you went to bed early."

I shrugged. "Bendomolena's snoring."

"Well, here's a bribe so you don't tell your mother," he said, handing me a box of cookies. Thin Mints, still cold from the freezer.

"Where have you been stockpiling these?" I said. "I didn't see them."

He wiggled his eyebrows and scooted over on the couch. "I'll never tell. C'mon, sit."

I sat.

After about ten minutes of watching one siege after another, I licked the remaining chocolate off my fingers. "Evan called me today," I said casually, trying to get a feel for the situation. My dad's pretty cool, I'll admit, and we talk, but we don't really . . . *talk.*

"Oh, yeah?" His eyes didn't leave the screen, but he turned down the volume a bit. "What'd he want?"

"Um, just to say hi. And that he wants me to come to New York to be on live TV with him and the rest of the band next Saturday."

Apparently that sentence trumped the Battle of Whatever, because my dad turned the volume down some more. "Oh, yeah?" he said again.

"Yeah. And there was this video today, too, of The Song, and it came out. . . ." And the next thing I knew, I was telling my dad about the video and the fight with Victoria, too, and how I hadn't told James anything about Evan calling or his offer, and my dad was listening and nodding while cannons kept exploding on the screen in front of us. (Not an inappropriate backdrop for the conversation, I had to admit.)

"So I don't know what to do," I finished, raising and dropping my hands in my lap. "I want to tell James but I don't, and I want to go to New York, but I don't."

"Wow," my dad said. I was really thankful he was taking such a laid-back approach to this. If it had been my mom, she would've been all momlike and sympathetic, which would've probably made me cry. With my dad, though, it was all business.

"It sounds like you need to make some decisions," he continued.

"Yeah, no kidding."

"So make them." He ate another cookie and glanced down at me. "C'mon, Aud, since when have you been a spectator?"

"Since I knocked myself unconscious on the balance beam when I was six."

"You know what I mean."

I did know. I had been hiding out and shutting up while everyone else talked about me. "So you think I should go to New York?"

"I didn't say that."

"You think I should stay here?"

"I didn't say that, either."

I sighed. "How come when you want your parents to tell you what to do, they don't, and when you *don't* want them to tell you what to do, they do?"

"Secret parenting classes," he said, then passed me the Thin Mints. "They teach you all sorts of things, including where to hide the cookies so your daughter can't find them."

Three cookies and a hug later, I went back upstairs. Bendy was still sawing logs and I threw a pillow over my head as I curled back up into bed.

I had to decide.

So I did.

The next morning, I found both my parents in the kitchen, looking oddly expectant. My dad must've filled my mom in on current developments. "So," I said. "Who's up for a trip to New York?"

37 "This is the long way down, and our lives look smaller now. . . ."

—AFI, "Summer Shudder"

I'VE NEVER BEEN TO NEW YORK. I've always wanted to go and I've imagined how it would be: buying little dresses at Marc Jacobs, dashing in and out of yellow taxis, and dancing at clubs so underground that they don't even have names. Forget the tourist sights. Catch you next time, Statue of Liberty.

It didn't quite happen like that.

MTV and Evan's record label and my parents hashed out the details of my appearance like they were on the Supreme Court. At first, my parents didn't want me to miss school on Friday to fly out, but then they relented, and then my mom refused to let MTV's wardrobe people get ahold of me because, as she put it, "I've seen what you people do to these girls." If my mother had her way, I'd be wearing a turtleneck, a parka, a snow hat, jeans, and boots on national television.

Um, no.

And then I had to tell James about my decision.

The day after the video first aired, we were in my car after school, sitting in the parking lot and waiting for traffic to clear out.

"God, don't do that," he said, pulling my hand out of my mouth as I chewed on a cuticle. "It makes me crazy when you do that."

I snatched my hand away from his but didn't resume chewing. "You could just say, 'Audrey, please don't do that,' you know. You don't have to lecture me about it."

Yeah, we weren't exactly in the best of moods. The video was still first and foremost on James's mind, while New York was on mine. "All these girls kept coming up to me in history class," he said, shaking his head at the memory, "and they were like, 'Was that really you in the video?' I mean, girls never spoke to me before in their lives, and now this."

I shrugged. "Welcome to my world."

"One of them even tried to sit in my lap!"

"Look, I have to tell you something."

"And all of her little friends were doing that stupid girl giggle, too."

"Evan called me last night."

James looked at me like I had shot him. "*Evan?* Ex-boyfriend Evan?" I think he was feeling the same way I had felt after I saw Sharon Eggleston getting all lovey-dovey on him.

"Yeah. Him." I took a deep breath. "MTV is doing this big thing in New York this weekend and they want me to come out for it. Do an interview with him on live TV."

James snorted and glanced out the window. "And you told him to fuck off, I hope." When I didn't say anything, James looked at me. It was like hearing a wave just about to crest in the ocean, the sort of silence that indicates all hell is going to break loose.

"I told him that I'd go and do the interview," I finally said.

I had thought that James would get all flushed and upset, but just the opposite happened: All the blood drained from his face. "You're *going?*"

"Yeah. My mom and I are leaving on Friday morning."

"You're going to see the same guy who made a video that basically trashed both of us?!"

"I'm not going to see him, I'm going so all of this will just die down! And besides, the video was probably the director's idea, not Evan's."

"Do not defend him," James shot back. "And you think by going on MTV that this will die down?" He laughed a short, bitter laugh. "Excellent plan."

"Yeah, actually, it is!" I said. "If people see me and Evan talking and not trying to kill each other, then maybe they'll get over it! Maybe they won't think I'm this evil horrible girl who cheated on her boyfriend with *you!*"

"You're out of your mind," James muttered. "This is gonna launch you through the stratosphere. Nothing's gonna die down. Quit lying to yourself!"

"Look, I'm doing this for *us*, okay?"

James turned to look at me. "No, you're doing this for *you*. But if that helps you sleep at night, fine. What the fuck ever."

"So what if I do it for me?" I shot back. "Is that bad? Is it so bad that I'm the one who finally gets to make a decision about what's happening in my life?"

But James wasn't having it. "Do you know how long I waited to date you, or even just talk to you? Months, Aud, okay? *Months.* And now this asshole comes back into your life and you're running back to him, like he never did anything to you! And here's me, standing like a fucking idiot at the Scooper Dooper, just like before, only now everyone knows me and they know my name and who I am. The moron who got dumped by you."

I was livid. "Um, excuse me? Did I say I was dumping you? It's just an interview, not a major life decision!"

"It's an interview with your ex-boyfriend!"

"Hey, here's an update, chief. You can't tell me what to do!"

"Yeah, no shit!"

It was terrible. It was a hundred times worse than our fight over Sharon Eggleston. We were both yelling by this point and people were walking past the car and trying to see what all the commotion was about. "All right!" I finally yelled and tried to catch my breath. "People are looking at us."

"People are *always* looking at us," he growled.

I sighed. "If this gets in the tabloids, I'll die."

James began gathering his bag out of the backseat. "The fucking tabloids. We're arguing about your ex-boyfriend and all you can think about is what everyone else will think."

"Where are you going?" I said as he shoved his history text into his bag.

"Home. I'll get a ride with Pierce. Or with Jonah. Whatever. I just want out."

I watched as he got out and slammed the door shut, then cut through the eucalyptus trees toward the street. People were still watching my car, and I started it up and zoomed home before anyone started to take pictures.

There was no way I was apologizing, either. The Sharon Eggleston thing was my fault, and I'd admitted it, and I'd gone way out of my way to fix it. But this one was all James. He could call me.

But the phone wasn't ringing.

For the next two days, school was the scariest place I had ever been (except for that one time two summers ago when I accidentally got stuck in the circle pit at Warped). Victoria and I still weren't talking, James was ignoring me, and walking through those school doors and not knowing who I was going to talk to that day was terrifying.

I was still seeing James and Victoria at school, but I was only catching brief glimpses. Jonah was by Victoria's side all the time as she studiously ignored me in the halls, but one time, when she was getting something out of her locker, he gave me a secret little wave and one of those "'Sup?" head nods. But instead of making me feel better, it made me want to cry. I couldn't even do that, though, because if anyone saw or heard, it'd be online in a matter of hours.

Thursday, the day before I left for New York, I was doing the same math problem in my SAT book over and over again, furious that I couldn't get the right answer, when I felt someone watching me. I turned around and saw Tizzy standing there with a gift in her hand, looking at me with shining eyes. "Hi," she said in a loud whisper. "Can you talk?"

I gestured around with my hand. "There's no one here. You don't have to whisper."

"Oh, right. Right," she added in a normal voice. "I just saw James walking down the hall. He's soo cute, Aud! You're so lucky!"

Apparently she hadn't heard. Not that it was strange to see James and me apart at school, since I was already apart from everyone, not just my boyfriend. "That's me," I said with forced cheer. "Lucky. Just too damn lucky."

"I know." She smiled wider and passed the gift to me. "Um, here. This is for you."

"Me?" I repeated. The box was beautifully wrapped, almost like someone had done it professionally. "Tizzy, you really didn't have to get—is this Christmas paper?"

"Yeah. I kept trying to give it to you before Christmas, but I couldn't find you, and then I got the flu and . . . well, I heard you were going to New York and I just thought, gosh, I better give it to you in case you love it there and end up staying!" She smiled wider. "So merry Christmas two months late!"

I could feel tears pricking at the corners of my eyes. I was officially the worst person in the world. I tried not to think of all the times I had made fun of Tizzy or just blatantly ignored her clumsy enthusiasm. "Um, Tizz, I'm really sorry, but I don't have a gift for you."

"Oh, that's okay! Really! It's not a big deal at all!"

But it suddenly felt like a huge deal.

"Can I open the gift now?" I asked her. I didn't care if there was a decaying head in the box, I was going to make the biggest deal out of her gift.

"No!" she said. "Don't open it now! I'll get all embarrassed and sweaty and weird! Just, you know, I thought you might like it! You can wear it on MTV or whenever you're mad at Evan. Or whatever."

"Well, can I call you after I open it?" I pulled out my phone and started to make a new entry for her, and she eagerly read off her digits as I programmed them into my phone. "Just don't call after nine," she warned, "'cause, you know, my mom goes to bed like *crazy* early." She shook her head and rolled her eyes. "Totally uncool."

I smiled. "Before nine. Got it." Then I stood up and gave her a hug. "Thanks again, Tizzy," I told her. "Really. That's so nice of you."

"Oh, you're sooo welcome! I mean, it's all good! Have fun in New York! I'm gonna be watching, don't worry!"

"I will," I said, then cleared my throat before my voice could crack.

"Okay, well, um, see you later!" She pulled her backpack higher up on her shoulders and waved goodbye like she was flagging down a plane. She waved until she turned the corner, and I fell into the chair with a heavy sigh and picked up her gift.

It was so nicely wrapped that it broke my heart.

I undid the paper carefully, like my mom always does when we have relatives over to open gifts. A pale blue shirt was inside, and when I shook it out and held it up, I saw the lettering on the front: I LIKED YOU BETTER BEFORE YOU SOLD OUT.

I spent the rest of the afternoon trying to keep tears from dripping all over my stupid SAT book.

By the time my mom and I boarded the plane to New York, I was ready to take off. It had taken me hours to pack the night before, since I didn't know what I wanted to wear, and I saw them fling my suitcase onto the plane from my window seat in first class. Say what you want about MTV, and I certainly do, but they know how to fly a girl and her mother in style. "They *should* be flying you first class," my dad grumbled when he found out. "They're gonna make millions in advertising off this."

Next to me, my mom checked her seat belt for the thirty thousandth time. I had forgotten that she was a nervous flyer and mentally braced myself for all the white-knuckled gripping she would be doing for the next six hours. "So," she said with false enthusiasm. "Are you excited? Ready to take off?"

I looked out the window again and thought of everyone else my age who was getting up, driving to school with their best friend, making out with their boyfriend or girlfriend before the bell rang. I thought of how much I wanted to be like them again.

And I thought of James's words to me.

"I just want out," I told my mom. "So let's go."

38

"Live through this and you won't look back. . . ."

—Stars, "Your Ex-Lover Is Dead"

"WHAT I DON'T UNDERSTAND," my mom kept saying on Saturday morning at our hotel, "is how you managed to get your entire closet into that suitcase."

"Lots of squishing," I replied as I flung three more shirts and a pair of jeans onto the floor. The room was big, but way too small for living with my mother, who liked neatness and order and sweater sets.

Let's put it this way: She's not an accessorizer.

"Just wear that nice pink sweater that Grandma sent you for Christmas," she suggested.

"Didn't bring it," I said, burrowing through to find my tights.

"The one thing you didn't bring," she sighed. "And it's so pretty on you. Hey, if you can, you should say hi to Grandma on-camera today. I know she's watching, she'd love it."

"Mom!" I finally cried. "Please! I'm about to be on national television! It's like my entire fashion life has been a dress rehearsal up to this point. I'm not going to look like I fell into the Gap, okay?"

She just looked at me. "You're nervous about seeing Evan, aren't you?"

How does she *do* that? Because until she said it, I didn't even know I was nervous about seeing Evan, but my mom was right. "I guess," I sighed. "Maybe. I don't know."

"Did something happen with James?" she asked. "Right before we left?" She already knew about my fight with Victoria, but it must have been dubbed a Sensitive Issue by my parents, because neither of them was bringing it up.

"We had a fight," I admitted. "About me coming here."

"What did he say?"

I gave her a brief and censored version. "So I don't know if we're broken up or what," I said as I flopped down on the bed. "We're not talking, which I guess is the same as breaking up. I don't know. Everything's all weird."

My mom sat next to me. "Aud," she said. "Sometimes you're gonna have to make decisions that not everyone is going to like. But if you think it's the right thing to do, you have to do it. Even if your boyfriend doesn't like it. Even if Victoria doesn't like it. Heck, even if Dad and I don't like it. You have to start trusting yourself."

I thought of how I had walked away from Evan as he called, "Audrey, Wait!" even though I knew I should have gone back to talk to him some more. I thought of how apprehensive I'd been about that *L.A. Weekly* interviewer and I how I hadn't wanted to talk to her. And then I thought of my cute, redheaded, possibly ex-boyfriend, who I thought was dorky just because everyone else thought he was dorky.

"I feel like I keep screwing everything up," I told her. "Every time a big decision happens, I choose the wrong thing and it just gets worse. And now I don't have a best friend or a boyfriend anymore."

"Are you kidding?" my mom gasped. "I'm so proud of you!

You've weathered all of this so well. Not many adults could handle this sort of pressure, and here you are, flying to New York with your head held high."

"Oh my God, Mom, that is so cheesy. You've been watching too many sitcoms."

My mom just smiled. "I'll let that one slide," she said. She pulled my hair over my shoulder and smoothed out the tangles. "Look, if you don't want to do this interview, you just tell me and we'll be on the next plane back to California, okay? But if you really want to, then I'm behind you one hundred and ten percent. Just make sure that you're making decisions for you, not because of what anyone else thinks."

"Will you still be behind me if I wear those turquoise boots that I got at the swap meet?" I knew she hated those shoes.

"Of course." She kissed the top of my head and went to stand up. "Way, *way* behind you."

39 *"MTV, what have you done to me?"*

—Arcade Fire, "Windowsill"

FROM THE MINUTE our car got to the MTV studios, some production assistant named Amy was put in charge of baby-sitting me. She was probably only a few years older than me and had two cell phones, a clipboard that didn't seem to have much purpose, a walkie-talkie, and a headset. She and two security guards got me and my mom out of the car and into a dressing room upstairs, away from everyone and everything.

And there were many, many everyones and everythings. The streets outside were lined with fans, some of whom had homemade signs and others who had signs that MTV had obviously instructed them to hold. The screaming was not like anything I had heard before, and it looked like the NYPD was brought in to control the crowd.

"So this is where you'll be until we're ready for you upstairs," Amy rattled on as she deposited my mom and me in a dressing room the size of a closet. She talked super fast and I acknowledged her as a fellow caffeine addict. She didn't look very New Yorky to me, either, which I confirmed later when it turned out she was from Kansas and a junior at NYU.

"Cute shoes," she said when she saw my turquoise boots, and I had to admit, I was having a stellar fashion day. I had paired the boots with this great black dress that looked like Edward Gorey drew it, and even though I was freezing to death, it was worth it. Plus I got to wear this very mod peacoat that I can never wear in California, so despite all the drama, I was totally loving my outfit. Even though my mom was all, "Are you sure about those boots?" about a million times.

I tried to relax on the ugly tan couch and not think about how I was about to be on live national television, but it was difficult. Mostly because the Do-Gooders had arrived and Amy's walkie-talkie kept going off with announcements like "The talent is five minutes away!" "The talent has arrived!" "The water for the talent is not in the dressing room. I repeat, the water for the talent is not in the dressing room!"

"The talent wants their M&Ms sorted alphabetically," I said at one point, rolling my eyes. "The alent-tay wants everyone to speak pig latin for the next inety-nay inutes-may." It still amazed me that Evan and the rest of the band were considered "talent," much less that people were falling over themselves to bring them water. (Keep in mind that these were the same guys who once had a contest to see how much bologna the four of them could eat. And let me tell you, in a bologna-eating contest, *nobody* wins.)

"Sshh!" My mother nudged my elbow and motioned toward Amy, who was apparently involved in the talent's water fiasco and was chattering into one of her phones. "You're gonna make that poor girl have a stroke right here in the dressing room."

"No, 'the talent' is," I said, but when I tried to go out in the hall to find a bathroom, Amy flung herself in front of me and motioned me toward a door in the dressing room. That's when I figured out that this girl was here solely to keep me from seeing Evan. I couldn't help but think that if Victoria had been here with me, not only would she have gotten past Amy, but she'd be telling "the talent" exactly where they could get their damn water.

And then the countdown started: "Sixty minutes to air!" "Forty minutes to air!" This must be why rock stars are so cranky, I figured. They have to get everywhere at o'dark-thirty and then cool their heels for hours afterward. No wonder so many dressing rooms have been trashed.

At "Ten minutes to air!" Amy took me and escorted me down the hall to a holding area that was very cold and hushed. "'Bye!" my mom said as I left. "Remember, say hi to Grandma!" She had been reminding me to do that every five minutes, but seeing as how my hands had suddenly gone numb with terror, Grandma was the furthest thing from my mind.

I glanced at Amy as we both stood in the holding area, surrounded by several other PAs and their useless clipboards. Everyone was watching the monitors that hung from the ceiling, and I could see the Do-Gooders getting interviewed and the in-studio audience laughing and listening at all the right spots. I recognized the interviewer as Dave, the guy who always asked the stupidest questions every time he interviewed a band.

"Just remember, be natural, just like in real life," Amy rattled on.

"This *is* my real life," I muttered.

She didn't hear me. "No gum and most importantly, no swearing," she continued, but I tuned her out and focused back on the band. The only images I had seen of Evan since we broke up had been videoized and airbrushed, making the whole band look as pinuppy as possible. With no computer effects to change them, though, they just looked tired. Evan, especially, looked so much older than he had a year ago, and I unconsciously reached out and touched the screen as my anger toward him slowly eased. "Hi, Ev," I whispered, but Amy didn't hear me say that, because someone was handing my cue cards to her.

Yeah, that's right.

Cue cards.

Amy gave me a brief rundown. "The camera with the red light on it is the camera that's on," she said, which I already knew. "And these"—she hoisted the cards up—"are what you're going to say."

"What I'm going to what?"

"Don't worry, it's just some guidelines to make the interview run smoothly," she said, her Kansas teeth practically blinding me with insincerity. "You know, just where your answers should go."

"But I thought I could say what I wanted to say," I told her, as the numbness traveled from my hands to my arms. I wondered if I was having a heart attack. *Wasn't that a sign of a heart attack? Numb arms?* When I wasn't struck down by staggering chest pains, I shifted my focus back to what Amy was saying.

"—like to have everything go as smoothly as possible," she chirped again. "Don't worry, these are just standard answers." But as she flipped through the cards to show me, I realized that they were all things I had said in the *L.A. Weekly* interview, how I loved The Song, loved being famous, *loved loved loved* everything about my life! I was surprised no one had drawn rainbows and teddy bears on the cards.

"Um, can I go to the bathroom?" I asked her. "I really have to pee."

Amy glanced at the clock attached to the monitor. "Six minutes," she said.

"I really, really have to pee," I said, sounding like I was in pre-school. "It'll be fast."

"Okay," she said, and since Evan was on camera I supposed, I was allowed to dash down the hall and into a bathroom. Once I checked to make sure that no one else was in there, I locked myself in a stall and started thinking fast. What could I do? I could refuse to go on air. I could play along with the cue cards and make every-one happy. I could say "fuck" on national television and shut the whole thing down in three seconds flat.

"—so glad when this is over!" a woman's voice suddenly said as two pairs of high heels clicked into the bathroom.

"Tell me about it," another woman said. "Believe me, we were *not* prepared for this. I haven't had a free weekend in six months."

They sounded official and professional, and I had a feeling they didn't know that I was in there. I had a feeling I wasn't sup-posed to be hearing this conversation.

So of course I stood on the toilet and eavesdropped.

"Well, you know we signed them just because someone's uncle or cousin or whatever knew their little manager, and it was this whole family-favor thing." The first woman sighed. "And then this song came out and it was like, 'Uh-oh, goodbye, free time.'"

"Do you know how long it took me to media train them?" the second woman said. From the way she spoke, I could tell she was applying lipstick. "We practically had to beat the Southern California out of them. Everything was 'dude' or 'fool' or 'stoked.'

It was terrible.

"And now they're like, 'When are we gonna record our album? We wanna make an album!' and I'm just like, 'Kids, you're lucky there's a fuckin' song! Grab your money and run!'"

"How was the contract they signed?"

"How do you *think* it was?"

Then they both giggled.

Ohmygod. Ohmygod. Ohmygod.

"But you know," the first one replied, "it's a good song. They'll have their moment, they'll be a VH-1 one-hit wonder or whatever it is. They'll have a story to tell their grandkids."

I couldn't believe this was happening. I had always seen the movies where the hero hides in the bathroom stall while bad things are being said, and I'd always be like, "Jump out! Confront them! *Do something!*" But now I totally knew why they didn't do that: They were in shock. Just like I was. I couldn't do things like burst out of the stall and say, "Aha!" because I was so surprised that it was all I could do to keep my balance. Forget confrontation. I just didn't want to fall into a public toilet.

But after they left, everything snapped into place. It was like someone had stretched out my brain and shaken off the dust. My arms lost their numbness, my vision was sharp, and when I climbed out of my stall and went to look in the mirror, I felt brave and clear and not scared at all.

Since when have you been a spectator? my dad had asked me.

"Not anymore, Daddio," I said to the mirror.

It was time to shake this game up.

40 "Something glorious is about to happen!"

—Bloc Party, "Positive Tension"

THERE ARE A FEW MOMENTS in my life that I'll never forget: meeting Victoria, kissing James for the first time in the freezer, and walking out on the MTV set to bright lights and the screaming applause of two hundred people I had never met in my life, but who all knew me. It was almost overwhelming. My breath did this weird hitching thing in my chest where it stopped and started and stopped again, and sparkles of adrenaline jammed into my heart and skin until I felt like I was shining.

I had to walk across the stage, which I managed to do without slipping and killing myself, and the interviewer was standing there with his microphone, even though I had already been handed a mic backstage. Next to him was the band, and when I saw Evan, he gave me a smile that meant too many things.

Hi.

I miss you.

Sorry about all this.

The rest of the band was smiling at me, too, and when I got close enough, I hugged Evan and the audience went bonkers. "You saw it here, folks!" the interviewer, Dave, shouted into the mic. "Enemies no more!" Like he was the one who was responsible for us reuniting on the stage. What a tool.

After the "Woo!" girls finally calmed down, Dave turned to me. "So, Audrey," he said, "thanks for coming out today."

Was that a question? Was I supposed to respond? Was my response already written out on those stupid cue cards? Ten seconds in and I could tell that Dave would be a real craptastic interviewer.

"I'm glad I could be here," I said, and three thousand miles away, I could hear Victoria making gagging sounds at how fake I sounded. Judging from Evan's face, he knew I was faking my enthusiasm, too.

"So let's jump right in," Dave continued. "The song 'Audrey, Wait!' has definitely changed your life. How do you feel about all of that? What'd you think of the song?"

There was a bunch of people standing off camera, looking both anxious and bored. Some woman was holding a stopwatch and wearing a headset, and next to her was my mom. Next to the camera that had the red light, I could see the cue cards that prompted me to answer Dave's question. GREAT! they read. I LOVE IT! ETC. ETC.! SMILE! ENTHUSIASM!

It was now or never.

"I wanted to throttle Evan when I heard it," I told Dave, "but he was onstage and there were too many witnesses."

The look on Dave's face was priceless. If you've seen the tape, you know what I'm talking about, that sort of frozen grin that said I was next in line to be throttled. I just grinned back as Amy frantically jabbed at the cue cards off camera.

"Throttle, hahaha!" Dave laughed, but his eyes were shooting death rays into my forehead. "It's been quite a ride for you, hasn't it? You dated Simon Lolita—"

"Oh, Simon Lolita's a liar," I said, making sure the microphone was directly in front of my mouth. There was a ripple going through the audience that I couldn't quite comprehend, and Amy was shaking the cue cards like there was no tomorrow. "We never dated. We kissed backstage at a concert while his tour manager hid in the bushes and made that video of us. And, you know, Dave, if you think about it, that's a dirty thing to do. Don't you agree?"

Evan was *so* trying not to laugh, I could tell.

"I mean, hiding out in the bushes to take pictures of a girl is pretty desperate," I said. "And it usually means you're not dating her. But you know, whatever. I guess the album's not selling well and they have to make money off of *something* to pay for all that cocaine." I shrugged and did my perfect imitation of a happy smile.

Only I realized that it wasn't an imitation. I *was* happy! In fact, I felt fantastic! Adrenaline was my new best friend! "C'mon, Dave, keep those questions coming!" I told him. "I'm having fun!"

Without any prompting, the audience started to cheer.

Off camera, my mom put her hand to her mouth.

I hoped those cue cards were recyclable.

"Well, ah, okay!" Dave said, and laughed toward the camera. I've seen the tape, and I can tell you that however panicked he looked on camera, it didn't even begin to show how nervous he was onstage. In fact, what with the bedlam of backstage, the deer-in-headlights look of the Do-Gooders, and the flushed and hyperventilating fans, I seemed to be the coolest cucumber in the room.

"So have you two talked at all since the song came out?" Dave said, and I could see a faint circle of perspiration spreading under his black thermal shirt. "Evan? What about you?"

"Well, we've been touring and stuff," Evan said before I could open my mouth. "And we haven't been home at all and—"

"And you changed your cell phone number, too," I interrupted. "That made it a bit more difficult to catch up."

"Well, yeah, there's that," he admitted with a sheepish grin.

"So you tried to call Evan?" Dave said, jumping on that new piece of gossip like a rat on cheese. "Was this recently or . . . ?"

"Oh, this was months ago," I said with a wave of my hand.

"So," Dave continued as if I hadn't said anything, "were you getting jealous of his success at all?"

Good God. Was this guy desperate for a scoop or what?

(Now, it should be noted here that due to adrenaline, jet lag, and delayed stage fright, I've forgotten most of what I said on camera. Luckily, a fan with a username of KatyWithAWhy from the "WeHeartAudrey" online message board transcribed the whole thing for a bunch of Connecticut fans, who lost their TV cable connection due to a freak snowstorm and missed the live telecast. So thanks to KatyWithAWhy for helping me fill in the blanks.)

"Look," I said to Dave. "Here's the story. Me and Evan, we dated, we broke up, and he wrote a song about it that became really successful. That's the story. That's all there is. If I have fans"—and here I gestured to three girls in the front row who were wearing homemade AUDREY, WAIT! FOR US! shirts—"I hope it's because they like me for being me. Or because they see me as someone who's just trying to survive high school like everyone else, and not because I'm some crazy hero figure or something."

"Now can you *really* say that you're like everyone else?" Dave said, one eyebrow raised. "Because this must have been pretty life-changing for you."

"Oh, believe me, I've changed," I told him. "But I would've changed even if none of this had happened. Right? I mean, I'm *sixteen*. I do stupid things, but c'mon, everyone does stupid things. I'm supposed to change and make mistakes and kiss the wrong guy and the right guy and fight with my friends.

"I'm a girl who broke up with her boyfriend. But I still have friends and parents and a really fat cat—"

"Her cat's *huge*," Evan interrupted.

"It's a glandular thing," I explained. "But I didn't do anything special or interesting. I just broke up with my ex-boyfriend. That's *all*. That's all there is."

"Well, speaking of breaking up, that's what's being reported this week." Dave was frantically flipping through his note cards and pulled out the right one. "Some media outlets are saying that you've broken up with your latest boyfriend, a guy named James? Care to shed any light on this? This would be the third boyfriend in six months, right?" *Booyah!* I could tell he wanted to shout at me. *Take* that *for screwing up my interview!*

Evan and the rest of the band swished their heads to look at me. "You broke up?" Evan said, not even speaking into the mic this time.

I took a deep breath, unsure for the first time since I had walked onstage. "I . . . I don't know," I said hesitantly. "I don't know what we are right now." Just thinking about James three thousand miles away was making me feel a little unbalanced, and then I thought of Victoria. Were they even watching?

I took a chance that they were.

"See, here's why I'm not perfect," I said, locating the camera with the red light. "I picked fights this week with two people that I really love, and it was all my fault. The biggest mistake I made in this whole thing was trying to be the same person I was before The Song came out. It's scary, you know? Everyone suddenly knew who I was and they knew where I lived, so I was trying to stay the same. But that just made me change *more*, and then I got even more scared and screwed everything up. My best friend and my boyfriend are awesome, wonderful people, and I hurt them. A lot.

"So, Victoria, if you're watching, I'm so sorry. I was scared and stressed and I'm saying on national television that you were right and I was wrong and . . . yeah. I screwed up. And James . . ."

My voice caught in my throat as I thought of how James's hair smelled, how he had smiled at me one afternoon as he emerged from the back of Pierce's car, how he had once whispered "I love you" when he thought I was asleep but I really wasn't.

"James . . ." I said again, and the whole studio was completely quiet. "I'm sorry. I really am. You were right, I've been playing into all of this, and I'm done. I'm coming home and I'm going to make it right."

"Fifteen seconds to commercial!" someone was saying off camera, and someone else muttered, "Thank fucking God." My mom still had her hand over her mouth and tears were streaming down her face.

Holy *shit*. I made my mom cry. At first I thought she was mad or something, but then she pulled her hand away and mouthed, "I'm so proud of you!" and I knew that I had finally made the right decision.

And the clock was ticking.

"The Do-Gooders are a great band," I said quickly. "And from what I overheard backstage, their label's gonna screw them over and not let them release a full album, so if you like the band, write in or do whatever you can to fix that. And just in case anyone at MTV wants to know, Amy is a great PA and had no idea that I was going to do this, so please don't fire her. Oh, and I think my grandma is watching, so hi, Grandma! I love you! I miss you!"

Then I looked at Dave and the Do-Gooders, who were now standing open-mouthed. Especially the Do-Gooders, who were just figuring out that their long-planned album was in danger of not happening. I walked over to Evan and kissed him on the cheek. "It's a really good song, Ev," I told him. "And I'm really proud of you."

And then I handed my mic to Dave, waved at my fans, and walked out of the spotlight for good.

41 "As streetlights sing on Audrey's song . . ."

—Anberlin, "Audrey, Start the Revolution!"

OF COURSE, though, the spotlight followed me for a while afterward. I mean, hello? You saw the scene at the airport when my mom and I landed that night. It was craziness defined, especially because one of the photographers ended up insulting another photographer, and then both of them went all macho and the police were called in. At least, that's what I heard happened. I didn't give two shakes about any of it—I just wanted to see Victoria and James and my dad. (And Bendomolena, too, just 'cause I had missed her.)

Getting from the gate to the baggage claim area required airport security, because everyone at the airport was pointing and whispering, "That's her, that's her!" I could tell my mom wanted to throw her coat over my head again, like she had at RPM Records, but she managed to restrain herself. I think if she hadn't been with me, I would have been locked into a small dark room at MTV by the producers, but after I walked offstage, she grabbed me and practically shoved me into an elevator and then into a cab outside. "What about our luggage?" I asked her. My latent stage fright had kicked in and I thought I would be sick. As it was, my hands couldn't stop shaking.

"We'll get it shipped to us," she said.

At the airport, my mom went to the counter to exchange our tickets for the first flight back to California. At first they refused to do it, but once they realized who I was, we not only got our tickets, but we got escorted to the gate, too. And when they offered us beverages on the plane, my mom got red wine, even though she doesn't drink that often. She was already sort of giggly, and kept looking at me and shaking her head, saying, "My daughter, my daughter."

In the baggage claim area in Los Angeles, this is what I saw: my dad, talking to another airport security crew; photographers half-holding their cameras up, waiting for that first shot; a small figure standing next to my dad, arms crossed, tapping her foot impatiently while her half-grown-out fauxhawk bobbed up and down.

And the back of James's head.

His red hair was peeking out from underneath his hoodie, and at first I thought it wasn't him. But then my mom said, "Is that James?" and I broke out of the pack, dashed down the escalator steps, past security, past the cameras, and I didn't stop until my arms were around his neck. As you've seen, he's so tall that I was dangling off of him like a baby monkey, which made for some really cute pictures.

And then I was crying all over the place. "I'm sorry!" I kept saying. "I'm so sorry, I'm so sorry, I love you, I'm so sorry!"

James was hugging me and even though he swears to this day that he wasn't, I know he was crying, too. In the pictures, his eyes are all red and swollen. "Shut up!" he finally said as we pulled away. "I can't kiss you when you're apologizing!"

So of course, I shut the hell up so he could kiss me.

Then Victoria and I started crying all over each other, so it got even messier, and then we were doing that weird thing where we were laughing and crying and talking at the same time, both of us saying what a shitty friend we were. "It's a terrible video!" Victoria kept saying. "I just said that to make you feel bad!"

"I know!" I said as I hugged her again. "Can we just not fight again? It's lonely without you!"

"I hate fighting with you! No more fighting ever!"

"Ever!"

"You were awesome!"

"Victoria," I said, nearly breathless from all I had to tell her about my backstage experiences, "wait until you hear what happened to me."

So that's kind of it. Victoria and I made up. (As if we wouldn't, though? Please. She's like my sister. I couldn't get rid of her if I tried.) She gave the BMW back, too, but not before we took Jonah and James on a joyride that ended with midnight drive-thru trips at both In-N-Out and Del Taco. It was awesome.

James and I made up, too. And James got a new job. We had one last kiss session in the freezer of the Scooper Dooper on his last day of work. ("Just for old times' sake," I told him.) But he and I also got all serious and mature and hashed out a deal where we would start going out in public, photographers or not.

The first time, we went to the movies and I was totally nervous, but I didn't run or flip them off or anything, and it just seemed less exciting. I guess the paparazzi are just like guys: They love the chase. The photographers and press were in a frenzy for the first week after the MTV experience, but then some movie star got busted for strippers and heroin and got sent to rehab. So that bumped me right off the front covers and onto page three.

(Coincidentally, the drummer of the Lolitas went into rehab a month later, claiming exhaustion, of course, but I'm sure it didn't help that I outed them on national TV. Either way, demos for their second album leaked online, but they didn't really do much for me. Or anyone else, for that matter.)

But what really changed everything was that Evan got a new girlfriend, some girl named Kayleigh who he met at a video game release party in Los Angeles, and all the attention went from me to her. I never thought I would be so happy to hear that my ex-boyfriend had a new girlfriend, but Victoria and I did the Happy Dance for like ten minutes when we found out about it.

"You're old news," James said as we glanced through all the weeklies at the bookstore, the ones where Ashleigh was featured. "You're a has-been."

"Her hair looks cute there," I replied, pointing at one of the photos.

Oh, and speaking of hair, Victoria's growing her hair out and I think she's gonna get extensions next summer, which is gonna look amazing on her. All of her finagling to get free stuff got her interested in PR work, so now she's thinking about doing some work with this local band, New Nostalgia, helping them get some press and booking shows. I might sell merch for them this summer, too, which is good, because I need cash to replace my car speakers.

Again.

Evan and I still talk, which James is cool with. Ev's in the studio a lot now. I guess that letter-writing campaign the fans launched really helped, because now the band's making an album and they're working with some crazy producer somewhere in L.A. We're talking about all of us getting together—me, James, Victoria, Jonah, Evan, and Ashleigh—and you *know* that Victoria and I are dying to meet Ashleigh. From what I've read, she seems nice enough. I told Evan to have her call me once her cell phone gets hacked into and I can advise her on what to do.

"Audrey, Wait!" doesn't get played as much on the radio anymore, but every once in a while, it comes on and I don't change the station. I wasn't lying when I told Evan it was a good song. It's even better now that I can enjoy it. James likes it, too. After our exciting first date at RPM Records, James got a new job there, and on his first day, Mr. Emo Glasses (whose real name is Kevin) played The Song over the loudspeakers to welcome him. And sometimes when we're being stupid and goofy, James sings it to me in this really awful high, warbly voice that sounds like a mouse crossed with a seagull.

It's funny. *He's* funny. And I love him.

I know this is like the longest story ever, but I really just wanted you to know the other side. (And besides, Bendomolena's been on my lap this whole time and once Bendomolena decides to sit on you, get comfortable, because you're not going anywhere for awhile.) Anyway, James is coming over in fifteen minutes so we can go with Victoria and Jonah to see New Nostalgia, and I still have to figure out what I'm wearing.

Like the Beatles said, "O-bla-di, o-bla-da, life goes on."

And it does.

Rock on.

Acknowledgments

Audrey, Wait! could have never happened if it wasn't for the friends and family who provided encouragement, read chapters, and asked me to please start drinking caffeine again. I know it's just a list of names, but trust me, these people are amazing.

Mom & Jack Schultz, Dad, Chris Benway, Adriana Fusaro, Maret Orliss, Johanna Clark, Kathleen Acosta Ekins, Heather Smith Siemons, Dallas Middaugh, Dan Smetanka, Tina Lee, Sheri Frouzesh Bennett, Katy Phillips, and Aaron Hartzler.

An extra special thank you to Rachel Cohn (Audrey's very first fan), Lisa Grubka, Ben Schrank, Kristen Pettit, and the entire Razorbill department, all of whom have taken such wonderful care of me and my book that it makes me smile to think of it.